Key ELEMENTS

Book Two of the Key Series

R O S I E P O L I T Z

Library of Congress Control Number: 2019915312

Published by Cypress Moon Publishing
8165 Rustic Rose Drive
Baton Rouge, LA 70818

First Edition

For Mamma Couvillion (Florence), Aunt Nat, and Aunt Isabelle.

There's a little bit of all of you in Aunt Mitzi.

ACKNOWLEDGEMENTS

Thank you so much for reading my work. I appreciate all the love and compliments I've gotten about my first book, *Key Moments*. It really means a lot and makes my heart feel good. I hope I continue to make you want to read more about Clay and Lynn and whoever else may come along in the future.

Big thanks to my editor, Billy, again for helping me fine tune this installment of Clay and Lynn's adventure. Your comments, suggestions, and wit were so beneficial in so many ways.

Marcus, thanks for your expertise and knowledge in helping me with the mental and physical part of Clay's inner demons and making sure they were as realistic as possible.

Erin and Chad, once again, huge thanks for getting me through the rough parts of war and Clay's battle with how to handle his behavior and reactions, as well as Lynn's reactions to his behavior. Thank you both immensely for your service. Much love and respect for y'all.

Cherie, thanks for always being you and for reading along as I wrote, sending me screen shots with circled typos and silly emojis. I couldn't have asked for a better sister. I love you all the popsicles in the world.

Ashley and DeeDee, thanks for your input and ideas on getting me through a few key scenes. I know I can always count on brutal honesty from both of you.

Terri, thanks a million for your feedback, sticky notes, and every 'LOL' you wrote on my manuscript. I appreciate it more than you know and I'm glad I could help you pass time on your flights.

To my Core Alpha Darlings, thank you again for your input and excitement with each chapter. Love y'all bunches.

Mom and Dad, infinite gratitude for being such great parents, helping to mold me into who I am, and for your unconditional love and support. I hope I've made you proud.

Tommy, my everlasting love and appreciation for you will never falter. Thank you for loving me in all the ways you do. I couldn't have gotten this far without your encouragement and belief in me. You are my boulder.

CHAPTER 1

THIS ISN'T HAPPENING. I must be dreaming, right? How could we have come so far, only to have the bottom pulled out from under us? As we stand here, looking at the empty lot where Big Red's Warehouse once stood, I feel an epic meltdown approaching.

Okay, let me give you a much-abbreviated bit of backstory. My great-aunt Mitzi died about a month ago, leaving her house to Clay (my husband) and me. We found a box of keys hidden in the stairs while we started doing some renovations. A cipher was in the box (along with a letter from Aunt Mitzi explaining everything about it) that had to be decoded and we discovered that each key in the box would open something in every state and Washington, D. C. So, we packed up Clay's truck and left our newly acquired house in our home state of Louisiana to come on this fantastic road trip.

Aunt Mitzi (and in some cases, my Uncle Sid, who died a few years before she did) had left us something in all the places we've been. We've traveled the states in the order she intended, and behind each lock, we obtained the things she left.

Gifts. The title to a 1957 Cadillac Eldorado Brougham (in need of restoration) that we received in Birmingham, Alabama. (We're still on the hunt for the vehicle itself, which we should come across at some point on our trip). One of Aunt Mitzi and Uncle Sid's old Victrolas that we acquired from a museum in Dover, Delaware. A charm bracelet with mementos of all the places we've visited so far, picked up in Lexington, Massachusetts. And more.

Knowledge. The fact that Aunt Mitzi was inadvertently involved with Al Capone. The fact that Aunt Mitzi bred her very own variety of prize-winning roses. The fact that Father Angelo was in love with Aunt Mitzi, much to the dismay of Uncle Sid. And more.

Heartbreak. It devastated me to learn that Aunt Mitzi and Uncle Sid tried to adopt two babies at two different times, only to have them taken back by the birth parents. It devastated me to find out that GiGi and Pops (my great-grandparents) forbade Aunt Mitzi to see Uncle Sid in the beginning of their relationship because they thought he was bad news. It devastated me to read the parts of Aunt Mitzi's diary where she wrote about the many pregnancies she had that ended in miscarriage. And more.

We've been through seventeen states and countless towns. We still have thirty-four states left with as many keychains and discoveries to make. But we've hit our first roadblock.

We're now in Bangor, Maine. We made our way up the east coast with a few hiccups, but nothing like our current predicament. Clay and I were supposed to find an old ballot box in this warehouse that no longer exists. But what was in the box? We may never know. Dammit.

We walk closer to what little remains of Big Red's Warehouse. There's nothing left but a slab of concrete, with dandelions shooting up through corroded rebar exposed by gaping cracks.

I stare at grass and weeds almost as tall as I am. A driveway that slopes where delivery trucks once backed in to offload supplies. Dilapidated fencing, bent and rusted. The empty parking lot that once held the cars of patrons and employees.

A gust of wind blows some of the dandelions' feather-like seeds into the air. It's nature's way of giving me a wish. Well, I wish this building were still here. But that's a wish that won't come true.

"Shit. Shit, shit, shit," I say, still staring into the empty space. "Clay? What now?" I look at him, and the second I see the blank expression on his face, I can't help it. I bury my head into Clay's shoulder and begin crying. Ugly crying. Blubbering. He binds me close to him and comforts me, rubbing his hand up and down my back. He must be so tired of doing this lately. I've always been such a complete emotional wreck in times of discontent. I go on for a few minutes before Clay says something.

"Babe, it'll be okay. I'm not sure where to go from here, but I know, no matter what, we'll figure it out."

Is he out of his ever-loving mind? Is he even on the same plane of existence as I am? I raise my head, shaking it, and stare at him. God, he has the bluest eyes. Even as upset as I am at him right now, I can't help but think about how sexy he is. "What the hell are you talking about? 'We'll figure it out'? How can you be so sure? It's gone, Clay! What the hell is left to figure out?" I scream through tears.

"Look, Lynn." His tone is completely opposite from mine. "I know this seems like a dead end, but we don't know the details." I take a few deep breaths and try to compose myself. "Come on. We'll go to the local library or maybe the city permit office and see what we can find out about the warehouse. Maybe we can track down some of the previous employees and find out what became of the contents. Maybe they got auctioned off and there are records. Maybe we'll even get to meet those guys from that show you like where they dig through everybody's junk."

I laugh with tears still in my eyes and voice. "*American Pickers*."

"Yeah. *American Pickers*."

Imagine that. He really does have a way to figure it out. Maybe. Hopefully. "That's a really good idea," I say as I wipe my face, which has clearly become nightmarish. "God, I'm a hot mess." Clay snickers. "What? What's so funny, Clay Sinclair?" I ask, a little perturbed.

"You're the furthest thing from a 'hot mess,' babe. You're just a mess."

I drop my jaw and playfully slap him. "Watch your mouth. I'm very vulnerable right now."

"Sorry. I'm kidding. You're a little disheveled, but you look fine. C'mon, let's get back in the truck. We'll start at the library. Saw one not too far from here on our way, so it's probably closer. Maybe there's an old article or public notice about the demo in the local paper."

We drive to the nearest public library, which was just down the street and around the corner from the slab of Big Red's. Walking in, that familiar 'old book' smell of brittle beige paper and glue hits me and I smile. I love the smell of old books. Is that weird? Plus, it reminds me of how Aunt Mitzi's diary smells, with those time-worn yellowed pages bound in leather.

Clay and I are directed to the archives section in the basement. We make ourselves comfortable and look for anything we can find on Big Red's Warehouse. He sifts through a bunch of papers from a file box and I look at old microfiches of the local paper, searching for any news about the warehouse. After a half hour of a bunch of nothing, Clay plucks a piece of paper with his fingers and the noise startles me.

"You found something?"

"I think so," he says. "Some sort of old tax document. Same address as the warehouse. It's got a list of employee names and phone numbers."

"Sweet. I'll take the top and you get the bottom."

"I love it when you take the top, babe," he says as he winks at me. "And oh how I love getting that bottom. Hey, it sure is quiet down in this section of the library." He cranes his neck to look around. "Nobody's here. You wanna—"

"Jesus, Clay. It's the library, for crying out loud. Oh wait, that's right… you have a thing for libraries. Are you having flashbacks?" I roll my eyes. Like I really need to be reminded of him losing his virginity in a library. And don't get me started on the bitch he gave it to.

"Shit, Lynn. I'm sorry. I wasn't thinking about that. And I was kidding anyway."

"Whatever. Let's just get to work on the list." I snatch the paper from Clay, make a copy, and tear it in half. I keep the bottom portion instead and throw him the top part out of sheer spite. I doubt he'll catch the metaphor.

Lucky for us, since there aren't any other people in the basement, we don't have to be especially quiet talking on our phones. I'm halfway down the list and I'm not having any luck with the phone numbers. They're either the wrong ones or disconnected. Don't you love the musical tone you get, followed by, 'We're sorry, the number you're trying to reach cannot be located.' Or, in cases with land lines, three ear-piercing tones and then that woman with the nasally voice saying, 'The number you've dialed has been disconnected or is no longer in service. Please check the number and try your call again.' They should at least tell you the number you actually dialed so you *can* check it instead of having to punch it in again just to hear the same damn message. So annoying.

Clay isn't getting anywhere either. Every time he finishes dialing, he sighs and shakes his head like an old man sitting on his porch watching street punks walk by with their pants halfway down their asses. Then I hear him speak. He's made a connection. I listen intently, but of course I only get half of the conversation. It doesn't sound promising though.

After he hangs up, he tells me that the lady he talked to, Katherine, worked there and knew about the ballot box. But she said her boss, who had only been there a few months at the time of demolition, decided to trash it and let it go with the junk stored in the building since it had been there for years with nobody claiming it, regardless of Aunt Mitzi's promise that one day, someone would indeed come for the box. Apparently, Katherine still felt bound by their pledge to Aunt Mitzi and planned to rescue the old ballot box, but then wasn't at work the day the warehouse was cleared. She had gotten a call from her brother out of state about an emergency with her mom who had taken ill. She left to tend to her mother and was away for three weeks. She knew the wipe-out of the warehouse was nearing when she left, so she put a bug in one of her trusted co-worker's ears: if the building was cleared before she got back, please snag the ballot box and drop it off at her church community center. Katherine told her she'd pick it up as soon as she could. Her co-worker agreed. All seemed right with the world. However, two days after Katherine's co-worker friend brought the ballot box to the church's community center for safe keeping, the building burned down. Katherine apologized profusely, as if it had been her fault, and said that if it was any consolation, the box had sounded empty.

"I'm sorry, love," Clay says. "I think this is the end of the road for us in Maine."

"Dammit. Well, you said this would happen. We've just been fortunate with everything before now. I guess it's back to the truck and the cipher to see where we go next. Just chuck this up as a loss."

"Hey, maybe not," he says. "Aunt Mitzi has been really smart with what she's left us. I'm sure we'll find out what we were supposed to discover here. If it sounded like there was nothing in the box, it may have been another envelope with something that will still be reviewed or at least touched on at some point in the future. Right?"

Clay. Always the voice of reason. "Yeah, that's true. Maybe so. You're probably right."

"That's my girl. Now, c'mon. Let's go figure out our next destination."

"Okay."

The roadblock at the library induces a bit of despair as I trudge back to the truck, but I try not to dwell on it. There is still much to figure out and a lot of ground to cover. I get the translated cipher out of my purse. "Alright, let's see where to now. It says—"

"Wait."

"What?"

"Since we're in Bangor, do you mind if we ride by Stephen King's house first? I hear it's really cool, with bats and spiders on his fence."

"He should call an exterminator."

"Ha ha. Statues of bats and spiders, goofball. Like sculptures or something."

"Sure. That does sound kind of intriguing. Maybe you'll get lucky and he'll be outside. You might meet one of your heroes."

"That would be surreal."

We drive by the horror author's massive nineteenth-century Victorian mansion. It's a beautiful home, close to street. The gray-roofed dwelling is painted red with white trim. It has turrets; balconies; porches; a porte-cochère; and many different styles of windows, as is the norm for most Victorian homes. It looks like a gigantic doll house. As Clay mentioned, the house is surrounded by a wrought iron fence. A web with spiders is fashioned into the ironwork of the gate, flanked by bats with large pointed wings at the top of the support posts. They remind me of gargoyles. This is a goth girl's dream home, though a goth girl would probably have painted it black.

We get out of the truck and I snap a picture of the gate and house. I take a photo of Clay in front of the macabre entrance, then we take a couple of selfies with the house in the background. No sign of King though. Maybe he's on a book tour, or inside churning out his next best-seller. I bet it's weird to have strangers come up to your house and take pictures, but I figure he's a little odd himself, so he probably doesn't mind. I must say, this was a fun side trip. Color me impressed.

"You about ready, Clay?" I think he could hang around here forever if I let him, hoping to catch a glimpse of his favorite author.

"I suppose," he tells me like a disappointed fanboy. "I was hoping to get my copy of *Different Seasons* signed." It's his favorite of all King's works, a collection of four novellas. He reads it at least once a year. I can't tell you how many times Clay has told me that *Apt Pupil* is the greatest horror story ever written. Even though I'm not much of a horror fan, out of the four novellas that make up *Different Seasons*, I actually read *The Body* because the movie *Stand by Me* was based on it, and that's one of my favorite movies. "I'll fix us some fresh Cokes while you read the clue," Clay says.

I climb in the front and Clay opens the back door to get the ice chest.

"Hand me our cups," he says.

"Here," I say as I hand them to him.

"And, hey."

"What?"

"I'm sorry about the library comment. I thought you were okay with what you found out about me and—"

"Okay with it?"

"Well, you made fun of me over it," Clay says, as he pours me a Barq's Red Creme Soda.

"I know. I'm not furious or anything. I was just in a bad place earlier. And she's the last thing I wanted to picture at that moment."

"Like I said, I wasn't thinking about that. About her. So again, I'm sorry." He hands me my drink and pours himself a fresh Dr. Pepper before he gets back into the front seat.

"It's okay."

"Read me the clue." He starts the truck and we wave good-bye to Stephen King's house.

"Okay, are you ready this time?"

"Yes ma'am."

"Alright. Pull into that gas station at the end of the street so we can figure this out before we wind up going in the wrong direction."

"Already on it."

"The clue says, 'Find the grand old home of the eldest son of our sixteenth president, and you shall find inside this residence, a secretary with a hutch, mostly filled with books and such. Pull the thickest one to see, what's inside page 333.' Wow, okay, something to do with Abraham Lincoln."

"What does the keychain look like?"

I dig in the box for the number nineteen keychain. "It's a penny, made into a keychain in a round, silver frame. Well that makes sense."

"Nice. Hey, did we ever look at the keychain for Big Red's?"

"No, we didn't, now that you mention it. Aunt Mitzi gave us the exact address and I forgot all about the keychain. I can't believe I didn't even get it out when we drove up to the fire station. That's not like me." I go back into the box and look for number eighteen. "It's a small silver key, maybe for a padlock, and the keychain says 'Vote' with an acrylic dome over it. Cool. Oh well. Too bad we didn't get to use it."

"Yeah. Okay, so do you know anything about Lincoln's children?"

"Well, I know he and Mary Todd Lincoln had four sons. Robert Todd Lincoln was the oldest. The second one, Edward, died of Tuberculosis, I think, when he was around four. Their third son, William, died from a fever when he was about twelve. Their last son, Thomas, died of heart failure at the age of eighteen. Robert was the only one who survived into adulthood and had the only descendants of Abe. But other than that, I don't have a clue about Robert himself."

"Well, Professor Sinclair, you're just a wealth of knowledge, aren't you?" He laughs. "You could have just stopped at Robert. How do you know all that anyway?"

"Well, Captain Smart Ass, I did a paper on Lincoln in high school. Some of the things you learn throughout life just stay with you. And I got an A plus, obviously."

"Obviously. Nerd. So, Mrs. Wikipedia, see what you can find out about Robert's house."

I playfully shove him for making fun of me and he laughs. I proceed to search online for Robert Lincoln's home. "There's a listing in Manchester, Vermont for a place called 'Hildene' that they say is 'The Lincoln Family Home.' Whoa, Clay. This house is incredible. It's massive. I can't wait to see it in person. Check it out." I show him the picture of the estate, which boasts twenty-four rooms and eight thousand square feet of living space.

"Sweet Jesus."

I read a little more about the house. "Holy shit. This was just their summer home. God, can you imagine their bank account?"

"Must be nice," Clay muses. "How far is that from here? I doubt we'll make it before sundown."

"About six hours. Yeah, we may need to call it a night about halfway. It's already almost five."

"Okay. Sounds good," he says, and he starts the truck.

CHAPTER 2

WE FIND A hotel in Hartford, Vermont and settle down into bed. I bring out the View-Master that we acquired from Hale House in New Hampshire. "Close your eyes and pick a set of reels," I tell Clay.

"Hmm, okay."

Eyes shut, he runs his finger up and down the lot and grabs the case labeled with the year 1968, then he hands it to me. I open it, insert reel number one into the slot, and take a look. "Oh my goodness. It's Aunt Mitzi's quilting circle. They're all sitting around, quilting the family tree quilt. And there's a tin of those shortbread cookies resting next to each one of the ladies." I flip to the next image. "Mom is there too, and Cecilia's in the corner in a playpen. I wasn't even born yet." Flip. "Mom is glowing. She must have been pregnant with me here and not even known it yet. She's not showing, but they usually only quilted in the spring and summer, so she would have been very newly pregnant with me." Flip. "Gosh, my grandmother was beautiful. I wish I could remember her more." I finish the reel and pass it over to Clay so he can see.

He goes through them. "Wow, Lynn. You look just like your Grams.

My heart literally skipped a beat when I saw her in this picture, looking right at the camera. Eerie."

"Aww…that just made my heart smile," I tell him. I do the math in my head and realize she was the exact age in that picture as I am now. Forty-eight.

He turns over a couple more frames. "The house looks almost the same inside as it does now. Even down to the curtains."

"Yeah. Aunt Mitzi and Uncle Sid were very proud of their house and always took such great care of everything they owned. I almost hate to change things up a bit, but it's what Aunt Mitzi wanted for us: to make it ours."

"You want to look at some more?"

"I do, but I'm really getting sleepy."

"Okay, love. Let's save the rest for later. Get some shut-eye." He kisses me goodnight and turns out the lights.

After breakfast, we get back on the highway and continue towards Hildene.

"What've you got for us, DJ Babealicious?" Clay asks.

I smile at his name for me. "What do you feel like?"

"Surprise me with something from one of your many playlists. We'll switch to mine after the next stop."

"Okay." I get my phone out and hit shuffle on my playlist titled *Name That Tune*. "Jack & Diane" by John Cougar starts playing.

"Oh, good one. Haven't heard that in ages," Clay says.

"Yeah. *American Fool* is one of my all-time favorite albums. I played it constantly when it first came out. That one, Queen's *Greatest Hits*, Prince's *1999*, Journey's *Escape*…you know, all the good eighties stuff. And whenever Annie spent the night, or the weekend (which was usually the case since she's always been my BFF), she'd bring her albums and we'd make a stack on my stereo until we thought it would break. Old-school playlists. I think that's where my love of playlists started. Anyway, we'd pretend we were music executives, like we owned a record label, and we had to determine if we would give them a contract. We would judge every song on a scale of one to ten. Of course, all of our favorite bands and artists made it on our label."

"Record execs, huh? That's hilarious. What did you call your label?"

"Promise you won't laugh?"

"No," he smiles.

"Neon Blast Records."

"Why would I laugh at that? That's actually a pretty cool name. Y'all might have been on to something there."

"You think?" I laugh. "We just loved neon stuff and figured it was brighter than gold or platinum, you know? Our artists went all the way to neon status."

"Very clever. So, nobody ever got turned down at this agency of yours?"

"Oh sure. We'd go get some of Mom and Dad's albums from way back. Stuff that wasn't our thing. So yeah, all their music got turned down. Motown, R&B, Doo-Wop. Golden Oldies."

"But you love Motown, R&B, Doo-Wop, and Golden Oldies."

"Yeah, now. Neon Blast eventually diversified. We made millions."

"That's so funny," he says. "I can't believe I never knew that. You two had quite the imagination."

"Yeah, that was all before we discovered boys. Not long after that, we'd just let the music play and practice putting on makeup so we could look pretty for the boys we liked at school. And sometimes we'd make mix tapes of all the songs we wanted played at our wedding. You know…typical girly slumber party stuff."

"Sounds about right," he says, as "Joanna" by Kool and the Gang sounds through the speakers.

We drive onto the Hildene property, and it's impressive. The home is a Georgian Revival Style, which basically means that it's symmetrical and proportional and has a ton of windows. The estate was built on a three-hundred-foot promontory which overlooks the Battenkill Valley. More than four hundred acres surround the former summer home of Robert and Mary Lincoln, including around twelve miles of hiking trails. It is simply stunning out here.

Fascinated, I read more about the place online. There is a Pullman car named Sunbeam on the property. The car has been restored and is available for touring. Robert Lincoln was president of the Pullman Palace Car Company, after the founder, George Pullman, died. The Pullman Company was the largest manufacturing corporation in the country at that time. Mind. Blown. No wonder he was so wealthy. The wooden luxury executive railcar came off the line in 1903, during Robert Lincoln's tenure as company president.

We park and make our way to the welcome center (which also serves as Hildene's gift shop) to check in for the self-guided tour. Clay starts looking around at stuff, but I tell him we'll come back when we finish our tour so we don't have to carry the bags all afternoon.

Once we're inside the house, we walk around and read about some of the pieces on display. The rooms have chained stanchions letting us know the furniture is off limits, but we can see everything. The interior is furnished with nearly all Lincoln family furniture. It contains items that belonged to Robert and Mary Harlan Lincoln as well as President and Mary Todd Lincoln. My favorite pieces are one of Abe's stovepipe hats, and Mary Harlan Lincoln's engagement ring. That hat though…completely surreal.

We have our eyes peeled for the secretary full of books. With a total of twenty-four rooms to explore, we don't want to rush, so as not to overlook it. We also don't want any attention drawn to ourselves. I imagine this place is under tight security. Like maybe borderline Secret Service style.

"Clay?"

"Yeah?"

I change my voice to a whisper. "I think we should tell somebody what's up. I know we like being sneaky, but this is not just any home we're touring. I mean, this is kind of a big deal."

"I was just thinking the same thing. I'm going to find a bathroom and you look for somebody to help us."

"Okay."

He leaves and I search around, half checking everything out, half looking for someone to assist us. I'm so focused on the furniture and my quest for a docent that before I know it, I bump into a man whom I nearly knock over.

"Oh my gosh, I'm so sorry," I tell him. "I should really watch where I'm going."

"Don't worry about it," he says in a voice as sexy as George Clooney's. "It's easy to get lost in here. This place is captivating."

"Yes, it sure is." He's around my age. Maybe a little older, closer to Clay's age. Dressed in jeans and a red polo shirt. Tall and well-built, with short dark hair. A lady-killer smile with dimples for days. Rugged, with a chiseled jaw and a five o' clock shadow. Strikingly good-looking. Like a model for men's cologne you see in magazines.

"Have you been to the observatory?" he asks.

"Observatory?"

"Yep. Robert Todd Lincoln had his own observatory on the property. He was quite the amateur astronomer."

"Wow. I didn't know that."

"I can show you if you'd like." He smiles and crooks his arm out, inviting me to grab it.

This guy is flirting with me. Right? I'm out of practice with anybody who isn't Clay, so it's hard to tell. But I don't believe that's normal behavior. "That's okay. I'm sure I'll make my way there at some point. Thanks though."

His smile slackens. Clearly, Romeo has never had to work so hard. "No problem." He lowers his arm back to his side. "Can you imagine the stars he saw out here a hundred years ago? I bet they sparkled as beautiful as your eyes do."

"Uh, thank you." Okay, now that was definitely flirting. One of the corniest lines I've ever heard, but I guess a guy with his looks can get away with it.

"Are you here alone?" he asks.

"No. My husband is in the bathroom."

"Husband." Casanova is disappointed.

"Yes." I smile, but inside I'm a bit nervous. I can't put my finger on why though. I guess because this man is so attractive and it's been a long time since anybody has flirted with me, besides Clay of course. Though I'm also a little flattered. I've still got it. Go me.

"Lucky man. Well, it's been nice chatting with you. Enjoy the rest of your tour. Don't forget the gardens. They're something. See you around."

And with that, plus a wink, the playboy walks off. I stand there stunned. What just happened? That was somewhat refreshing, though more uncomfortable than anything else I'm feeling right now. My heart starts fluttering. Clay comes back in, none too soon, and I immediately hug him.

"Well, hello to you, too. Missed me much? Did you find somebody to help us? Lynn? You okay?"

I let go of him. "Yeah, I just…I wasn't watching where I was going, and I bumped into a guy who flirted with me." Of course, I leave out the part about how eye-catching he was. Is. "It was a little awkward. I'm just glad you're back."

"Wait. *What*? Who? Where? Did he touch you?"

"No, no, nothing like that. I ran into him. By accident. He left. It's fine. I'm fine. Let's just go find somebody that can show us what's in the book."

"Are you sure you're okay? What did he say to you?"

"Nothing, really, I'm probably just overreacting. He said I had pretty eyes."

"He did, huh?"

"I'm sure he was just being nice."

"Well, you do have pretty eyes. But I'm not letting you out of my sight for the rest of the day."

"Okay." I smile at him and he grabs my hand, interlacing our fingers.

We see one of the tour guides walking around and go up to him. According to the badge attached to the lanyard around his neck, his name is Gregory. Clay and I introduce ourselves and relay the short and sweet version of our story.

Gregory scratches his temple. His thick, dark brows crinkle in confusion. "I'm sorry, I'm not familiar with anything you're telling me. Though the name you mentioned, Santini, rings a tiny little bell. Could be a coincidence. But, I'm new. Only been here about a year. Let me fetch someone else that will probably know more about your quest. I'll be right back," he says, and jets up a set of stairs. About ten minutes later, he returns to us with a much older gentleman at his side.

"We've been waiting quite some time for you," the elderly man says. "I'm Sammy." We shake hands and exchange pleasantries. "Right this way." He leads us to the secretary. "I assume you have a key? Not that you really need it. I can open it for you. But if you don't have the key, I'm afraid I'll have to ask for some ID. This is a historical site, after all."

"Sure," I tell him. "That's perfectly fine." I show him the key, along with my ID as a gesture of trust. He inspects both the key and my license. Sammy nods with approval.

We stand in front of a lovely piece of furniture, a chain separating us from reaching it. I see three shelves inside the upper cabinets that are visible behind doors of diamond-shaped glass panes in a wooden lattice. The cabinets are full of books.

The cabinet doors under the open writing surface are solid wood, so I can't see what they hold. My gut tells me we're looking for one of the books in the top half anyway.

Standing at the corner near the secretary, Sammy unhooks the chain from the wall and waves us in. People start to gather, whisper, and take pictures. I suddenly feel like a rock star, especially when Sammy replaces the chain across, blocking the rest of the patrons from gaining access. He unlocks the glass doors to the cabinet and gestures for me to go ahead and pick a book.

"Which one do you think it is?" Clay asks. "There are a couple that are pretty thick."

"Well, the clue stated that we need to go to page three-thirty-three. Several of the books appear to have over three hundred pages. Let's start with the one all the way on the bottom right with the tan spine." I reach for it and it's heavy. I carefully hold it open over my left arm while I flip to page 333. I don't see anything written on the margins or hi-lighted. I look at Sammy and he smiles. He knows it's the wrong book.

"Here, let me have it, dear. Pick another one," Sammy tells me.

I hand him the book and he replaces it on the shelf as I turn my attention to Clay.

"The top red one?" we ask each other. As we laugh, Clay reaches for the book. He gives it to me and I proceed with turning to page 333.

CHAPTER 3

A N ENVELOPE NEARLY falls out of the pages before I even get there. I catch it at the edge and flip the book open to where it's been nestled for so long. I take the envelope and hand the book back to Sammy. The envelope is like a little package cushioned in my hands, like there's something soft inside. I open it and find a timeworn handkerchief. It's white, albeit a little yellowed, and edged in Battenberg lace. I don't recognize it. As I unfold it, I notice one corner that's nearly threadbare, no doubt used to ease someone's worries. I bet this handkerchief has dried many tears over many decades. Examining it further, I see that it's embroidered. It simply states, 'To Mitzi from Rita with Love.' It takes my breath away.

"Wow," I whisper.

"Your grandmother made that?" Clay asks.

"She must have. At the least, I bet she made the lace and I know she stitched the endearment. I've never had anything that my grandmother made. Everything was lost in her house fire. Cecilia has a small blanket Grams embroidered, but I don't have anything. This is super special."

"That's awesome, babe. I know you'll hold it close to your heart." I nod. "You ready to see the rest of the property? I'm itching to see inside that Pullman."

"Ahh," Sammy interjects. "The Pullman. One of our most popular attractions. It's grand."

"Oh, Sammy," I say as I turn to him. "Thank you so much for allowing us access back here and letting me hold the books to look for this memento."

"No need to thank me. The Santinis set this up for you. Years ago. I'm assuming your presence here means they've passed away."

"Yes. Uncle Sid a few years ago, and Aunt Mitzi just last month. How did they come to leave the handkerchief here?" I ask.

"I was here the day they came to Hildene," Sammy says. "Was working the floor back then. They took the tour, spoke with a few higher-ups about what they wanted to do, and after a hefty donation, they were granted permission to leave the item in the book. They fell in love with Hildene. Who wouldn't? And they wanted to make sure you and Clay experienced it as well. And, speaking of the Pullman, that's something you'll get to see that they didn't. Sunbeam didn't come to us until the year twenty-eleven. Long after Mr. and Mrs. Santini visited."

"That's a great story," I tell Sammy. "Thank you for telling us all of that. I'm so glad you were here and that you remember them."

"I remember them well. Such a nice couple."

"Yes, they were," I say.

"I was delighted by the look on your face upon seeing the handkerchief. Mrs. Santini told me you'd love it and that it would be dear to you."

"It definitely is."

Clay claps his hands and rubs them together. "Can you point us to the Pullman?"

"Of course. There should be a tram along any minute now that will take you there. It was a pleasure meeting you both. Enjoy the rest of your day."

"Thank you. And thanks again for everything," I tell him.

"Yes, thanks a million," Clay says.

"You bet."

Clay shakes Sammy's hand and I give him a hug. Sammy unhooks the chains and we step into the small crowd that has gathered. As we go outside and head to the Pullman, Sammy gingerly locks the secretary back up.

Clay and I make our way to the Pullman via the tram that Sammy mentioned. Sunbeam has been exquisitely restored. The interior is lavish, bathed in what appears to be rich dark walnut. It's some of the shiniest wood I think I've ever seen. I bet the inside of this car is polished daily. The transoms above the passenger windows and the clerestory windows above the pull-down berths are made of stained glass in light colors of yellow, green, and cream. The sleeper beds are quite large, and I'm surprised of the extravagance of everything. This railcar is over a hundred years old, and yet, still very luxurious.

"Babe," Clay says to me after taking everything in. "We should take a train trip one day. I think ever since we visited the B&O Railroad Museum in Baltimore, and now this Pullman, I've become more fascinated with trains. I mean, I've always liked trains. I had train sets when I was a kid and played around with building the tracks up with my dad and Stone. But something about seeing all these cars, up close and personal, I want to experience this other kind of venture with you."

"Add it to our bucket list," I tell him. "After we recover from this cross-country expedition, we'll look into it. It sounds fun."

We tour the rest of the grounds, including a restored schoolhouse that's nearly two hundred years old.

There's the observatory I pretend to know nothing about, not wanting to bring up the hot guy from earlier. I take special care not to say anything to Clay about the flirtatious man wanting to escort me here. No need to worry my husband unnecessarily. Moving on.

A school group looks through a glass-walled beehive, as a docent educates them about the life cycle of bees. He mentions that the Hildene staff collects the honey from the bees and sells it in their gift shop. I'll have to remember to buy some.

So much to see. We mosey over to Hildene's Nubian goat farm.

"Aww, Clay, aren't the goats precious?"

"Sure. Except for having Satan's eyeballs."

I smack him lightly. We continue walking through the stables. "Look how cute this black and brown goat is, with its pretty golden eyes."

"Golden eyes of Satan."

The goat stands up on a bale of hay inside its pen and lets out a bleat. I swear it sounded like it said my name. "Did you hear that, Clay? It said 'L-eh-eh-eh-nnn.'"

"You're damned."

Clay and I laugh. When the goat 'says' it again, I go up to it. "It just wants some attention." I give the goat a few pets on its head.

"Great. Now you're damning your soul to hellfire for eternity."

I can't help but crack up at that. "The sweet thing likes it. It looks like it's smiling at me."

"Of course it is. It just captured another unsuspecting soul for its dark master."

I laugh and shake my head. "You watch too many scary movies."

"No such thing."

My eyes wander to the nameplate on the wall of the pen and I freeze. I can't believe it. "Oh my God, Clay. Her name is Mitzi. What are the odds? Maybe she really did say my name. Maybe this is Aunt Mitzi in spirit animal form," I chuckle.

"Jesus, I hope not. Let's get the hell out of here. Literally. It's creeping me out."

"What? I didn't think anything could creep you out. You watch and read so much horror and scary stuff."

"All fiction. This weird goat coincidence is too much."

"You're such a goofball." I take a picture of Mitzi the goat and we walk on.

There's still so much to see, but I'm growing a bit tired. We could easily spend a second day here walking the trails. We decide to wrap up our time at Hildene for now and make our way to the gift shop. I'm thrilled to see that there's an ornament of the Pullman car. I show it to Clay with a smile on my face.

Clay scans the rack. "You mean there are no ornaments of inverted pentagrams showing the demon lord Baphomet? I can't believe you find Satan's minions so cute."

I nudge him and roll my eyes as I put the ornament into my basket. I also get a pack of postcards and some of the goat cheese made onsite with the goats' milk. I add some fresh honey and maple syrup to my lot of goods. The syrup is also made at Hildene, with the sap collected straight from the Maple trees on the property.

"You about ready to check out, love?"

"Yeah, almost. I just want to look at their books on President Lincoln."

"Okay. If there's one about him being a vampire hunter, buy it for me," Clay says, poking fun at the movie released a few years ago with the same ridiculous theme. I actually enjoyed the movie though, crazy as the premise is. And it wasn't really scary, so I was able to watch it without putting my hands over my face and peeking through my fingers.

"Sure thing." I walk towards the books and pick one of several biographies for sale, then head to the cashier and check out. "I'm getting hungry," I tell Clay. "We can grab a bite on the way to our next destination, wherever that is."

I hand Clay one of the bags to carry and he walks ahead of me. As I start to exit the gift shop, there's a tap on my shoulder.

"You dropped this," a low voice says.

I turn. It's the gorgeous guy from earlier. The hairs on the back of my neck stand up.

CHAPTER 4

THE FAMILIAR STRANGER hands me a five-dollar bill. That's funny, I didn't pay with cash, but I suppose it could have fallen out of my wallet without me noticing.

"Oh. Thank you," I tell him. Clay turns around upon hearing my voice that's not directed at him and starts walking back towards me. I don't let on that this is the guy from earlier.

"What's wrong, Lynn?" Clay asks as he eyes the dude up and down. He even bows up a little bit.

"Nothing. Apparently, I dropped this money and this guy saw and gave it back to me."

"Nice of you," he tells the man. "Thanks. Come on, babe. Let's go."

The guy looks at Clay from head to toe, like he's evaluating him, and then does the same thing to me. Weird. "Did you enjoy the tour?" he asks as we start to leave.

Oh no. Don't give yourself away, Lynn. Clay will have a shit-fit if he knows this is the man that was hitting on me a couple of hours ago. "Yes, it was great," I say.

Clay puts his arm around me and ushers me out, a bit on the hasty side. "I don't like that guy," he says once we're outside.

"What? He was nice. He gave me my money back."

"He was undressing you with his eyes."

"You're crazy. You're the one he was scanning up and down. He's probably gay." He's probably not.

"Lynn, I think I know the difference between the look of a guy sizing me up and the look of him wanting to get into your pants and…is that the guy who you said was flirting with you earlier?" Oh shit. "Never mind. We're leaving, so it's over and done with."

Thank God. "Then, we're dropping this right? Forgetting all about it?" Please.

"About what?" He smiles as we make it back to the truck and he opens my door.

I smile back at him. Whew, that was close. I am not in the mood for a fight.

Clay puts the bags with my souvenirs in the back seat and rearranges a few things. I get settled in the front and look back towards the gift shop. The man is there, right outside the door, looking in our direction as he lights a cigarette. He sees me and waves. I look away and dig out the number twenty keychain. Clay climbs into the driver's seat and situates himself behind the wheel.

"We have another coin. This one is a quarter. A bicentennial quarter."

"Hmm. I bet we're headed to Philly," Clay says.

"Probably so." I get the list of clues out of my purse. "Ready?" I ask.

"Lay it on me."

I clear my throat. "Ahem. 'In the city where our country became unto itself, the salvage of Carpenter has many a shelf. Go inside, and take a gander, there's much to see as you meander. Look for an object innate to a pachyderm. Inside at the bottom, a thing for a worm.' Well, I'm at a loss. Except for the Philadelphia part. A pachyderm? Isn't that an elephant?"

"It can be. Or a hippo or rhino. It means 'thick skin.'"

"And something for a worm? What do you make of the rest?"

"I'm not sure about the worm part. But I think we're looking for a trunk. Since trunks are a fundamental part of elephants."

"Ah. Yes, that has to be it. Or maybe it's a grand piano with ivory keys."

"Hmm…possibly. Could be a tusk." Then he starts quoting and acting like Groucho Marx, mumbling about how in Alabama, the 'Tuscaloosa,' but that it's entirely 'irrelephant.'

"Let's just keep going, Captain Spaulding."

He grins at me. "Proud of you, babe. You got the right character," he says, thankfully in his normal voice.

"That would have been funny if we were actually in Alabama."

"That's funny no matter where you are."

"Can we just get back to the clue, please?"

"Okay, what's the part about a carpenter?" he asks.

"She says 'the salvage of Carpenter has many a shelf.' So, what's that mean? The 'C' in Carpenter is capitalized."

"Okay, so maybe it's a shelf inside somebody's garage with the surname of Carpenter?"

"No, I don't buy it. That's sending us on a wild goose chase. To go around Philly knocking on the doors of everybody named Carpenter, asking if we can look in their garage? What else you got?"

"You're probably right. That's too broad. Let's try to think of some other things that are capitalized, besides people's names. Businesses…monuments… titles…"

"Street names," I add.

"Ooh. Yeah. Street names. That's good. Let's start there."

"Alright, so what do I search for? Carpenter Street Garage? Maybe it's an auto repair shop? The trunk of a car?"

"Maybe," Clay says. "But we already found something in the trunk of a car. Aunt Mitzi's Bible in Tallahassee. Do you think she'd repeat types of places for us to find her treasures?"

"She hasn't so far. We can't rule it out though."

"But there's another key word she mentioned. Aunt Mitzi specifically said 'salvage' like it's debris, or something reclaimed."

"So, like a junkyard?"

"Not exactly. It might be some sort of restoration place, especially if we're looking for a trunk. Look for a salvage yard on Carpenter Street in Philly and see what you come up with."

I do. "There is a place called Philadelphia Salvage Company. But it's not on Carpenter. Should we just go there?"

"Hmm. Try—"

"Oh wait. Scrolling down, I see a magazine article that says they got too big for their shop on Carpenter and had to expand. So that must be it." I show Clay the address and he punches it into the GPS.

He starts the truck and I watch beautiful Hildene recede in our rearview mirror.

"Nice sleuthin', babe. Off to the City of Brotherly Love."

"Can we go by and see the Liberty Bell while we're there? And tour Independence Hall?"

"Sure. I'll trade you that for the Rocky statue." He starts singing "Eye of the Tiger" by Survivor, punching the air in front of him, like he's Rocky Balboa himself.

"Cheralynnnnn," he yells my full name out in a slurred voice, just like Sylvester Stallone. I crack up laughing.

Clay's phone rings. It's Stone.

"Huh. Speaking of 'brotherly love…' Wonder what he wants." He pushes the button on his steering wheel and answers the call. "What's up, bro?" Clay asks.

Stone's voice fills the cab. "Hey, man. Just checkin' in on y'all. How's it goin'? You found that Brougham yet? I'm dying to get my hands on that baby."

"No, not yet," Clay tells him. "I did find out that it's somewhere in the Midwest though. I promise when we find her, I'll let you know. Now, why are you really calling? You're not the type to just 'check in,' dude. What's going on?"

"Are you alone?" he asks. "Or can Lynn hear me?"

Clay looks at me and puts his finger over his lips, signaling me to be quiet. I give him the universal sign that I understand by 'zipping' my mouth shut.

"Don't worry, man. You're good. Go ahead. What is it?"

"Dude. I'm freaking out over Annie."

"What? Why? How? I thought things were going hot and heavy."

And now I'm the one who's freaking out. Annie is going to be devastated if he breaks things off with her. Shit.

"Yeah, 'hot and heavy' is a good way to put it. Wait, how would you know?"

"Do you really have to ask? My wife is Annie's best friend. You know that. You don't think they talk about that shit?" Clay grinned. Even over the phone, I can picture Stone blushing. "Don't worry, you got a good review. Apparently, we Sinclair boys are excellent lovers."

"I know I'm a good lay. You don't have to tell me."

"So why are you freaking out?"

"Her birthday's coming up and I don't know what to get her. It's too soon for something like jewelry. But I don't want to fuck it up with something stupid like a coffee mug."

"How about a bejeweled coffee mug?" Clay jibes.

"Cut the shit. I'm really sweating this." He half laughs. "This is a first, huh? Me coming to you for chick advice instead of the other way around? I've been out of the dating game for so fucking long. What do women want? What do they like?"

"Well, let's see…they like long walks on the beach, gelato, anything with Ryan Reynolds…"

"Fuck you. I'm being serious."

"Dude. Get a grip, man. Are you seriously stressing over this shit? Why didn't you just call Lynn? She knows Annie better than anybody. Let me get her."

"No, no, no, don't. I don't want her to know I'm losing my cool."

Clay cracks up laughing. I put my hand over my mouth to keep from releasing my own laughter. "Losing your cool? What are we, in high school, Fonzie?"

"Fuck you, man! It feels like fucking high school."

"Why don't you make her a mix tape then? Maybe Lynn will let you borrow her Lionel Richie CDs."

"Got dammit, Clay. Stop being such a dickbag. I'm telling you, this is making me nervous as fuck."

I, however, am smiling ear to ear. This is greatness. Stone really likes Annie. I've never heard him act like this. I get my pen and notebook out and scribble down a couple of ideas Clay can give Stone for Annie's birthday present.

"I get it. You're falling for her."

"What? No way, not this soon. Daisy and I have only been divorced for six months. I mean, yeah, I like her. A lot. But I wouldn't say I'm falling for her just yet."

Clay looks at my notebook and gives me a thumbs up sign.

"Right. Sure. Whatever, man. Look, just get her a book of poetry or something. Chicks dig that shit. Lynn likes Emily Dickinson, so I bet Annie does too. Or find out who her favorite author is or favorite book and buy a first edition. That could set you back though. I don't know how much you want to spend."

"Jesus, why didn't I think of that? Fucking poetry. Of course. Soft kitty, cotton candy, mushy sappy, fucking chick flick shit. Thanks, man."

"'Ayyy," Clay says, in his best Fonzie impersonation. "No sweat, daddio."

"Asshole." Click.

And with that, the both of us laugh hysterically for about five minutes.

"Oh my God, that was so funny," I say. "The mix tape suggestion was perfect. I thought I was gonna lose it right then and get you busted."

"Who cares? I'm sure he knows I would have told you anyway. But for real, don't you dare say anything to Annie."

"Never. I want her to be genuinely surprised when she gets her bedazzled coffee mug. Seriously though, I hope he gets it right."

"He will. And if he gets any more confused, he'll probably just straight-up call you since I was apparently such a dickbag asshole to him."

"Classic brotherly banter. I don't think I've ever heard the two of you talk back and forth like that to each other. So much cursing and name calling."

"Yeah, well, you weren't supposed to be listening, remember? That was mild compared to some of our past conversations. Arguments. Fights."

"I can only imagine."

"So," Clay says in a subject changing tone, "we've got about six hours till Philly. It's my turn for the radio, right?"

"Yep. Whatcha got?"

"Well, let's see. Anything could pop up. Whatever it is though, it'll be good."

He presses the music on his phone and "Thunder" by Imagine Dragons starts playing.

"Oh, you're right," I say. "That is a good one."

CHAPTER 5

THE NEXT MORNING, we drive through the Hunting Park neighborhood of Philadelphia and into the section of Nicetown-Tioga. We pull up to the salvage yard, where there is not much room for parking. We find a place in the driveway of an abandoned building across the street.

The Philadelphia Salvage Company building must be at least a hundred years old, but the rust-colored bricks don't give it away. It's in very good shape, save a few broken windows near the roof. Painted on the side wall at the top is a previous business' name, though it's been chipped away by weather and time. I can barely make out the words 'bronze' and 'aluminum.' I bet it was once a foundry for those metals. This place has so much character. I love it already.

My eyes wander around the outside of the building. The yard is divvied into sections of reclaimed lumber, sinks, bathtubs (many of them claw-foot), doors, columns, church pews, piles of bricks…all of it saved from demolished buildings. The yard has a dusty smell of tar paper, copper, and old wood.

Clay and I walk in and it's more of the same. The tang of Brasso, turpentine, polyurethane, and ammonia mix in with the construction air of the yard. Everything has been rescued by the owners of the salvage company who are helping the items find new homes.

Beautiful glass doorknobs glint from bins of galvanized tin, reflected by ornate mirrors. Overhead, a canopy of fancy light fixtures illuminates cabinets, desks, shelves, and furniture, to the buzz of neon signs. Antique iceboxes flank a vintage Chromaray color energy therapy machine, a crazy medical device from the 1930s that looks like a heavy spotlight on wheels, with thick panes of interchangeable colored glass filters. Need to cleanse your aura? Look no further.

I could easily spend the day here checking out all the exquisite salvage. Ideas float in my head. Some of this stuff would be best used back home in my art projects.

Clay and I look around for a trunk. No idea what kind it is. It could be a vintage wooden steamer trunk of leather or cardboard panels reinforced with metal and leather at the seams. Or it might be one like I took to summer camp when I was ten: a big enamel box with chrome buckles and latches.

Aisle after aisle of shelves crammed with prodigious relics that I would love to snatch up for myself. Mental notes are planted on several pieces as we walk through the rows. What I could do with that stack of old doors and shutters…so much potential. Not to mention the entire section of antique crates and barrels. Most of the crates (which once held fruits of grapes, pears, apples, and peaches) still have their colorful labels applied, although they are somewhat faded and peeling around the edges.

From the corner of my eye, I spy a trunk resting near a row of stained-glass windows hanging on the wall. I nudge Clay.

"Sweet," he says. "Let's check it out. You got the key?"

"Right here." I tap my pocket as we walk over to the chest. But then we see that this isn't the only trunk here. We've merely reached the trunk *section* of the shop. There must be at least fifty of them.

"Whoa," Clay says. "It looks like the warehouse at the end of *Raiders of the Lost Ark*," he laughs.

"This could take a while. We can't even eliminate any since the brand name on the key has been worn off through the years." I can't help but sigh.

"Might not take as long as you think. I bet most of them don't even have keys and are already unlocked. So, I'll start on the other end and check to see if any of them are open. I'll raise the lids of the ones that are, so you'll be able to see. You start here and look for the ones that are secured. We'll cover more ground that way. Let's start poppin' some trunks, babe."

"Okay. Good plan."

Clay walks to the space catty-corner from where I am. I crouch down at the trunk in front of me and the key doesn't work. I scoot to the next one and can see that it's already open, so I move down again. This one is locked, but the key fails again: not the one we're looking for. I see Clay lifting the lids of all the trunks that he can.

After about a dozen more trials, I come to a trunk with a 'Not for Sale' sign on it that seems to shine. In my gut, I know this is it. It's beautiful, leather-bound, wooden, and dome topped. A steamer trunk—the kind that looks like a big treasure chest. It has dull brass dowels, latches, and corners. The handles are made of leather. The trunk is not in the best condition, as some of the wood has cracked and is peeling away. All the straps are missing, but some of the slats remain. It's a gorgeous piece even if a little worse for the wear. It's in good shape for as old as it probably is. And it would be just like Aunt Mitzi to leave us something in a trunk that looks like a treasure chest.

I insert the key into the lock. With a twist of my wrist, it clicks. A smile crosses my face. "Clay!"

Clay looks to me, and after seeing my expression, he bounds over in long strides, closing the lids of all the trunks he'd opened. "You found it. I knew you would. Nice job."

"Okay, here we go." I lift the heavy lid and the inside is in near mint condition. The tray is here, as well as the hat box and its cover. The lithographs typically embedded in the compartment lids are missing, but the floral border is still intact. I'm shocked at how well it's been kept.

A staff member comes to check on us and asks if we're interested in the trunk. I tell him that we're just looking and if we decide to buy it, we'll let him know. He gives me his card and returns to sorting sink fixtures.

I lift the lid to the hat box, wondering if we're going to find our prize under it, but there's nothing.

"You want me to take the tray out?" Clay asks.

"Yes please."

Clay lifts the tray and I see what we're here for. 'A thing for a worm.'

Chapter 6

"Oh wow, Clay. Check it out." I pick up the item. It's a book. But not just any book.

"A cookbook," Clay says. "I get it now. Bookworm."

I read the title out loud, with pride. "'*Chauvin Family Recipes: Foods for Your Holiday Table and Then Some.*' I've heard about this family cookbook, but I don't remember ever seeing one. I'd asked Mom about it before because I knew she used to have one when I was a toddler. She said it fell apart and told me that one of her housekeepers threw it away, thinking all the loose papers were trash. She was so mad. I'm glad we have one now."

The book is about an inch thick, spiral bound, and has a line drawing of the same family tree that's on the quilt we got from the old house in South Carolina. I take a photo of the book cover and text it to Mom. She'll be so happy we have one in the family again.

"Hey, I wonder if Aunt Mitzi's long-lost strawberry pie recipe is in here," Clay says.

"I bet it is. I'll look through it when we get back on the road. Right now, though, I want to look around some more at all the fantastic pieces in this place and reclaim some for myself. Is that okay with you?"

"Of course. What do you have in mind for these 'fantastic pieces'?" I can tell by his tone of voice that Clay is leery of the vision-lust in my eyes.

"Who knows? There's so much promise. An inconceivable amount of art to be crafted. Canvas everywhere you look. I'm definitely snagging some of those glass doorknobs. Maybe some old marquis letters I saw a few rows back, a couple of those ancient card catalog drawers, a handful of drawer pulls, and whatever else I fancy."

Clay laughs. "Well, you can never have enough card catalog drawers. We certainly don't want our stack of library cards left uncatalogued, do we? Just how fancy can you get with the Dewey Decimal System?" He starts singing Iggy Azalea's "Fancy."

I playfully shove him in the arm and join him in song. "I'll find something to do with them. They're just so retro, you know? I love them. Love the nostalgia."

"Don't go crazy," he says. "The back seat is nearly stuffed, and the bed is a quarter full. We still have thirty states to go."

"Clay, look around. This warehouse is an artist's dream. I bet they ship. But don't worry, I won't get a heavy load."

"I'll give you a heavy load," he grins.

"You and your innuendoes. Lord, help me."

"Hey, speaking of heavy loads," he says with a wink, "can we get that discarded 'Hooters' sign?" He points towards the door that leads outside where a bunch of old retail signs lean against a fence.

"Let me think about it. No."

"Come on, Lynn. It'll go great in my—"

"It's too big."

"That's what she said."

"Baby Jesus, give me strength," I say, trying to hold back a smile.

"I'm just screwing with you. I know we don't have room in the truck for it, obviously. But you said they probably ship, right?" I roll my eyes and walk ahead of him. "It would be really cool to have though. Total badass addition to my future den of seclusion."

I spin around. "I'm sorry…your what?"

"My den of seclusion. You know, like a man cave."

"Why didn't you just say, 'man cave'?"

"Because everybody has a man cave. Nobody that I know of has a den of seclusion. Plus, it sounds classier."

"Nothing classes up a place like an old sign from a titty restaurant."

"Touché," he laughs. "You'll never even see it. The den of seclusion will be like my clubhouse, where no girls are allowed."

I laugh at his childish description. "You join the He-Man Woman-Haters Club? Bringing *The Little Rascals* back together, are ya? Give my regards to Spanky and Buckwheat."

He snickers. "Both are no longer with us, sadly. Looks like it'll just be me and my buds."

"So tell me, what'll go on in this tower of testosterone?"

"You know, guy stuff. But, you're always welcome to bring us cookies and lemonade in your bikini," he says with a laugh.

"I thought there were no girls allowed."

"Grown-ass women bearing snacks in bikinis are welcome. Always." He raises his eyebrows up and down.

"You can be such a caveman sometimes, Sinclair. Especially when it's just you and Stone together, which I know it will be, rebuilding that Brougham in your female-free fortress. You two are a couple of Neanderthals. Annie and I will make ourselves scarce while y'all scratch, burp, and spit. I'll make my own diva domain, lady lair, chick chamber, or whatever I decide to call it."

"Woman, the entire house is your diva domain."

"You got me there, so touché back atcha."

He smiles. "Your lady lair is another story though. That's for me. Only me."

"What?" I crinkle my brow at him in confusion and he looks down at my crotch. I burst out laughing. That was actually funny.

"Come on," he laughs. "Let's go find you some artsy stuff and get back to the truck."

A few decorative doorknockers, gorgeous glass tiles, antique buttons, and other random items later, we head back out to the truck.

"Wait a second," Clay says. "You can have knockers, but I don't get my Hooters sign? That's just not fair."

I roll my eyes. "Goofball," I mumble under my breath, but loud enough for Clay to hear.

Clay laughs. "Where to now? Independence Hall or the Rocky statue?"

"Let's do the statue. That won't take long and then we can take our time at the museum without you rushing me to get to the statue."

"I would never do that," he says with a sly grin.

"Bullcrap. Drive." I shake my head at him.

Clay and I make it to the Philadelphia Museum of Art, where the Rocky statue stands. Of course, Clay does the whole song and dance of running up the stone steps, 'training' as a boxer getting ready for the fight of his life. I thought people would stare at Clay's antics, but then I noticed about half the people there are middle-aged men running up the steps, punching the air, and humming the Rocky theme song, "Gonna Fly Now." We take a couple of pictures by the bronze monument of Sylvester Stallone's Rocky Balboa. It's an exciting moment for Clay, *Rocky* being his all-time favorite movie.

Having been lucky enough to get tickets to Independence Hall, which I didn't even know were only available first-come, first-served, we head over to the esteemed building where the Declaration of Independence was signed. Clay and I revel in some of the most profound aspects of our nation's history. One of my favorite things to see was the Rising Sun chair, the only piece of original furniture that remains in Independence Hall today. It's a high-back chair with a gilded sun carved at the top. I also loved the beautiful silver Syng inkstand, used to sign the Declaration of Independence and the Constitution. Another surreal moment for the Sinclairs.

We browse the visitor center's gift shop and Clay buys a pewter Rocky statue. It's a foot tall and he says it'll go great in his estrogen-free zone at home. There are several Christmas ornaments to choose from, but I can't make up my mind, as usual. Clay finds a keychain with both the Liberty Bell and Philadelphia's LOVE sculpture that I can make into an ornament instead.

After wrapping up at Independence Hall, we walk over to the real Liberty Bell for some more history lessons and photo ops.

Back in the truck, Clay wants to know the next clue. "Okay, babe. What does the next keychain look like?"

Sifting through the box of keys, I find number twenty-one. "It's a picture of a cardinal."

"Cool. You think we're going to St. Louis? Maybe it's a key to a locker in Busch Stadium."

"Good guess, but I doubt it. Missouri is too far east from where we are. We'd have to skip over too many states. Plus, the key is too small. May be for another diary."

"Okay. What's the clue say?"

I grab the clue sheet from my purse and read it. "You listening? Here we go. 'The town where Mary Lou Retton is a native, is where we had to get creative. One Type roasts on an open fire. Another? The second word of the band that sang Elvira.' Well, not sure what any of that has to do with cardinals, but we have—"

"Wait. What? Was there a question in there?"

"Yeah. 'Another?' But is she asking us for something or telling us that the last part of the clue is the other half of the preceding line? Am I making any sense?"

"Yeah, I think so."

"Also, the word 'type' is capitalized."

"Okay, let's break it apart. First of all, I don't think any of that has to do with cardinals. I bet the cardinal is the state bird of whatever state we're going to next."

"You're probably right."

"So, you can search for that or look up where Mary Lou Retton is from. I had a crush on her, by the way," Clay says with a smile.

I smile back at him as I look up her birthplace. "I'm guessing that was about the same time I had a crush on Mitch Gaylord."

"Well, look at us. A couple of gold medalist gymnast crusher-on-ers," he laughs.

"Yeah, how 'bout that? I'm sure we weren't the only ones. Okay, here it is. Fairmont, West Virginia. Now, I'm sure we can agree about a type that roasts on an open fire would be a chestnut. Right?"

"It would appear so. And the Oak Ridge Boys sang 'Elvira,' so we have something with a chestnut ridge in Fairmont, West Virginia."

"Dang it. How did you know about the Oak Ridge Boys? I was sure that was gonna stump you and I would look like a genius, figuring out the clue. Hmph!"

"Hey, just because country music's not my thing, doesn't mean I don't know it. I'm just disappointed that we don't get to meet the smokin' hot Cassandra Peterson."

"Sorry. Wrong Elvira. I don't blame you though. If I were a guy…" I trail off.

"Oooh, you get a lady boner for the 'Mistress of the Dark'? That's hot, babe."

"I'm just saying, I can appreciate her sex appeal, even when she's not dressed as Elvira. She's a gorgeous redhead."

"Dang right." He smiles and nods his head, then looks at me and clears his throat. "She ain't got nuttin' on you though."

"Nice save."

Clay laughs. "Anyway, my parents had that freaking Oak Ridge Boys record on all the time. *All the time*! It burrowed into my brain. But I must admit, it's a catchy tune." He starts singing the deep voiced part of the chorus and I crack up laughing at him. It's just so out of character for Clay.

After I catch my breath, I look up chestnut ridge in Fairmont, West Virginia. "Ah. Now I see why the word 'type' was capitalized. We're going to the Chestnut Ridge Typewriter Museum."

"Finally. Sounds like a qwerty cool place." He laughs at his pun as I roll my eyes. "How far are we from the museum?"

I pull up directions on my phone. "It's a little over five hours away. Too far to drive today. Let me see what might be on the way where we can stop." I zoom in on the map and I see not one, but two places to go. "Clay, you're gonna love this."

"What is it?"

"Intercourse."

"Yes, let's do it."

"No, goofball. Intercourse, Pennsylvania. I've heard about that little town. We're so close, we might as well stop and at least take a picture of the sign for the fun of it, right? Plus, it's Amish country. I've always wanted to go to an Amish settlement and see how they live. It's fascinating. And,

I bet there's an authentic general store where we can pick up some home-made goods."

"Sounds great, love. But now I can't stop thinking about intercourse."

"Well, it's not far, only like an hour."

"No, I mean intercourse with you."

I whack him with the clue sheet, and he starts the truck with a laugh.

We drive the hour to Intercourse, and I take a snapshot of the welcome sign.

"See? It says so right there. We're welcomed to intercourse," Clay muses.

"You're terrible."

"That's not what you said last night."

"Jeez." I roll my eyes and shake my head at him.

"As a matter of fact, I think your exact words were—"

"I know what I said."

"Really? Because that was a first. You never talk like that when we're—"

"You took me to another level…that's where that came from."

"So…not terrible then?"

"Far from terrible." I wink at him.

We drive around town and come to the Kitchen Kettle Village. There are tons of quaint little shops. We walk around for a while and almost every store we go into has something to taste: jams, relishes, balsamic vinegars, olive oils, wines, cheeses, fudge, cured meats, and more. I buy some of the fig balsamic jam, Amish butter cheese, and cured bacon, while Clay chooses a few kinds of exotic jerky and beef sticks.

"Ostrich and kangaroo? Are you serious?" I ask him.

"I'll try anything once."

"How is that not illegal?" I ask with a slight smile.

"Beats me. Guess they're not endangered. Wonder how the Amish have access to all those wild animals."

"I don't think everything in this shopping village is made by the Amish. Just some of the stuff. They got any 'gator jerky?"

"Hell yeah. Already had that before though, so don't need to buy any."

"What about nutria?"

"Not that I saw. Hold up. You'd eat nutria rat?"

"No." I make a yuck face. "I don't care how 'so-ugly-they're-cute' they are. I was just curious."

"I didn't think you would eat that. You know, back home they'll pay you five bucks a tail for those invasive rodents. They're eating up all the plants that hold our marshes together."

"Yeah, I heard about that. Maybe you and Stone can rent an airboat and do your part in saving our state's coastline."

"Hmm…maybe so. Killin' rats and savin' Louisiana's wetlands. Win, win."

"Hey, Clay?"

"Yeah?"

"You feel like something sweet?"

"We finally gonna have intercourse?" He winks at me.

"No. Ice cream." I point across the way to an ice cream shop.

"Ooh, that sounds perfect right about now."

"Good. I hope they have peppermint stick."

"It's just called peppermint, Lynn."

"Whatever. Let's go."

We're getting our fill of some of the most delicious ice cream I've ever eaten, made with milk from a local dairy. They didn't have peppermint stick, or 'just peppermint' or what-the-hell-ever you call it, as Clay so sarcastically pointed out, so I chose the next best thing: mint chocolate chip. Clay got homemade strawberry. After our treat, we mosey back to the truck and put our goods away.

"Where to now?" Clay asks.

"Well, we've still got some daylight left. There's one more place I want to go before we head to Fairmont. But it's slightly out-of-the-way."

"Do tell."

"Let's spend the night in Hershey. Won't that be fun? It's less than an hour from here."

"Sure, babe, whatever you want. I could use a good chocolate fix."

"Sweet. Wait, why didn't you get chocolate ice cream then?"

"Because homemade strawberry is way better."

"Ah. Agreed."

"Are there any songs we can listen to about chocolate? I mean, that aren't kid songs?" Clay asks.

"I'm sure there are. Um…" I rack my brain trying to think of one.

"How about 'Candy Man' by Sammy Davis, Junior?"

"Nah. Not in the mood for the Rat Pack today."

"You sure aren't. First you say 'no' to nutria and now you're turning down Sammy, Frank, Dean, and that other guy nobody can ever remember."

I laugh. "Okay, the only song that pops into my head is 'You Sexy Thing' by Hot Chocolate. Probably not exactly what you're looking for."

"But it's perfect, considering the name of the town we're in," he says, as we head towards the exit of Intercourse. "Play it."

So I do. Clay rolls down the windows and cranks up the music. We're singing along at the top of our lungs like crazy people as we stop at a light next to an Amish family in their horse-drawn carriage waiting to turn left. The father, a lanky man with a graying chin curtain beard, surprises us by belting out how he believes in miracles, right at the appropriate time in the song.

His kids giggle and his much younger-looking wife gives him a disapproving look from beneath her white bonnet. "Just witnessing for the Lord," he tells her. "Do you not believe in miracles, Mother?" He winks in our direction. That's the icing on the cake for our day.

"He must have had quite the rumspringa," Clay says as the light turns green and we pull away.

Once we get to Hershey, Clay and I get a kick out of the streetlights. They are all topped with giant Hershey's Kisses. Super cute.

Clay voices his reservations. "I keep thinking a bunch of Oompa Loompas are going to jump out and sing a song about my biggest character flaw."

I laugh. "Don't be ridiculous, babe. That's the wrong chocolate bar, so you're safe."

We check into the beautiful and historic Hotel Hershey, which is situated on a hilltop overlooking the town. Its architectural style boasts Spanish and Italian characteristics, with mosaic tiles and arched doorways.

After we settle in, Clay and I have some of the best chocolate desserts and martinis after our delicious dinner at the Trevi 5 restaurant on site.

"I've never been one for chocolate martinis," Clay tells me, licking some intoxicating chocolate from his upper lip, "but, when in Rome, right?"

"Hits the spot, doesn't it?"

"That it does."

Now, as Clay is sleeping next to me, I'm lying in bed reading the local tourist magazine. I see an attraction that's not too far from here, a place I've always wanted to visit, and not at all off our course. I'll tell Clay in the morning.

CHAPTER 7

MY EYES OPEN. I check the time. It's almost eight in the morning. I hate waking up five minutes before my alarm goes off. I lose the grip on my phone and it falls to the floor. "Shit," I whisper as I reach to pick it up. I feel Clay stir. He stretches and lets out a loud grunt.

I turn my head back to look at him over my shoulder while I disable the alarm on my phone. "Hey, babe," I say, my voice thick with sleep.

"Mornin', love," he says.

"Didn't mean to wake you."

"Don't care that you did. What are you doing way over there?"

"Sorry, I just—"

"Your raspy morning voice makes me…" He wraps his arm around my waist and pulls me into him. "Hard." He emphasizes his last word with a push into my backside. Jesus.

"Well. Good morning."

"Mmm. It is," he says into my ear, waking the rest of me up.

He reaches for my underwear and pulls them down to my knees. I grab them and throw them on the floor. He raises my tank top, exposing my breasts. Clay takes the tip of one into his mouth while his hand finds the other one. He positions himself on top of me and rips my shirt off over my head, tossing it over his shoulder. I pull the elastic on the waistband of his boxer-briefs and let it go, snapping him with it. He flinches and we laugh. After taking them off, he kisses down my belly and spreads my legs. When his mouth reaches my center, a long moan escapes from me. Minutes pass as Clay works wonders with his mouth, tongue, breath, and fingers. And when he lets out a moan of his own, the vibration of his voice right there sends me over the edge. It is definitely a good morning.

Clay works his way back up my body. "You okay, babe?" he whispers into my ear, sending tingles down my spine.

"Mmm hmm," I answer with my eyes closed.

He takes his time entering me, inch by precious inch. My limbs are so lax that I can barely wrap my legs around him. When he's finally all the way inside, he stays there, motionless.

"What are you doing? Or rather, not doing?" I ask with a smile, opening my eyes.

"I'm enjoying the feel of you." He slowly pulls back, almost voiding me completely of his length, then moves in again, just as slow as before. Languid thrusts. In. Out. In. Out. In.

"Mmmmm." My eyes close again.

"Oh god, Lynn. It's so good. I love being inside of you. You always feel so fucking good."

I open my eyes and meet his. "So do you."

"Yeah?" he smiles.

"Yeah."

His measured plunges continue. "God, I could do this all day, babe."

"I like it slow like this. It's nice."

"'Nice'? Just 'nice'?" he teases.

"Okay, delightful. Better?"

He snickers. "I'll see your 'delightful,' and raise you an 'unbelievable.' What do you think about that?"

"I'm all in. Bring it, Sinclair. Gimme all you got."

He picks up his pace, thrusting a bit faster now. His eyes are locked on mine and I can see how much he loves me. I rake my nails up his back. He shudders. "God, I love it when you do that." I smile and he speeds up. Wilder. Harder. Deeper. I give him some more fingernail action a few minutes later, followed by squeezing his tight chiseled ass. He's done for, letting his release go inside of me and bellowing out, "Fuuuuuck!" Panting, he collapses on my chest. "Shit. That was intense," he huffs. "I love the hell out of you. You know that?" He kisses my neck.

"Right back atcha, babe," I say, also trying to catch my breath. I kiss his temple.

He rolls off me and we lie there, holding hands, until our breathing stabilizes.

I look over at Clay and his eyes are closed. I wonder if he's fallen back to sleep.

"You awake?"

"Yeah." He opens his eyes and looks at me.

"I found another side trip for us. It's on the way to the typewriter museum."

"Cool. What is it?"

"Frank Lloyd Wright's Fallingwater."

"Seriously?"

"Seriously. You know how bad I've always wanted to tour it. I didn't realize it was around here."

"Me either. How far is it?"

"About three and a half hours. And then the museum is only about an hour from there. If we get an early start, we can finish the day in West Virginia."

"Alright. I'm going to make some coffee and then take a long, hot shower."

While Clay is in the shower, I think about my purchases from the salvage shop yesterday and imagine what I'll do with them once I get home. Remembering everything else we saw, and wishing we'd had room in the truck for so much more, an idea pops into my head. I make a phone call and then join Clay in the shower.

❦

I take out my phone and pick a playlist by giving it a swift scroll and stopping on one at random. My finger lands on the list entitled *Rap It Up*, and LL Cool J's "Going Back to Cali" starts.

I look over at my husband. With his freshly shaven face, sunglasses on, and his head bobbing to the music, I reflect on our life together and what led us here, to this moment. I feel like I know everything about him, but that can't possibly be true. Even after all these years together, I want to know more.

"Tell me something about you that I don't know," I tell Clay.

"What do you mean?"

"You know, the other day, when I told you about playing record execs and stuff. You thought that was funny, and never knew that about me. So, tell me something about you that I probably don't know. Or about you and Stone. Like something from when y'all were younger."

"Babe, there's nothing that exciting. Just the usual brother stuff. Fishing, camping out in the backyard, kicking each other's asses. There was this one time though, when we went hunting with Dad. I was about twelve I guess, so Stone would've been fourteen."

"Well, there's something already. I didn't know you liked to hunt."

"I don't."

"Why not?"

"Are you going to let me tell the story?"

"Sorry."

"So, we're—"

"What season was it?"

"Lynn."

"I'm sorry," I chuckle, "I'm just trying to picture the time of year. What the trees in the woods looked like, and how you're dressed. Long or short camo sleeves?"

"Long."

"So, deer season then?"

"Yeah. Okay. So—"

"Daylight or still dark?"

He sighs. "Daylight. About seven in the morning." His tone of voice changes like he's reading a story to a child. "There was a slight crisp in the air, and I could smell a campfire off in the distance beyond the horizon of a cloudy sky, with birds chirp-chirp-chirping all around. Any more questions?"

I give him a sarcastic look, knowing he totally made up that last part. "No, ass, but I can't promise I won't stop you again."

"Fair enough," he laughs. "Just let me get started."

"Fine. Proceed."

"So, anyway, you know, we're sitting in the deer stand, bored, freezing our asses off. And out of nowhere, this guy comes running past us from behind, freaking out, looking back. Something was obviously chasing him. I can still see him, like it was yesterday."

"Oh my God. Did he see y'all?" I turn the radio down. This is getting good.

"No. We were like, fifteen or twenty feet up in the stand. When we heard him running our way though, we thought it was a deer, and Dad whispered at us to be quiet. Then we saw that it was a young guy, in his twenties or so, with blonde hair, wearing a flannel shirt and faded jeans. Dad still told us to be quiet. The guy hid behind the biggest tree he could find. Dad got his gun ready to shoot whatever was chasing him. Then we heard another guy holler, 'I know you're out here, boy!' Dude had the thickest redneck accent I'd ever heard. 'You better hope I don't find you, you sum'bitch!' So then, the other guy comes scurrying past the deer stand, and I shit you not, he looked just like Bluto from *Popeye*."

"Oh crap." I'm hanging on to every word.

"Right? And he's got a gun. A hunting rifle, kind of like the one Dad had. But the man can barely move, he's so big. He's shuffling along, looking for the young guy. At this point, Dad made us sit on the floor of the deer stand so we couldn't see anything. He got down too but kept watch.

"Now, Bluto keeps on with his yelling for the young guy to show himself. I think it's just because he was too out of shape to be running around looking for him. The younger guy…I don't know his name either, so I'll call him Jack…so Jack had to have known that Bluto wasn't much for running, so Jack stayed put behind the big tree."

"How have I never heard this story, Clay?"

"I don't really like to talk about it."

"Oh. Well, then what happened?"

"Bluto finally catches sight of Jack behind the tree. 'I see you, boy!' he yelled, and Jack starts running again, so Bluto fires at him."

I gasp. "Oh shit! Did he kill him?"

"Bluto's a lousy shot. Hit a tree nearly ten yards from where Jack was. Bluto's still yelling. 'I'mma git you and hang you from a limb by yer balls, asshole! I done tole you, stay the fuck away from my sister!' Then he shot again. And missed again. He's running, barely, chasing Jack, stopping every few seconds to catch his breath and fire shots at him. He's bumbling along and gets tripped up over a cypress knee. We hear another gunshot, followed by a thud, and then silence."

I gasp again. "Oh my God. He hit Jack?"

"No. Shot himself right in the neck when he fumbled over the tree root. Killed himself instantly. Idiot was running with the barrel pointed up."

"Jesus."

"Obviously never had a firearms safety course. Anyway, at this point, Jack stops and turns around, since Bluto stopped yelling, and sees him laying on the ground. He darts over and stares at his dead body on the floor of the woods. Then he spits on him and runs off."

"Holy shit, that's awful. I don't know who I feel more sorry for. What did y'all do? Did you let Jack know you were there?"

"No. With us there, Dad didn't want to put us in the middle, in case Jack had a gun too. I doubt he did though, since he never fired back at Bluto. But I think Dad just didn't want us involved. We went home and Dad called the cops and made an anonymous tip. Told them the whole story of what he saw, and that Jack was innocent."

"You don't know who they were or what happened after that?"

"No. Dad told us not to ever say anything to anybody since he'd made an anonymous phone call to the police. It wasn't in any of our local newspapers or anything. I checked. I assume that's because we were at our camp in Mississippi. I asked Dad if he'd heard anything back at the camp, and he said he hadn't. It's like it happened in *The Twilight Zone* or something. Nobody knew anything about it. If Stone and Dad hadn't been there, I would think I'd dreamed it."

"Oh my God, Clay. No wonder you don't like hunting."

"Yeah. That was the last time I was in a deer stand. First time I've thought about that incident in years. Stone and I have mentioned it a couple of times since then, but never really talked about it."

"Wow. I'm sorry you've had to keep that in for so long."

Clay takes a deep breath. "Feels good to get it out to somebody else. Please don't bring it up to Stone though. Or tell Annie."

"I'd never. But damn, Clay. That is one crazy story."

Clay 'sings' the instrumental theme song to *The Twilight Zone.* "So, is that what you had in mind? For something you didn't know about me?"

"Not what I was expecting, that's for sure. I was thinking more along the lines of something fun and silly. But that will suffice. Thank you for trusting me with it." I give Clay a reassuring smile and he winks at me as he adjusts the volume on the radio, filling the cab with Run DMC's "It's Tricky."

We turn onto Fallingwater Road from Highway 381. The drive is beautiful, with blooming trees of star magnolia, dogwood, redbud, and crabapple, along with hints of their fragrant and sweet-smelling blossoms in the air. We park and walk about a quarter mile to the house. I'm getting giddy, imagining what it's going to be like inside. I've seen pictures of course, but this will be another surreal moment for me. I've always been fascinated with architecture and design styles, and this is one of the most famous houses in the country. Its cantilevered floors and prominent vertical and horizontal lines give the house its distinctive look, not to mention being built on top of a waterfall.

The tour takes us about two hours. I'm in awe the whole time. We're not allowed to take any pictures inside, but I take about a zillion outside. I can tell Clay is getting bored with my capturing so many different angles of the house.

"Okay, Julius Shulman," he says, "as much as I love watching you work that camera, I'm going back inside. Meet me in the café when you're ready to eat, but try not to take too much longer because I'm starving."

I chuckle at his calling me the name of my favorite architectural photographer. "Okay. Sorry, babe. You know this is a once-in-a-lifetime opportunity for me. I'll be up there in a little bit."

"Okay. Watch your step when you walk back. Love you."

"Love you too." Clay gives me a peck on the lips and leaves for the café. It's just me, my camera, and the beauty of the woods surrounding me. As I'm snapping away, I get chills. Not the good kind of chills, like when something awesome happens. It's the freaky kind of chills, like someone is watching me. I turn around and hear rustling a few yards away behind some trees, but don't see anything. Must have been a deer. Either way, I'm done playing Julius Shulman. I trek back to the house with a little more pep in my step than I would normally apply.

We eat lunch at the café onsite at Fallingwater and then hit the gift shop. I won't have to make an ornament out of any of the photos I snapped, as there are several to choose from with various scenes and perspectives of the house. I buy two, plus a book. And a bookmark.

Clay and I get back on the road towards our destination in West Virginia. We're there before I know it. The typewriter museum is nestled in a secluded area off the highway. It's a log cabin with a cobblestone chimney, reminiscent of the Glade Valley Bed and Breakfast we stayed at in North Carolina.

"Is this somebody's house?" Clay asks.

"Kinda looks that way. I don't see a sign. Right address though."

"You got the typewriter keys?"

"Right here." I've been keeping them in a pillbox in my purse ever since we found the first one back in Roanoke, Virginia. We've found four keys total, each one at a corresponding clue destination, not knowing what in the world they were for until we figured out the clue that led us to the typewriter museum. We knew they would come into play at some point on our road trip. I take the small round box out of my purse and put it in my pocket, along with the keychain.

We make our way to the porch. A small table separates two red rocking chairs with chipped paint and worn patchwork cushions, an indication that they've been sitting here for years, and no doubt have rocked hundreds of hours.

Clay knocks on the heavy wooden door. Footsteps approach, and a gentleman opens the door, puffing on a pipe, its aromatic cherry-vanilla blend lingering after the smoke dissipates. The man's gray hair sticks out from underneath a fedora.

"Can I help you?" he asks, pushing the bridge of his horn-rimmed glasses and sliding them up his face about an inch.

"Is this the Chestnut Ridge Typewriter Museum?" Clay asks the man.

He stares at us for a few seconds before he answers. "It is. But, I'm sorry, it's by appointment only." His face wrinkles. We've clearly annoyed him.

"Oh," I say with defeat in my voice.

He starts to shut the door, but Clay stops him by putting his hand on the door before it closes.

"Well," Clay says, "can we make an appointment for thirty seconds from now?"

The guy chuckles. "Sure, come on in. I'm not really doing anything anyway."

We smile and follow him inside.

"Thanks," I tell the man.

"Mighty docent of you," Clay puns. I grimace. The old man chortles, a gesture that I'm sure he only makes as a courtesy to Clay.

The room is stocked with dozens of shelves and cases full of antique typewriters and other odd apparatuses that I've never seen before. One looks more like an old rotary telephone than it does a typewriter. I get a whiff of ink, combined with metallic components sheened with oil. Déjà vu. I'm back in seventh grade typing class. I can hear the *clack, clack, clack* of each typeface striking the thin paper on the platen, the bell dinging at the end of the line, and having to manually swing the carriage over with the protruding silver carriage return. Having to learn typing skills on those old donated dinosaurs gave me a slight impediment when I got into the real world. It was at least a month before I stopped swatting dead air when the bell would ding on an electric typewriter.

"You're not my typical demographic."

"And who would that be?" Clay asks.

"Old ladies that used to be secretaries, steam-punks, hipsters, historians, communications majors, and Tom Hanks."

"Tom Hanks?" I ask.

"He's a fellow collector. What brings you here?"

Clay looks at me. "Love? Wanna show him?"

"Sure." I take the pillbox out of my pocket and open it up, flipping it over into my palm and displaying the keys.

"Oh, for heaven's sake. Why didn't you just tell me you were Clay and Lynn? Goodness gracious, come here, both of you." He engulfs us in a giant hug, his demeanor the complete opposite from when he answered the door. He releases us and says, "Come on, I know exactly what you're here for. I'm George."

"Hi, George," I say to him with a bit of laughter in my voice. "Nice to meet you."

"Yes, sir," Clay says as the two of them shake hands. "Pleasure."

"Pleasure's all mine. Right this way."

He leads us into another room with more of the same, but this area includes a lot of antique typewriter stands and tables. I also see some vintage adding machines, calculators, and a contraption that reminds me of those devices that shoe salesmen used to measure your foot, back when there were actual shoe salesmen.

"Your collection is incredible," I tell George. "I never knew typewriters could be so collectible."

"Thank you. I've been an enthusiast since the sixties. I'm an author with over forty books under my belt. Wrote one a year when I started out of college. Now, I'm lucky to get one out every few years. I was actually trying to come up with something new when you knocked on the door, which is why I'm wearing my lucky brainstorming hat." He points to his head.

"Really?" Clay asks. That's great. I love to read. What kind of books do you write?"

"Thought you'd never ask. Mostly mystery, with a few horrors mixed in. Those never sold as well though. Mystery's my favorite. Have you ever heard of the *Metalmark Moe McCoy* series about the typewriter repair man who helps the FBI solve crimes?"

"No, sorry," Clay says. "Not really my *type*."

I roll my eyes at Clay. He gives me one of his goofy smiles.

"I see," George says in a disappointed tone.

"I've heard of that series," I tell George.

"You have?" he asks, a pleased smile across his face.

"Yes. I haven't read any, sorry to say, but Aunt Mitzi loved mysteries. There are a few of your stories on her huge bookshelf at home, amidst a bunch of Agatha Christie novels."

"Well, glad to hear she hadn't sold any of mine in yard sales over the years," he laughs. "I've also written a couple non-fiction books about type-writers." He continues his account about how he came to be a collector. "Anyway, I was always looking to upgrade to the next best typewriter. Kind of like kids nowadays do with these new-fangled cell phones. I never wanted to get rid of any of my previous typewriters though, knowing so many of my books came off of those machines. I'm a little sentimental." He pats his heart. "So, I just kept them in a closet. They started to take up too much space. My wife, God rest her soul, begged me to get rid of them. I couldn't, so I had to think of a purpose for them and began researching primitive typewriters. Started collecting, and here we are."

"Wow. Very interesting," Clay says.

"Thanks."

"So, tell me how Metalmark Moe McCoy solved crimes with typewriters," I say to George.

"Mostly by examining typewritten ransom notes through a combination of ink-stain analysis and forensic typography."

"Awesome," Clay says. "I'd love to read your horror stories. That's my favorite genre."

"I'm on Amazon." George still seems a little annoyed that Clay has never heard of his popular mystery books.

We round a corner and my eyes focus on one of the strangest typewriters I've ever seen. It's missing four keys. The same ones that are in my hand.

"This is it," I say pointing to it.

"Whoa. This thing?" Clay asks. "It looks like some kind of medieval torture device with typewriter keys."

"Yep. This is it," George says. "One of my favorites. It's a Remington Standard. Number eight. Remington is credited with producing the first commercial typewriter."

"Remington as in the gun company?" Clay asks.

"One in the same. Well, in a way. It was in fact the same company that manufactured guns, but by the time this version was made, Remington had sold its typewriter business to Standard Typewriter, allowing them to use the Remington name. Hence 'Remington Standard.' In later years, they changed it simply to 'Remington Typewriter Company.'"

"Interesting," Clay says.

"No, what's really interesting, is that it's rumored that Mark Twain was the first person to turn in a typewritten manuscript. And he used a Remington typewriter."

"Okay, yeah. That's pretty freaking cool."

"That's awesome," I say.

Looking closer at the Remington, it stands over a foot tall, including the carriage, which is located on top of the entire machine. It's sitting on what I guess would be considered the modern-day cover plate, though it looks more like a stage, so that's what I'll call it. Underneath the stage is where the typebar is, but Clay is right. It does look like some sort of torture device from the Middle Ages.

"Did you lose the cover plate?" I ask. "It seems to be missing."

"No, they were built like that."

"Didn't the works get gummed up with dust and stuff?"

"Yeah, that's why they started using cover plates on later models."

"So," Clay says, "what do we do here?"

"Just put the keys on and press?" I ask.

"Surely, Mitzi gave you some sort of direction, did she not?"

"Uh, no, not really. I mean we found them in a certain order, but she didn't specify if that was significant," I tell George.

"Well," he says, "I would lead with that."

"Okay. We found them in the order of B, C, S, and L. Clay, you put them at the missing places on the keyboard and I'll push them down in order."

As I push each key down, the stage pops up a bit. On the last stroke, the machine opens to reveal a black velvet box.

CHAPTER 8

THE SMELL FROM the inked silk ribbon invades my nose, reminding me of elementary school, when the teacher would hand out worksheets fresh off the ditto machine.

I remove what we came here for, what we've been wondering about for weeks. It's one of those larger velvet jewelry boxes for a necklace with a pendant. It's about six inches square, and it has a tiny lock on it. I take the small key from my pocket and open it. Gasping, my hand finds my mouth. There are four brooches, all of them Aunt Mitzi's.

"Wow," Clay says.

"'Wow' is right. I haven't seen these in years."

"Well, they've been here," George chuckles. "Mitzi and Sid brought them. With the typewriter, which they donated, under the condition that I not mess with it. I knew what was in there, and that it would only open at your hands. Sid rigged it that way." He ran his hand along the machine. "Still a fantastic display piece though. For the most part, his alterations were undetectable. Really nice work. He could've done restoration work here. We kept in touch over the years, got to know each other. I went to both of their funerals. I saw you there. And now you know, I knew who you were the minute I opened the door," he smiles.

"Are you serious?" I ask.

"I am. Sorry for giving you a hard time earlier, but I wanted to keep a little mystery and excitement going for you."

"Good one," Clay says.

Aunt Mitzi had a huge collection of brooches. Back at the house, there's a big jewelry box just for them. She wore one on every occasion. Some were fancier with real jewels and gemstones while others were more playful costume jewelry.

I look down in the velvet box, pick up the pins, and reflect on them, one at a time. Of all Aunt Mitzi's brooches, these have always been my favorites, because of what they represent.

One has two pear-shaped rubies, stacked vertically with their points touching, the one above larger than the one underneath. There are curved spikes of diamonds and marcasite jutting out from the rubies, creating a flame effect. Another is of a tree, with a diamond encrusted trunk, and leaves made of jade and emeralds. The next one is of a hot air balloon, with bright fun colors of orange, purple, green, and pink. There are small diamonds draped on the side of the balloon. The last one is a diamond bow with sapphire water droplets dangling from it.

Clay sees me inspecting them. "Are they significant, babe?"

"Yeah, they are. Fire. Earth. Wind. Water. The four classical elements of nature. Aunt Mitzi knew these were my favorites. They aren't even a set, really, but I dubbed them her 'Elements Collection' since she had one to symbolize each. She said she never meant it that way, didn't even get them at the same time or place. She just bought them because she liked them. Most of these stones probably aren't even real."

"They're not," George says. "You think she would have left thousands of dollars' worth of jewelry with a stranger?" he laughs. "But they are sparkly."

"They definitely look like Aunt Mitzi," Clay says. "So, I guess that does it for us here."

"I guess so. George, thanks so much for keeping these safe. And for letting us in," I smile.

"Of course. It's been wonderful meeting you both. You have no idea how bad I wanted to speak to both of you at her funeral. But I knew, well, I hoped anyway, that I'd be seeing you soon, and here you are. Do you know where you're headed?"

"We're not sure," Clay tells him. "We like to figure out the clues one by one, as we go."

"Yeah, so you're guess is as good as ours."

"Well," George says, "I actually do know where you're headed next, but I'll let you figure it out." He smiles.

"You know?" I ask.

"Yup. Asked Mitzi and Sid when they were here if your next stop had been planned yet. I was fascinated by their story, and I was curious. They told me. It was hard not to turn all the information into a book. Of course, I would've added in a few murders, or a heist, or even a couple of ghosts. I ended up not writing it though because I was worried that Mitzi might think it was a betrayal of her trust. But I did base the character Michelle in *A Shot of Lead and Ink* on her."

"Really? I'll have to check it out," I say. "So, do you know the rest of the clues?"

"No, just the one for your next stop. If you get stumped, you can call me." He smiles.

"Never know. We might," Clay says.

"Thanks for the afternoon company. Can I get you a pop for the road?"

Pop. We're definitely not in Louisiana anymore.

"Thanks, that would be great," I tell him.

"Mountain Dew alright?"

"Perfect," Clay says.

George leaves to get the drinks and then yells out, "I'll be right back. Gotta fetch something upstairs."

"Okay," we shout in unison.

He finally brings our cans of 'The Dew' and a little lagniappe for Clay.

"What's this?" Clay asks, accepting a cardboard box decorated with images of graveyards, leafless trees, and gothic mansions in thunderstorms.

"All four of my horrible horrors, just for you. Inscribed of course. I'll admit I was a little miffed when you said you'd never heard of my well-known mystery series, but I forgive you. I realize that most people have a go-to genre," he chuckles. "After spending some time with you this last hour or so, you both feel like family. So, this is my gift to you.

"One Christmas, my wife had a bunch of these specially crafted boxes printed up for me so I could present my horrors as a boxed set, thinking that might help boost sales. I hope they don't disappoint. Don't expect too much though. I'm no Stephen King."

Clay and I smile at each other. He looks at the spines of the novels in the box George gave him. "Wait. You're Fox Winthrop?"

"I am. One of my pen names."

"Holy crap." Clay surveys the titles of the books in the set. "I've actually read *Nightmare of the Rancid* and *Rogue Visions*."

"You have?" George is genuinely surprised.

"Yes. And I really enjoyed them. A little campy, but I love that stuff. One of my favorite movies is *Killer Klowns from Outer Space*, if you can believe that."

"Well I'll be damned," George says. He chuckles. "Didn't realize my stuff was in such august company as *Killer Klowns from Outer Space*."

"These are great," Clay says. "Thanks so much, George. I look forward to reading *Wretched in the Chasm* and *The Maniacal Magistrate*."

"Glad to hear it." He turns to me. "Lynn, darling, I know I have a copy of *Lead and Ink* around here somewhere, but I couldn't put my hands on it. If you give me your address, I'll send it to you soon as I find it."

"Oh, that's so sweet. Thank you. It's the same as Aunt Mitzi and Uncle Sid's. Do you have it?"

"I do indeed. Great. All set then." George walks us out to the porch. He gives me a hug and shakes Clay's hand with a clap on the shoulder.

"Thanks again, for everything," I tell George.

"You bet. You kids be safe."

We get in the truck and Clay starts the ignition. As we back out of the driveway and wave good-bye to George, he tips his hat to us.

I pull up the internet browser on my phone and search for something I forgot about earlier. "Hey, Clay?"

"Yes?"

"Just in case you were wondering, the cardinal is the state bird of West Virginia."

"Well, that's good to know. Mainly because it was kind of random."

"What do you mean?"

"Because neither the clue nor the destination itself actually involved cardinals. It was more of a silent symbol."

"But she's given us keychains like that before, remember? With New Hampshire? The keychain was a piece of granite and it's known as the 'Granite State.'"

"Yeah, but she mentioned it in the clue she gave us. 'Go to the Granite State and find the Hale House.' Or something like that. See what I mean?"

"I do. So, this tells us she's getting trickier."

"That it does."

Before Clay gets back on the main highway, he turns the truck into a side street and pulls off to the side of the road. That's my cue. I get the set of clues out of my purse and unfold the worn papers.

"What've we got?" Clay asks.

"Let's see. 'Where the Guardians of Traffic watch over the city, there's a famous hall with many a ditty. Inside you'll find, Papa was one of these. The wizard engages a mean one with ease.' Huh. What the what?"

Clay laughs at me. "Okay. There's lots to pick apart here. Let's start at the beginning."

"Guardians of Traffic is capitalized if that helps. Any idea who or what they are?"

"No. Maybe stoplights?"

"Stop signs? Police?" I add.

"Crossing guards at busy intersections?"

"Hey, did you ever work safety patrol in elementary school and wear one of those bright neon-orange body-cross belts with a badge?" I ask.

"No. But I remember the ones that did. They were all dorks."

"Oh really?" I raise my hand. "I was a patrol guard."

"And you're still a dork." I playfully punch him in the shoulder, and he pulls me in for a kiss. "But you're my dork. And I love you." I smile, a little turned on, as that kiss came from out of nowhere. "I bet you looked cute in your patrol belt."

"I was in the fifth grade. I was hardly cute then. That was the beginning of my awkward stage."

"We all had our awkward stages. Now, Mrs. Sinclair," he says, and then gives me another sensual kiss. "Are you ready to finish going through this clue?"

Cheeks flushed, lips millimeters from Clay's, I whisper, "Yes."

He takes my hands and kisses the backs of them. "Okay. Where were we?"

"Um," I'm still reeling from those hot kisses, "crossing guards."

"Okay, let's shelve that for now and move on. 'Famous hall with many a ditty.' Monty Hall? Arsenio Hall? They aren't really musicians though. I got it. Daryl Hall. From Hall and Oats."

"That's a good track to be on," I tell him, thinking clearly now, "but 'hall' isn't capitalized, so I doubt it's a proper name. And I'm sure Aunt Mitzi didn't know jack about Hall and Oats."

"Maybe. But she's getting trickier, remember? We're almost halfway through the states. She's throwing curve balls left and right."

"True. But what if it's not a person? Like it could be Carnegie Hall."

"We've already been to New York," he says.

"That's just an example."

"Hall of Presidents."

"We're way passed D.C. and Disney World, and too far from Disneyland."

"There could be other famous halls of presidents in a museum or something."

"But then where do the ditties come in? You know any presidents that were famous for singing?"

"No. Clinton played the sax though."

"Alright, so maybe it's got something to do with that. The next sentence talks about Papa being one. My great-grandfather was a grocer, so you think that's what she means? That she's talking about her Papa?"

"Maybe. What else defined his life?"

"Christian. Husband. Father."

"Too broad," Clay says. "Let's go with grocer. What's the next part again?"

"'The wizard engages a mean one with ease.' How many famous wizards can you think of besides Harry Potter?"

"Wizard of Oz."

"Good one. That's obvious, I can't believe that wasn't my first thought."

"Merlin."

"Another obvious one. Jeez, where is my head? What about the 'mean' part? A mean wizard?"

"Maybe. The mean ones in Harry Potter were called Smithereens, right?"

I burst out laughing. "No, goofball, the house they lived in was called Slytherin."

"Were they called Slythereens then?"

"No."

"Slytherinians? Slytherites?"

"Don't be such a muggle. It's just 'Slytherins.' Besides, Harry and his crew were in the house of Gryffindor," I snicker.

"Gryffindorians? Gryffindites? Gryffindoids?"

"They just called themselves 'wizards,' Clay. So, we have something along the lines of a stoplight at a famous hall near a grocery store selling Harry Potter merchandise."

"No way in hell that's it," Clay muses with a laugh. "What's the keychain look like?"

I dig it out. "It's a flipper." I dangle the miniature swim fin in front of him.

"Well that's random."

"The key doesn't really give us much help either. It's pretty modern."

"Didn't you say that Guardians of Traffic was capitalized?"

"Yes."

"Search for that."

I pull up Google and key in the phrase. "Well, we should have totally started with that. The Guardians of Traffic are huge Art Deco figures carved out of sandstone on the Hope Memorial Bridge. There are eight of them. They—"

"So, where is it?"

"I'm getting to that. They stand on the pylons of the bridge spanning the Cuyahoga River, connecting the east and west side of…Cleveland."

"Cleveland. Cool." He keys Cleveland into the GPS and starts the truck.

"I'm not finished. Listen to this neat tidbit of info. The guardians symbolize progress in ground transportation, and each one of them holds some sort of vehicle."

"Interesting. So, now that we're headed to Cleveland, let's reevaluate. Knowing what I know, the famous hall has to be the Rock and Roll Hall of Fame, which is in Cleveland."

"Oh my gosh, that's right! I've always wanted to go there."

"Me too," Clay says. "Thanks, Aunt Mitzi. And, thinking further, I bet 'Papa was one of these' doesn't have anything to do with groceries. I bet it's the Temptations' 'Papa Was a Rolling Stone.'"

"One of Aunt Mitzi's favorite music groups."

"So now I think I know what the wizard part is."

"What?"

"Pinball Wizard. I can't believe that wasn't my first guess. I should have known that off the bat."

"Elton John?"

"Well, it was originally by The Who, but Elton John covered it in the movie based on their rock opera, *Tommy*."

"I've seen it."

"I think we'll be looking for a pinball machine. But with all these music groups, I don't know exactly which one. The Temptations? The Who? Elton John?"

"Makes total sense now. I love pinball. Guess we're staying in Cleveland tonight," I say.

"Yeah. Because it'll probably be time for the museum to close when we get there. And because," he starts singing "Cleveland Rocks."

"I didn't realize you were that big of a Drew Carey fan. You know that was one of the theme songs for his TV show."

"What? No. I mean, yeah, I like Drew Carey, but I was singing it because I like the song and it fits our current situation. Ian Hunter was the original artist, but I actually prefer the cover by The Presidents of the United States of America."

"Ah. I see. Well, me too. I guess, anyway. I don't think I've ever heard the original."

CHAPTER 9

W E MAKE IT to Cleveland in record time (no pun intended) and
check in to our hotel.

"What's the nightlife like here?" Clay asks as we set our
stuff down.

We plop on the bed and I take my phone out of my pocket. "No idea.
Let me look." I scroll down the menu of things to do in Cleveland, and
there's a lot. One of the first things I see gets me a tad bit excited. "Clay!"
He jumps at my shouting his name.

"Shit, Lynn," he laughs. "What? What did you find?"

"The house from *A Christmas Story* is here!"

"You call that 'nightlife'?"

"No, silly. But we have to go tour it. You know that's my favorite
Christmas movie. And their museum is conveniently located right across
the street from the house. Both are closed for the day, but we've got to go
before the Hall of Fame tomorrow."

"You got it. What else is there? Read me a list of stuff to do."

I keep scrolling. "Bars, boat tours, breweries, comedy clubs, escape
rooms, food tours…" And then I see it. Something that we haven't done

yet on this trip, something that we haven't done since one of our first dates. "This is it."

"What is it?"

"It's a surprise."

"How are you going to surprise me? I'm the one driving."

"You're going to close your eyes while I put the address into the GPS. That's how."

"Hmm. Should I change?"

"Nah, let's go."

"Can't we rest a minute?"

"No, I want to see the Guardians of Traffic and get some pictures before it gets dark. You know I love the Art Deco style of architecture, so I'm anxious to see them. Plus, the fact that they were part of the clue will bring them to life for me."

"I don't know if the Clevelanders will appreciate those things tromping through the city. Kudos to Aunt Mitzi, though. Bringing those things to life is some powerful voodoo. Especially from the grave."

"Bring them to life, figuratively speaking, goofball. I'll feel closer to Aunt Mitzi."

Clay makes a noise that can only be described as a half sigh, half grunt. "You're lucky I love you." He gets off the bed and calls the valet for our truck.

I reroute the directions to take us on a detour across the Hope Memorial bridge. We drive past Progressive Field, home of the Cleveland Indians, and hop onto the bridge. I spot the Guardians immediately, a pair on each side of the highway. They are massive structures, sternly beautiful. At least to me. I can appreciate the architecture and the time it took to carve the details into the sandstone. I tell Clay to slow down as much as possible. Living a little dangerously, I pop my head out of the sunroof to get a better view. Holding the shutter down on my camera, it continuously snaps photos until we pass them up. I turn to capture the other side of the Guardians. I slip back inside the truck and review some of the shots.

"Not half bad," I muse, a bit shocked at how well most of them turned out.

"We're almost to the end of the bridge. The other sets are coming up. Get ready."

I pop back out of the sunroof and repeat my actions. Surprisingly, they came out decent as well. "I'm so excited about these pictures. I can put them in a matted collage frame for the house. I love it."

As we drive towards the night's destination, Clay gets antsy.

"Where are we going, Lynn? Give me a hint. It's taking forever."

"Hold your horses. It's just on the other side of the city, that's all."

"Hold my horses? Is that a clue?"

"Uh, no. Not really."

"What do you mean, 'Not really'?"

I ignore his question. "We're almost there. Start slowing down. I think it's to the left across the tracks."

Clay veers into the turn lane and sees the sign on the black-and-white checkered tower next to the gray brick building where we will be spending the next couple of hours. "Go-kart racing?"

I smile and nod with excitement. "You like?"

"Me like. So, telling me to hold my horses was a clue. I get it. Horsepower."

"That was a coincidence. I wasn't even trying to give you a clue. That's funny." I smile.

He parks and kills the engine. "Why is it so quiet?"

"It's an indoor track."

"Whoa. Hope we don't get carbon monoxide poisoning."

"They're electric cars, so no fumes."

"Sweet. Babe, this is awesome. We haven't done this in forever."

"I know. The last time was on our fifth date. Remember? At Celebration Station?"

"Holy crap, that seems like a lifetime ago. That was a fun date." He pauses. A wide grin spreads across his face.

"What's so amusing, Sinclair?"

"That was the night I knew I would fall in love with you."

"What? You never told me that. What happened that made you feel that way?"

"Well for starters, you agreed to a night of go-kart racing on a date without hesitation. And when I picked you up, you were dressed for the part, wearing a black-and-white checkered bow in your hair with matching dangling earrings."

"Oh, my god. You remember that?"

"Yeah," he says. Blushing, he looks down with a smile, as if he's embarrassed that he's admitting this to me. "It was perfect, that you thought enough about go-kart racing to throw some checkered flag symbols in with what you were wearing."

"Good thing I did, then. Wait. So, you're saying that if I had not done that, we wouldn't be having this conversation, right here, right now?"

"No, love. It was more than that. You were so relaxed, being yourself, not trying to impress me. After about six rounds of racing, you yelled out, 'Pizza!' I loved that you would eat like a normal person and not like a crazy woman starving herself."

I laugh. "I do like my pizza every now and then."

"Then, to top it all off, you saw that little girl crying because she wanted the big stuffed teddy bear and didn't have enough tickets."

"I remember. It was like, a bazillion tickets to 'buy' it. Ridiculous."

"Agreed. Anyway, you gave her all the tickets we won from playing games, and when that still wasn't enough, we played more Skee-Ball, racking up more tickets to give her so she could get the bear. That was all your sweet idea, and I knew your heart was big. It made mine grow. Opened it up. It's like you took a sledgehammer and tore the walls down that had been built up around it. I pretty much knew that night that you were the one."

"Oh my God, Clay." I lean over the center console in the truck and kiss him. "Now see, that's the kind of story I was looking for the other day." I tear up.

"Yeah, well…that makes two things you didn't know about me. Now, let's go kick some butt on that track. Best two out of three gets to pick."

"Pick what?" I ask as I get out of the truck.

"Which position we'll be in before we go to sleep tonight," he says with a wink. Clay drapes his arm around me, and we walk towards the entrance of the go-kart arena.

The next morning, we make our way to the house from *A Christmas Story*.

We learn that the house was bought on eBay and had to be gutted and restored to its movie splendor. It opened for tours in 2006.

Inside, the famous leg lamp glows in the front window. In the corner sits the open crate in which the leg lamp was delivered. Sadly, the three original lamps that were used in the film were all destroyed (obviously, since part of the story is that it broke). Around the living room is a Christmas tree, a bowling ball, a Red Ryder BB gun, a mess of tangled electric cords, a big standing radio like the one where Ralphie sat and patiently listened to the *Little Orphan Annie* show, so he could translate the cipher with his secret decoder pin, and more.

The kitchen is set just like in the movie as well, including a fake turkey roasting in the oven. Pots and pans on the stove and in the sink are the same kind that a family would have used in the 1940s. Replicas of Mr. Parker's newspaper and Randy's bib lay in wait on the table.

Upstairs, the room that Ralphie and Randy shared has sailboat wallpaper and twin beds with blue bedspreads, just like in the movie. Next to their bedroom is the bathroom. A bar of Lifebuoy soap with teeth marks in it rests on the sink. Oh, fudge.

After we finish with the tour, which was a total fan-girl pilgrimage for me, we head over to the museum. Inside the museum is a plethora of memorabilia from the movie: original props (the chalkboard from Ralphie's classroom, Randy's actual bib, Ralphie's original Red Ryder BB gun, and more), costumes (Mrs. Parker's robe, Randy's tight snowsuit, plus others. But not the pink bunny suit. I read that Peter Billingsley, the actor who portrayed Ralphie, has it in his personal collection), and a ton of behind-the-scenes photos.

And what would a museum be without a gift shop? Except this gift shop is so big, it gets its own house, which is located next to the museum. We mosey over next door to peruse the movie merch.

I get in line at the register with a leg lamp ornament and a couple of pieces for my Christmas village at home. Clay wants to buy the full-size leg lamp, of course. Truth be told though, I want one too.

"Look, Lynn. Electric sex! Let's get one," he says, hauling the lamp to the register behind me, complete with its wooden box marked 'FRAGILE.'

"Clay, you know we can't fit that in the truck. We'll order one online."

"Okay, good. I was hoping you'd be on board."

"Are you kidding? I want it in the front window for all our company to see as they drive up."

He laughs and brings the awkward package back to where he got it from in the corner. "Fra-gee-lay," he says, as he's walking across the room.

I step up to the counter and put my items down, shaking my head at Clay. I smile at the poor clerk behind the register as if she doesn't hear quotes from the movie a thousand times a day. She smiles back and greets me with the next line. "Must be Italian." What a great sport she is.

On our way to the Rock Hall, Clay says, "You know, I was thinking earlier…the part in the clue about 'Papa Was a Rolling Stone,' even though The Temptations sang it, it might actually be about—"

"The Rolling Stones," I interrupt.

"Yeah."

"That just occurred to me as you were saying it. I guess we need to add them to the list of pinball machines we could be looking for."

"How many keys are on the keychain? Maybe we need to be looking for all of them."

"Just one," I tell him.

"Well, that answers that then. Oh! A flipper! I get the keychain now. It's a homonym for the flipper in pinball machines."

"Nice. And very tricky. Man, she had all kinds of antics up her sleeve with this clue and keychain combined. We need to stay sharp."

"That we do. Thank goodness we don't have to go scuba diving in Lake Erie to find what we're looking for," Clay quips with a small chuckle.

The legendary Rock and Roll Hall of Fame building is right on the shore of Lake Erie. An architectural maverick, the museum is a dramatic combination of geometric shapes and cantilevered sections which are anchored by a tower that supports a dual glass pyramid entrance. We enter the atrium and one of the first things we see is an exhibit called *Rolling Stone/50 Years*. I get excited, thinking this is where we need to be. But then I realize it's a showcase for the music mag.

Clay and I get in line for tickets and make our way to level zero for the start of the tour, eyes peeled for pinball machines. There are seven floors to this museum. My senses overload on musical icons.

Elvis is definitely in the building. His music, his 1975 Super Trike motorcycle, his outfits. "A Little Less Conversation" is spilling from speakers hidden somewhere above my head.

Clay grabs me by the arm and startles me. "What?" I ask. "Do you see the pinball machine?"

"No. Better than that." My eyes follow as he points to a row of glass cabinets filled with mannequins dressed in David Bowie's Ziggy Stardust costumes.

"Oh, cool. Let's go check it out so you can relive your youth." David Bowie is Clay's all-time favorite artist. As we move towards the display, a childlike expression appears across his face. A smile that cannot be contained. Eyes wide and glowing. "Let's Dance" pours from the speakers. Clay's in a little corner of heaven right now. He snaps a couple of pictures with his phone. You'd think he was looking at David Bowie himself. I guess it's as close as we'll ever get again.

Clay turns to me. "I still can't believe you think Steven Tyler is the greatest rock star over David Bowie. Bowie's music covered the gamut of rock."

Here he goes again. This should be fun.

Clay continues. "Bowie would get so into his music that he'd adopt a whole new personality. Ziggy Stardust, Major Tom, Aladdin Sane, The Thin White Duke, Halloween Jack, The Blind Prophet. I mean, don't get me wrong, you know I like Steven Tyler and freaking love Aerosmith's music, but what'd Tyler ever do except swap out the rags on his microphone?" he huffs.

I should tell him the truth. "Well…" I look at him with a bit of apprehension. Why am I afraid to reveal this silly little white lie?

"'Well' what?" he asks. "Have you finally come to your senses?"

"Not exactly. I've always had them."

"What do you mean?"

"I mean I have a confession to make." I pause.

"Spit it out, Lynn."

"I've always thought David Bowie is the greatest rock star of all time."

"Wait. What?"

"It's true. I'm sorry." I give him my best puppy dog eyes.

"Holy shit. Are you serious?"

"Yeah," I say with my tail between my legs. "Are you mad?"

"Mad? No. Relieved? Hell yes. But really, why? Why keep on about Steven Tyler? That's so dumb," he half laughs.

"I just love the playful banter between us, arguing over who's number one. I love getting you worked up, how you always try to do your best to convince me. I love hearing and watching you talk about Bowie, how passionate you get."

"You're insane, woman. I can't believe you sat on that for more than twenty-five years. I'm so turned on right now." He lowers his voice. "So… oddly…turned on."

"That's not odd. That's just you."

He flashes his infamous coy smile at me. Uh oh. "Now, I've got a secret to tell *you*." He puts his arm around me and whispers in my ear. "You're not doing this to me again. I want you as turned on as I am right now with nothing to do about it until we get to our next destination." My toes curl. "I know what this does to you. My hot breath in your ear, traveling through your body, landing right at the center of your being, making you so wet that you won't be able to stand it." He follows that with a soft blow and a tiny lick with the tip of his tongue. My knees buckle but he keeps me upright. "That's right, Lynn Sinclair." His voice is just above a whisper now. "Take that. Hold it for me, and know I'm going to handle it later. I will possess you. Bewitch you. Fatigue you." Jesus. I'm Jell-O.

"Let's find that pinball machine. Now," I whisper back.

Two hours, six floors, and countless flirtatious looks between each other later, we finally come across the Rolling Stone pinball machine. The only other pinball machine we saw was a Guns 'N Roses one that once belonged to Slash. We didn't even try to get into it, as Aunt Mitzi never alluded to anything about GNR. She probably had no idea who they were anyway.

The Stones machine was hiding from us in a corner on the lowest level. The side art on the cabinet has the 'Sticky Fingers' tongue logo between the band's name, which is in big red letters. The front of the cabinet depicts a Union Jack. A cartoonish drawing of the band from the '60s era is plastered across the backglass in brilliant colors of orange, purple, and blue.

Mick Jagger is posed front and center, shirt unbuttoned, mouth wide open. Meanwhile, the front and center of Mick Jagger is swinging a little to his left. I don't know how we missed this machine the first time we were down here, hours ago. Well, we were a tad preoccupied with ourselves. "Beast of Burden" falls from the overhead speakers. That's my second favorite Rolling Stones song, after "Wild Horses."

"The dreaded velvet ropes," Clay murmurs. "Any ideas?"

"We could ask for help."

"That's so boring though. I'm all about sneaking around and seeing what we can get away with. Asking for help is a last resort. Always."

"Alright. I suppose I'm with you on that. It's fun playing Scooby-Doo with you."

"We're more Fred and Daphne than Scooby and Shaggy."

"True. Hey, didn't we pass an equipment room back there?" I point.

"What are you thinking?"

"Maybe there's something in there you can use. A mop bucket, one of those big rolling garbage bins, anything that might give the illusion you work here."

"I'm no David Copperfield, but I'll do my best."

"Come on, goofball."

He follows me and we approach the supply closet in the dark corner near an emergency exit. Clay turns the knob and it opens. The stockroom gods are on our side.

"What now?" he asks.

"Find a disguise and put it on. Duh."

"A disguise? I don't think Groucho Marx glasses will suffice. Not that they keep any of those in here," he laughs.

"You know what I mean," I whisper. "Look for anything that says you're employed here. Get in there. I'll keep watch."

He returns ten minutes later in an oversized Dickies jumpsuit and a toolbox. "Let's get to work."

"Lose the hat."

"What? No. It helps to hide my face."

"There's no way any employee in here is wearing an LSU ballcap. You'll get made inside of a minute."

"Oh. Right." He hands it over and I stuff it in my purse.

"Go ahead. I'm right behind you."

"I need the key."

"Here." I dig it out of my pocket, turn his hand sideways and put it there, giving him a light tickle in his palm with my middle finger before I let go.

"You are so wrong for that," he deadpans.

"What'd I do?" I smile.

"You know what you did."

I do know what I did. I gave him the discreet sign that tells him I can't wait to get him alone. That's the nice way to put it.

"Hurry, Sinclair." I give him a wink.

Clay carries the toolbox like he's large and in charge. Stepping up to the pinball machine, he doesn't think twice about unhooking the red velvet rope from its stanchion. So far, so good. I stroll in his direction, feigning interest in some of the other memorabilia nearby. He lifts the lid of the toolbox for authenticity, unlocks the giant game, and opens the door.

Three boys, about ten years old, come up to Clay as he starts looking inside. "Hey, mister," one of them says. "What are you doing? Is it broken?" Shit. They're going to blow our cover.

"Uh, no," Clay replies. "Just doing some routine maintenance."

"Can we see inside?" another one asks.

Clay looks at me with a cry for help. "Hey," I say to the kids. "Don't bother him. Let him do his job so he can concentrate. This is a very special and valuable artifact of the museum. We wouldn't want him to break it. Come on. Check this stuff out over here with me."

"Are you the boss of him?" the third one, red-headed with freckles, asks.

"Pretty much," Clay says.

I smile, and the kids follow me to the display case holding several guitars that once belonged to The Beatles.

Clay gives me a thumbs up. Out of the corner of my eye I see him reach into the mechanics of the pinball machine, grab something, and put it in his pocket. As he is locking it back up, a real maintenance man rounds the corner and catches him.

"Dude. What are you doing?" he asks Clay. Clay looks up, eyes wide and face ashen. I don't think I've ever seen Clay so frazzled. So much for 'large and in charge.' He takes a wrench from the toolbox and waves it.

"You can shake your tool at me all you want, bro."

Clay stifles a laugh, but can't help saying, "That's what she said."

"Whoa. That didn't come out right." The real maintenance man catches himself. "Don't say nothin' to nobody about that." They both laugh. "Maintenance check isn't till Wednesdays. Didn't you get the email? They moved it. We don't do that one anyway. It's just for show. Shouldn't you know that the Stones machine is off limits?"

"Oh. Uh…"

"Are you new?" the guy asks. "Haven't seen you in the break room before. I thought I knew everybody."

"Yeah. Sorry. Wednesdays. No Stones. Got it. Thanks, man. You mind keeping this on the DL?"

"Sure. Consider it on the down low. Our secret. I'm Big Joe." He holds out his hand for Clay to shake and Clay takes it. "Looks like they gave you one of my work suits. What's your name? I'll call and tell them upstairs." He reaches for his radio.

"No, it's okay. I'll tell them," Clay says.

"Suit yourself." Big Joe can't help laughing at his own joke. "See you around." He walks away shaking his head.

Leaving the kids, I scurry back over to Clay. "Well that was freaking close. Let's get the crap out of here."

"What about the clothes and tools?"

"Just leave them."

Clay disappears behind a wall tucked around the corner from the pinball machine and strips himself of the coveralls, kicking them into the shadows. Guess it was a good thing Big Joe left a spare uniform in the equipment room.

We get back to the truck as fast as we can without bringing any attention to ourselves.

"Home free," Clay says.

"So? What did you find?"

The color drains from his face. "Son of a bitch," he whispers.

CHAPTER 10

"No. No, no, no. You've gotta be shitting me, Clay! You left it in the pockets?"

His deep sigh answers the question. He grabs the steering wheel in frustration, giving himself white knuckles in the process, and lowers his head. "I'll go back. I'll go back and get it. Shit, Lynn. I'm so sorry. I was just trying to hurry and it slipped my mind."

"Jesus, Clay. No. Screw that. I'll go back and get it."

"No. I did this. I'll fix it."

"It's fine, Clay. I'll do it. You've been noticed by personnel. Just stay here," I say, exasperated. I get out of the truck and slam the door, sprinting towards the glass pyramid entrance. How could he forget to take whatever it is out of the freaking jumpsuit pocket? I stop in my tracks. What *am* I looking for? Having been so aggravated when I got out of the truck, I forgot to ask Clay. And as the luck of Lynn Sinclair would have it, I left my phone on the seat. I can't text him and I'm closer to the entrance now than the truck. I don't want to turn back. I can't. I need to get this over with, and time is of the essence. My nerves are shot. Dammit to hell.

I make my way back inside and down into level zero again. Big Joe is standing by the pinball machine talking to a couple of other workers. He

nudges the abandoned toolbox on the floor with his foot. Great. Just great. Hopefully they haven't discovered the discarded work clothes dumped in the shadows. A security guard walks over to the small group of guys. All their backs are turned towards me, so I slink into the corner. I'm eclipsed by the darkness. The uniform is still there. Praise the lord. Crouching down, my hands rove over the large empty coveralls and find a pocket. Nothing. Now the other one. Got it. I don't even look at what it is, but it feels a tad bit smaller and thinner than a tin of Altoids. I slip it into the back pocket of my jeans. God, I hope this is it.

"I didn't get his name," I hear Big Joe say. "He was just here. White guy. Light brown hair. A little over six feet tall. Had a Kevin Bacon sorta vibe going on. Said he was new."

Peering around the corner to check on the huddle of men, the little red-headed boy from earlier spots me. "There's that boss lady," he tells his friends. Wonderful. I stoop down. "Are you hiding?" he asks, making my presence known.

"Uh…I was just…" I smile. Big Joe and the other guys amble over to me. "Just tying my shoe," I lie as I stand up. Big Joe and crew surround me, and the kids run off. "Excuse me," I beg. I try to move past them, but they don't budge.

Big Joe takes a step forward, invading my personal space. "You lost or something?" His breath smells like spearmint. Not what I was expecting.

"Yeah. I was just looking for my friends." Another lie. "If I could just squeeze by you, I'd appreciate it."

The security guard spots the jumpsuit behind me and picks it up off the floor. "Looks like one of yours, Joe."

"That's it. He was wearing it. Where did he go?" He turns to me. "Hey lady, did you see a guy around here wearing this suit?"

"No. No I didn't." I hate lying. "Can I go? I got lost looking for the bathroom. My friends will be worried." Lies, lies, lies.

"Can you explain why you were obviously hiding in the corner there, with this work suit?" the security guard asks.

"Hiding? I was tying my shoe." He can see right through my fibbing.

"Right. Why did that kid call you 'that boss lady'? Whose boss are you pretending to be?"

"Nobody's." That's the truth, right? I mean, since Clay said I was 'pretty much' his boss.

"Empty your pockets," he demands.

"My pockets?" No. Not my pockets. Please no, not my pockets. "Why?"

"Under suspicion of conspiracy to commit a misdemeanor of the first degree."

"What?" Is he serious? "Is that even a thing?"

"Your pockets. Let's go."

I pull out the insides of my front pockets, as there is literally nothing in them. My back right pocket holds a piece of gum along with my ticket stub for the Rock Hall, and as I pull out the treasure from my left pocket, I see that's it's a cell phone. An old cell phone. An old red Motorola Razr. I used to have a Razr, about ten or twelve years ago, which would be at least five or six phones ago. This particular red Razr must be Aunt Mitzi's first cell phone. I smile to myself, remembering when I brought her to the Verizon store, browsing the different phones until she settled on this one. It was such new technology back then, at least for Aunt Mitzi. She kept calling it her 'Razzer,' no matter how many times I told her it was pronounced 'razor.' If I remember correctly, my Razr was the first cell phone I had that was Bluetooth-enabled.

Big Joe brings me back to the present. "A Razr?" He laughs. "Who still uses a Razr?"

"I do," I tell him with as straight of a face as I can muster. The chorus of the song "Liar" by The Rollins Band is my own personal hell of a soundtrack on repeat in my brain right now. "I don't have a smart phone." *Cuz I'm a liar.* "I try to stay off of social media as much as possible. I don't even have book-face, or whatever they call it." Two more big fat lies. "It's a hinderance to life and family. People are such slaves to their phones, it's sickening." That part is one hundred percent true. But I'm guilty as charged. "Takes you away from what's most important. Like making memories with your loved ones and friends, visiting museums." I point my hands at the displays in front of me.

"My wife is like that," the security guard says. "Won't let me get a smart phone for the same reason. Alright, ma'am. You're free to go."

"Thanks," I say as they part to let me leave.

"Way to wear those pants," Big Joe says. I turn around, almost ready to slap him. Turns out he was just ribbing the security guard about his wife.

"You are so p-whipped, dog," I hear another guy say as I walk towards the exit.

I high-tail it back to the truck, Aunt Mitzi's cell phone in hand. What in the world could possibly be on this thing? How are we supposed to find it? God, I hope it's charged up. Can juice drain out of a phone left turned off for years, even if it was fully charged when it was powered down? Jeez, I sure hope not. Will any stored info be lost? All of this is running through my mind when I finally get back in the truck.

"Tell me you got the phone," Clay says.

"I got it. By the skin of my teeth. They busted you. Almost busted me. Drive. Find us somewhere to eat. I'm starving."

Clay punches the food category on the GPS and a bunch of nearby eateries pop up. "How does Shooters on the Water sound?" He asks me like I've heard of it before.

"It's perfect, whatever it is."

"Then to Shooters we shall go." He picks that one and follows the navigational directions. "What happened in there?"

"In Shooters? How should I know?"

"No, woman. In the Rock Hall. Smooth sailing or what?"

"Hardly." I relay what took place while I was inside. Clay cringes with nearly every detail.

"Oh shit, Lynn. I'm so sorry. God, I'm an idiot."

"It's okay. I seriously thought they were going to take me in for some major questioning. It's a good thing you didn't go. They would have hauled you back for sure. Thank God they didn't pull any surveillance tapes or anything. Oh no. You know they're going to do that. They'll put an APB out on us."

"Relax, Lynn. Somebody knows that cell phone was there. Nobody will be hunting us down."

"I guess that's true."

"Turn on the phone."

"Ah. Yes." I say a quick prayer and press the power button. "Nothing's happening. I don't suppose you have an old charger in the black hole of your center console, do you?"

"As a matter of fact, I just might."

I start rummaging through the small crypt of Clay's truck, where things get buried. "Jeez. How old are these Tic Tacs? They're stuck to the inside of the container."

He laughs and grabs my purse to get his LSU cap while we're stopped at a red light. "No idea. If you can't find a charger, I'm sure we can find one at the nearest cell phone store. Surely they'd have an old one in their back storage room or something."

My hand tangles with a coiled cord. I pull it out from underneath a pile of napkins, CDs, fast food receipts, sticky loose change, and various shapes and sizes of multi-tools. You'd think as immaculate as Clay keeps his truck (at least when he's not taking a cross country road trip with his wife), this compartment would be a little less junky.

"This looks like it might actually work. How do you even still have it? Your truck is only two years old."

"I don't know. Got left in there some way or another."

I plug the big end of the car charger into the dashboard socket and the small end into the phone. "Holy shit. It fits." I press the power button and the phone boots up. "We're in business."

"Sweet. Is there a banner message scrolling across the top?"

"Yeah. It says, 'Lynn, check texts.' Is this going to be another clue? We don't have another key."

"Check the texts and find out, silly."

I go into the phone's inbox and see one unread message…from Uncle Sid's number. "It says, 'Tell Joshua the swordfish has landed.' What the hell? Who's Joshua?"

Clay mumbles the words to himself. "Huh," he muses. "It does sound like another clue."

"To what? To where?"

"Or, more than likely, it's a passphrase."

"A passphrase? You mean, like a password? How so?"

"Well, for starters, we don't know any Joshuas, right? At least not any Joshuas that Aunt Mitzi or Uncle Sid would have known. But, 'Joshua' was the password in *WarGames*, with Matthew Broderick. Remember that movie?"

"Of course. I love that movie."

"Uncle Sid and I watched it together not long before he died. I kind of made him. He said he enjoyed old war movies and I asked him if he'd ever seen any of the newer war movies, like *WarGames*. Even though it's not exactly the kind of war he was talking about. Figured I'd start with that since it's one of my favorites too."

"I remember that day. I was helping Aunt Mitzi in the garden. What about the rest of the clue there?"

"'Swordfish' was a password used in that Marx Brothers movie *Horse Feathers*. The one where they're in college. The word 'swordfish' used as a password has been parodied throughout pop culture ever since."

"I've never seen that Marx Brothers one. But I have heard about 'swordfish' being used as a password. Plus, in the movie *Swordfish*, Hugh Jackman was a hacker. So, I get it."

"I'm sure they got the title for that movie from *Horse Feathers*, which, by the way, I can't believe you've never seen. We're going to have to do something about that. It's a classic. It's got all four Marx Brothers in it."

"There were only three Marx Brothers. Even I know that."

He sighs. "Poor Zeppo. You probably think Harpo wore a blond wig, don't you?"

"He didn't? That was his real hair?" I'm shocked.

Clay shakes his head. "How have I let you persist in such ignorance? That's on me. Anyway, he wore a light-red wig. We have a date to see *Horse Feathers*, and then maybe *A Night at the Opera* so I can build up your tolerance for *Duck Soup*."

"Deal."

Clay pulls into the restaurant parking lot and we walk inside. There's a long bar with tables on one side and a stage with a dance floor on the other.

The hostess greets us. "Hi, welcome to Shooters on the Water. Table for two?"

"Hi there. Yes," Clay tells her.

"Inside or out?" she asks.

Clay looks at me. "You wanna sit outside?"

"Sure." He takes my hand and we follow the hostess towards the patio.

"Hey, check it out." Clay points to a few glass cases hanging on the wall containing antique guns of all sizes. He slows down to admire them.

"That must be why they call this place Shooters."

We're seated at a table on the patio overlooking the Cuyahoga River. The sky's a little overcast, but the weather feels great. The temp is in the low seventies, the breeze blowing. My long hair insists on wisping across my face, so I put it up in a ponytail.

We watch the boat traffic go up and down the river, some going into Lake Erie. A vertical lift bridge opens its jaws to let a huge barge through. Clay and I watch, fascinated by the power of both industrial marvels.

"That's the 'Iron Curtain,'" our waitress, Jeannie, tells us. "It replaced that swing bridge mid-century when the river was widened." She points behind her and we see exactly what she's talking about. The old swing bridge is still there, in its upright position.

"Oh, wow," I say. "I was wondering about that."

"That original bridge was built by B&O Railroad."

"Impressive," Clay says. "Most waitresses just tell you about the daily special."

Jeannie smiles. "You can go check it out if you like, after your meal. The railroad tracks are still there."

"Count me in," Clay says.

"Me too," I smile.

"B&O, huh?" Clay winks at me, no doubt remembering the two fabulous days we spent in Baltimore. "Makes perfect sense, seeing as how we're in Ohio."

"Yep," she says with a proud smile.

"Ever been to the museum in Baltimore?" I ask her.

"No. On my bucket list though. My grandfather worked for the railroad."

"It's a great museum," Clay says. "We were just there a couple of weeks ago."

We give Jeannie our orders and Clay turns his attention back to me as she leaves.

"Love?"

"Yes?"

"You ready to interpret the next clue?"

"I'm still stuck on Joshua and the swordfish."

"That sounds like a great title for a children's book."

"Ha. It kinda does. But seriously, I'm stumped."

"Well, maybe we're supposed to be. Maybe Joshua's swordfish has something to do with the next place. Or the next. Or ten states from now. But I know we'll figure it out."

"You're right. Once again."

"So? Clue sheet time?"

"Clue sheet time."

CHAPTER 11

"What do we have?" Clay asks.

I fumble through my purse and dig out the translated cipher. "'Head to the city Antoine Laumet founded. Land with your skewer and your catch at D-Ham—"

"Dee ham? What ham? We don't have a ham. Where's the ham? Who's got the ham?"

I laugh. "That's the capital letter D, hyphen, capital letter H in Ham. D hyphen Ham. I think it's a place. It says 'at' not 'with' so…can I finish?"

"Sorry. I was just confused."

"Moving on. 'The place is nearly surrounded.' See? It's a place. 'Watch out for a traffic jam.'"

"Who is Antoine Laumet? Sounds French."

"I dunno. Look it up. I'll see if I can figure out what this D-Ham is."

We both dive into our phones and search for our respective subjects. Several odd and obscure results come up for D-Ham: a Twitter handle, a rapper, a software engineer, and a pilgrimage site in India. None of which I believe is what we're meant to find. Then I see it. One that makes the most sense. D-Ham is shorthand for Detroit-Hamtramck. It's the General Motors Assembly Plant. The last remaining plant in Detroit that manufactures…Cadillacs. This is what Clay has been waiting for. The Brougham.

"Babe," he says with bright eyes. "Guess what?"

"Detroit. The Caddie."

"Damn. How did you know?" He slumps. I've burst his bubble.

"Sorry. D-Ham is short for Detroit-Hammatrammack. I'm not sure I'm pronouncing that correctly." I show him the paper.

"I don't think anybody can pronounce that without knowing any better. Kind of like Tchoupitoulas Street in New Orleans," he laughs. "Lucky for you though, I've heard of that place. It's pronounced, 'Ham-TRAM-ick.' A guy I served with was from around there."

"Cool." I tell him what I found in my quick research. "They also build cars for Chevy and Buick."

"I should have known the clue would have something to do with Cadillacs, given our current location and how close we are to Detroit."

"So, this Laumet founded the Motor City?" I ask.

"Yep. But that was his birth name. As an adult, he changed it to a crazy long French name with prestigious titles but is usually referred to as Antoine de la Mothe…" he pauses. "Cadillac."

"Wow. That's still a mouthful. So, Cadillac founded Detroit. I take it the makers of the Caddie named it after him."

"That's not the only car named for an explorer. Besides Cadillac, there's DeSoto and LaSalle. I'm sure there are others, but those are the only ones I can think of off the top of my head."

"Interesting. Alright, we know where we're going. I think I understand the last half of the clue. According to the map, the city of Hamtramck is surrounded by Detroit, except for a small portion of the western border. So that's that. And the part about the traffic jam is probably because it's a car manufacturing facility."

"A traffic jam of cars coming off the line. I get it. But what do you think the part about landing with the skewer and catch mean?" Clay asks.

"I don't know. Let's talk it out. Skewer. Something sharp. Pointy. Like a knife maybe? A safety pin?"

"Could be. Or an arrow. But what about 'catch'? We haven't caught anything. Have we?"

"No. Oh my god, Clay. What if this has to do with what we were supposed to find in Bangor at Big Red's? Whatever was inside the ballot box might have been a clue for this place."

"We don't know that. Let's keep talking. Back to the skewer."

"All I can think about is shish-kababs and those metal skewers we have at home that look like little swords."

"That's it!" Clay exclaims. "Swordfish. Swords are skewers and 'catch' refers to fish. Like 'catch of the day.' All the words are there: land, skewer, catch. It's cryptic for 'The swordfish has landed.'"

"Well done, babe. Aunt Mitzi's cell phone clue *is* for the next place."

"I think the plant in Detroit is where we give the passphrase to this Joshua fellow. Then we'll get the keys to the Brougham. I better call Stone and tell him to get ready to meet us. It'll take him a couple of days to get there." He picks up his phone.

"Don't. We need to be sure first. If the Brougham is there, we'll just wait for Stone. Use those couple of days to get acquainted with Detroit."

"I like your idea. We can go to Berry Gordy's old house and tour the Motown Museum."

"From one music museum to another."

After the three-hour ride to Detroit, we check into a hotel and settle in.

"Long day today," Clay says. "I can't believe how late it is. I'm beat." His voice betrays how fatigued he is.

Clay plops down on the bed and closes his eyes. I'm a serpent, as I slink out of my clothes and slither under the covers.

"You know," I say, running my fingers through his hair, "we never did get to pick up where we left off at the Rock and Roll Hall of Fame."

"You're right. We got thrown off track, didn't we?" He opens his eyes and stares at my cleavage peeking out from under the sheets. "You little sneaker."

"You too tired to follow through?"

"Too tired for sex with you? Never." He stretches his long fit body, takes a deep breath, and exhales.

"You getting a second wind?"

"I'm getting a hard-on, thank you very much."

Clay rolls over in my direction and smiles, tracing a finger along the line between my breasts. Then he stands up and removes his shirt in that sexy one-handed way only men seem to know how to do, by grabbing the back of it at his neck and pulling it off over his head. He slips off his shoes and socks, unbuckles his belt, and slides his shorts and boxers down, kicking them away when they reach his ankles. He joins me under the covers.

"I love you," he whispers, brushing my hair away from my face.

"I know," I whisper back with a smile.

Closing the gap between us, Clay places his lips on mine with gentle pressure, and glides his hand along my body. Our kiss grows deeper. Stronger. Hotter. His mouth moves to my ear, his tongue skims along the outer edge and inner ridges. My nerves tingle in the best way. He reaches between my legs, sliding a finger up and down my slick center. I moan.

"Oh, god, Lynn," he whispers between kisses. "You're so wet already."

Clay squeezes my core with his hand, and inserts a finger into me, swirling it around. Then he barely touches that perfect spot, over and over, teasing me. Damn him. "Clay…please," I whisper, and he releases a low maniacal laugh. "Jerk," I laugh back. He finally gives in, circling with perfect pressure. Not too fast, not too slow. I reach for him. Hard-on is an understatement. I take hold and slide my hand up and down the length of him. He groans. The speed of his hands and fingers increase. Inside, swirling. Outside, circling. I'm on the brink.

"Jesus, Clay." My voice is breathy. "I need you in me. Now."

He doesn't hesitate. Clay enters me with ease. His movements are powerful but gentle. His kisses are deep but soft. His words are sharp but loving. In the midst of this intense passion, he takes me over the edge, right along with him.

CHAPTER 12

"**Y**OU READY?" CLAY asks. "What's the keychain?"

I find the one with 23 on it. "It's a rock with the word 'city' painted on it. Looks homemade. The key is small. Could belong to another diary."

"Detroit Rock City," Clay says, and starts belting out the chorus of the tune by Kiss. "How did Aunt Mitzi know about that song? That's greatness. She just went up a million cool points in my book. I would have gotten the clue just by the keychain. At least where we'd be going."

"Me too. Isn't it funny how sometimes we forget to look at the keychain first? We drive ourselves silly trying to figure out the clue, when it's right there on the keychain. And then other times, it's opposite. We look at the keychain and are dumbfounded, while the cipher tells us where to go."

"That's Murphy's Law at work."

"If we hadn't already been to Georgia, I might think this was a clue for Rock City. But we're much too far north for that right now anyway."

"True. I wasn't even thinking about the Rock City attraction down south. Probably because we're already in Detroit so my mind just automatically went there. Let's roll, babe."

We make a beeline for the Detroit-Hamtramck Assembly Plant. After driving around the huge campus a couple of times, we finally find the street that leads to the visitor center.

Walking into the lobby, we are greeted by a blonde receptionist named Haley, according to her nametag.

"Good morning. How can I help you?"

"Good morning, Haley. We're here to see Joshua," Clay says.

"Joshua? You mean Mr. Matthews? Do you have an appointment?" She starts clicking away on her computer, probably looking up his appointments for the day.

"Sort of," I answer.

"What do you mean by that? I'm afraid I can't call him if you don't have an appointment."

"We don't have an appointment," I say, "but he's expecting us."

"I'm sorry. He doesn't take drop-ins."

"He'll take this one," Clay tells her. His voice is firm, bold, and absolute. "Make the call, Haley."

Where did this attitude of his come from? It's like he's been possessed by Heisenberg, the alter ego character of Walter White from the television show *Breaking Bad*.

"I need your names."

"I'm afraid we can't give them to you," Clay says in Walter White's chilling and intimidating Heisenberg diction.

"Why?" she asks, her voice shaky.

"Just make the call, Haley."

I put my hand on Clay's arm and shoot him a look that begs the question, 'What the hell are you doing?' and I get a returned expression that says, 'Let me handle this.' I roll my eyes.

Haley stares at her phone system. She dials three digits. I hear a man pick up on the other end. "Security." Clay reaches over the counter of the desk and terminates the connection before Haley has a chance to speak. He scans the buttons on her switchboard and presses the one labeled 'Matthews.' Clay gives Haley an expectant look. What has gotten into him? Is he insane? Having been a police officer, he knows the dangers. Why did he hang up on security? He really shouldn't have done that.

Haley presses her headset closer to her ear so we can't hear the other end of the conversation. "Um, Mr. Matthews? There are a couple of people here to see you. … No, sir, they don't have an appointment, but they said you're expecting them. … I'm not sure, forties maybe. A man and a woman … Um, okay. Thank you. … Yes, sir. I'll let them know." She hangs up. "He'll be with you momentarily. You can take a seat, if you please."

"We'll wait here. Thank you for your cooperation, Haley," Clay says.

I pull my husband to the side and yell at him in a whisper. "What is wrong with you? You could get us thrown out! Arrested. Or worse, killed!" My pulse is racing.

"You have a better idea of getting Joshua's attention? Anyway, relax. It worked, didn't it?" he whispers back.

"You don't know that. I swear, if you screwed this up by acting like a complete ass, I'll—"

A door bursts open behind the front desk and a group of men rush through, guns at the ready. Ah. Security.

"You okay, Haley?" the leader asks. He doesn't take his eyes off us. "Matthews called. I thought—"

"Yeah. Sorry about hanging up on you, Murph." Haley looks at Clay, then back to the guy she called Murph. "I'm not sure what they're here for, but they need to see Mr. Matthews."

"You sure you're okay?" another guy asks, checking us out as well.

"Yes, I'm fine, Sully. Mr. Matthews said he'd see them."

"He told us to verify first," Sully says.

"I'm sorry," Clay says to Murph. "This is my fault. We need to see Mr. Matthews and it's urgent. I guess I gave Haley a scare."

"You *guess*?" Haley looks at Clay and rolls her eyes.

"What the hell, man?" the third guy asks Clay. He makes a move like he's about to attack Clay, but Haley pulls him back. He jerks out of Haley's grip and pulls his gun on Clay.

I gasp. My heart rate soars.

Clay puts his hands up in a flash. "Whoa, man. Everything's cool."

"Get on your knees! Hands behind your head!"

Holy shit, what's happening? This sure escalated quickly.

"Okay, okay," Clay complies.

"You too, missy!" the man yells to me.

"Oh my god, okay, I'm sorry."

"Don't you fucking touch her!" Clay yells.

He cuffs Clay and slams his body to the ground. Clay lands with an "oomph" and the guard pats him down.

"Oh shit, please don't hurt him!" My voice is weak and shaky. "This is a misunderstanding!"

"It's about the swordfish!" Clay yells. "My name is Clay Sinclair. Just tell Matthews. Please."

"You're not the one in charge, asshole." The guard pokes his gun into Clay's side, and I start crying.

Haley yells, "Sawyer! Stop! Oh my god. I'm calling Mr. Matthews."

Sawyer holsters his gun and I breathe a sigh of relief as I wipe the tears off my face.

"He's clean," he says to the other guys. He uncuffs Clay. "You can both stand up now, but don't fucking move," he tells us. Sawyer returns to Haley while keeping his gaze on Clay. "Hales, I can hold him for harassment."

"That's not necessary. Mr. Matthews is on his way. I'm okay. You guys can go back to your dungeon."

"I'm not leaving you alone with them. We're just doing our job, baby," Sawyer says.

"I know, thank you. Don't call me 'baby.'"

"But—"

"Not at work."

Sawyer walks closer to Haley and brushes her cheek with his knuckles. "You sure you're okay, Hales?"

"Yes. Nothing happened. I'm fine." She takes his hand away from her face and says in a low voice, "I told you, we should remain professional here. No public displays of affection."

"Sorry, baby," he murmurs. "I'm still new at this boyfriend thing."

She gives him a small smile. "It's okay. You'll learn."

An elevator to the left of the reception desk dings. A distinguished gentleman with white hair and Ben Franklin glasses exits and makes his way over to us, a look of curiosity across his face. He's wearing a coffee colored, double breasted, pin stripe suit, topped off by a brown derby hat. A taupe silk handkerchief matching his tie sticks out of his suit pocket. It's not every day you see someone dressed so debonair. Mr. Matthews, I presume.

"Are you Joshua?" Clay asks. His *Breaking Bad* act has vanished. Thank God.

"Yes, I'm Joshua Matthews. What's this about a swordfish? Who are you, exactly?"

"My name is Clay Sinclair. This is my wife, Lynn. We have a message for you," Clay says.

"A message?"

"Yes." Clay turns to me. "You should be the one to relay it."

Adjusting my posture, I try to stand tall and confident, though my body still trembles from the actions of the last few minutes. My voice is flimsy at best. "The swordfish has landed."

"I'm sorry?" he asks.

I repeat myself, but with assertion this time.

Joshua tilts his head to the left in confusion and his brows furrow. "I don't understand."

"Christ. Don't tell me we're in the wrong place," Clay says, mostly to himself. "Not after everything we've been through here this morning." He lets out a long sigh.

I try a different approach. "Mr. Matthews, we were given a message that led us here. The message said, 'Tell Joshua the swordfish has landed.' I hope we're in the right place and this isn't a crazy coincidence. Does it jog your memory if I tell you that I'm Sid and Mitzi Santini's great-niece?"

A flash of recognition hits him. "Oh! *That* swordfish!" He snaps his fingers. "I'll be right back." He pivots and walks back towards the elevator. "You guys can relax," he tells the security guards. "Everything is totally fine."

After Joshua disappears behind the elevator doors, Clay walks over to Haley. Her mouth is open and her eyebrows are up. The security guards surround her with their arms across their chests, not relenting.

"A little quick on the draw there earlier, huh, cowboy?" Clay directs his question to Sawyer.

"I'm not going to apologize for protecting my girl, or this company."

"I hope for Haley's sake that's not an indication of how things are in the bedroom."

"Fuck you, asshole."

"Jesus, Clay!" I yell at him. "That's enough. Shut your mouth."

"Now I understand why you took me down for no good reason. Trying to show off in front of your girlfriend."

"Clay!"

"Okay, look. I'm sorry," Clay tells them all. "Truly. I'm not an asshole, really. I just couldn't tell you our names, Haley. I thought it would have given it away. We're on a mission. Things just got out of hand. I should have never given you the impression that you were in any danger. I was way out of line. I sincerely apologize. To all of you."

The security guards nod (except for Sawyer, whose guard is still up) and their arms retreat to their sides (again with Sawyer being the exception).

"Okay," Haley says, "but I beg to differ. You are an asshole. You scared the crap out of me. Why are you here?"

I step up. "We're not exactly sure yet." My voice is steady and composed now, and my body has stopped trembling. "I think we're here to pick up a package or something. And please excuse my husband. He can definitely be an asshole from time to time. I'm sorry that he scared you." I slap Clay on his bicep. "Are you alright, Haley?"

"Yeah, fine. Just a little freaked." She looks back at Clay.

Clay gives her an apologetic expression.

The elevator dings again and I'm thankful for the distraction. Joshua exits carrying a briefcase.

The security team retreats, but not before Sawyer whispers something into Haley's ear, causing her to blush a hot shade of pink.

Joshua holds the briefcase out to me and I take it. "I believe this belongs to you, Lynn. Clay." Clay and Joshua shake hands.

"A briefcase?" So that's what the tiny key is for. "Thanks, Mr. Matthews. Sorry for dropping in without an appointment, but—"

"No worries," he says. "I understand. But you must also understand my need for security to check you out."

"Of course," I tell him.

"I'm sorry about the way you were manhandled, but I won't apologize for my security team. We've had a few incidents in recent months, so I've instructed them not to take any chances. I'm waiting on a walkthrough metal detector to be delivered any day now."

"I can appreciate that," Clay says. "As a retired police officer, I get it. You may want to have one of your guards in the lobby at all times though, just as another precaution."

"We usually do, but all the guards were working with my Information Technology department today, in the control room going over new computer software for our surveillance system."

"Gotcha. The good ol' IT department. What would we do without them?" Clay says.

"Exactly. I have one of the best. Can I offer you some lunch? We're preparing for a catered meeting upstairs. Plenty to go around."

"No, thank you," I tell him. "But that's so nice of you to offer."

"No problem. Sid told me years ago that you'd be coming to pick up the briefcase. Just didn't know when. My condolences to you, regarding Mitzi."

"Thank you."

"She was a fascinating woman."

"Agreed. How did you know them?"

"My father and Sid go way back. School days, I believe."

"Wow. How wonderful that they kept in touch."

"It is. And you know, you almost missed me. I retire next month."

"We would've tracked you down," I say.

"Yes," Clay says. "We're good at that. So, are the keys to the Brougham in there?" Clay asks, pointing to the case.

"I don't know. That's for you and Lynn to find out. You have a key, yes?"

"We do," I say. "Thanks again. We'll let you get back to work. It's been a pleasure meeting you."

"Pleasure's been all mine. You two take care." He tips his hat to us and retreats into the elevator.

We wave good-bye to Haley, exit the building, and head back to the truck.

"I could've taken that Sawyer guy," Clay says with a confident smirk on his face.

"*What?* Clay Weston Sinclair, that is not the response I was expecting from you after we walked out of the doors. Promise me you won't act a fool again."

"I promise."

"I'm serious, Clay. I can't believe the way you acted in there, knowing the risks employees face in public buildings these days." I stop and jerk his arm back. "You fucking know better than that!"

"Jesus, Lynn. I'm sorry. Okay? I know you're right. I realize I shouldn't have been such an ass."

"You risked our lives. I mean…are you crazy? You could've gotten us killed."

"I get that. I'm sure if they'd called the local police, I could've gotten out of it, given my background and all, but I wasn't really thinking of the immediate consequences. I'm getting caught up in the thrill of the hunt. It was a stupid move. No more of that. Pinky swear."

He holds out his pinky finger and I take a few seconds before I crook mine into his. He pulls them to his lips and kisses our joined pinkies, a gesture that tells me he means it. He never does that. I'm usually the one that invokes the pinky swear. "I'm sorry, love."

"Okay," I say with a heavy sigh, as we climb inside the truck with the briefcase.

"Can we please move on from this? Will you lighten up? Everything is fine."

"Telling a woman to 'lighten up' is no better than telling her to 'calm down.' You do know that, right?"

"Noted. And I'm sorry. Again. Please, Lynn. Let's just git'er done. The Brougham keys have gotta be in here," Clay says.

"Fine. Whatever. Apology accepted. I'm over it." I let out a huff and put the key into the case, popping the lock. Lifting it open, I see four things. None of which are what Clay wanted to see.

CHAPTER 13

"**W**ELL, SHIT. No apparent key. But, open the box. Open the box," Clay says with anticipation. "Or that envelope." He points a finger at said envelope. "The key could be in either one of those items."

"Hold on a minute, Sinclair. Let me take inventory. We have a small wooden trinket box, an envelope, a large gold thimble, and…" I pause. "What is this? A tiny bottle of liquor? I don't know about you, but I could definitely use a drink right about now," I laugh. The bottle is the size of those miniature ones they give you when you order a drinky-drink on an airplane. This one is an upright rectangle with a square black cap. It reminds me of Disaronno amaretto.

"Let me see that." I hand the bottle to Clay and he takes a closer look. "Holy shit, Lynn. Holy. Shit."

"What? What is it?"

"This isn't alcohol. Well, it probably is by now, but this is the original bottle of perfume that came with the vanity items in the Brougham."

"What?" I snatch the bottle from Clay and examine it. Putting on my best French accent, which isn't that great, I read the label. "'Arpège Extrait de Lanvin. Paris, France.' Oh my god. Is that really what this is?"

"Yup. And from the looks of it, it's never even been opened."

"Well, Aunt Mitzi always wore the same perfume. She probably put this one away under the bathroom counter or something." I pick up what I thought was a thimble at first, but see now that it's not. "What's this?"

"That's the atomizer that goes on top." Clay takes the two items from me. "You have to unscrew the bottle cap and replace it with this." He demonstrates without removing the cap of the perfume. "Pfft, pfft." He makes the sound of the bottle spraying, acting like he's spraying it on his neck. I snicker. Clay is completely in awe of what he's holding. "Do you have any idea how much this set is worth?"

"It's priceless to me."

"Of course. I'm just saying, these bottles practically don't exist anymore, let alone unopened. And with the atomizer? This is the holy grail of the Brougham. It's worth a small fortune."

Out of curiosity, I ask. "How much?"

"Probably anywhere from seven to ten thousand."

"*Dollars?*"

"No. Yen."

I smack him. "Damn. Seriously?"

"I don't joke when it comes to the Brougham. Could be worth more, depending on how desperate someone is to have the complete set of vanity items." He stares at the bottle.

"Do I need to leave you alone for a minute?"

"No," he laughs. "I just can't believe what I'm looking at. I'm so proud to have this."

"I had no idea it was so valuable. I'm glad we have it too. Let's see what else we have here."

I pick up the trinket box. Made of wood, it's the smallest trinket box I think I've ever seen: about two inches long, one inch high, and one inch deep. Its leather covering displays the pattern of a vintage map, with grids of latitude and longitude. Fitting. I unfasten the tiny swing hook clasp and open it to find another keychain with another key.

"What the hell?" I ask.

"Lynn, check out the keychain. It's the Cadillac logo. Maybe we're going to find the Brougham here after all."

"You think so?"

"Open the letter. See what Aunt Mitzi has to say."

Lifting the envelope from the briefcase, my finger slides under the seal. I unfold the paper and we read her words.

Dearest Loves,

I bet Clay is chomping at the bit wondering exactly where his 1957 Cadillac Eldorado Brougham is, so I'll get right to the point. You'll find it at your next destination. Make provisions now on how to get it home safely.

The key in the keepsake box belongs to the glove compartment and trunk. I happened upon it in our kitchen junk drawer several years back. I showed it to Sid and we reminisced about our beautiful Brougham and the places we'd gone in that wonderful car. After seeing the key, Sid came up with the idea for this stop on your quest. He thought of the clue and everything else for your Detroit stop. I hope you were able to meet with Joshua. He is the son of a friend of Sid's from school. In fact, his father, Jed, was the one who got Sid interested in Cadillacs in the first place. Suave fellow, that Joshua.

As for the perfume bottle, it was part of the vanity items that came with the Brougham, but you may already know that by now. I never opened it or wore it. I knew I'd never stray from my signature scent of Chanel No. 5, so I put it away in my closet and forgot about it. When Sid thought of this idea as one of your stops, a light bulb went off and I remembered I still had the perfume. I was thrilled that I'd be able to add it to your findings. And now you're probably putting two and two together. The powder puff that was in the ballot box in Maine also goes with the vanity items. I'm sure you were scratching your heads at finding a vintage powder puff at your stop at Big Red's Warehouse, not realizing the significance until now. That's another thing I can't believe I still had after all these years. Found it in an old purse in my closet. Surprised it hadn't disintegrated. At least it's barely used, otherwise I'm sure it would have been tossed decades ago.

When you get to your next destination, you'll receive more details on the Brougham and how I was able to track it down. Clay, I hope you enjoy bringing her back to life, and Lynn, I know you'll enjoy helping to keep her alive.

Love to you both,

Aunt Mitzi

"Oh my gosh," I say. "Thank goodness the ballot box only had a powder puff inside. Not that I wouldn't have loved to have it as part of the vanity collection for the car, but I'm just glad it wasn't something really important and majorly sentimental, you know?"

"Yeah, we dodged a bullet with that one. No wonder Katherine said the box sounded empty."

"Can you imagine what we'd have thought if we'd gotten it? I'd probably have thought it was a mistake or a joke or something. Now, back to the matter at hand. You ready to go find your new baby?"

"So ready. What's the clue say?"

I dig the folded sheets of paper out of my purse and flip to page three. "'In the city of Colts and Pacers, you're sure to find lots of racers. People are there you'll be happy to see, from the paternal side of your family tree.'" Looking up into Clay's blue eyes, I smile. "We're going to my grandparents' house."

"That was an easy clue."

"I wanted to go visit them anyway. I'm so glad we don't have to make an extra trip." I have a sudden realization. "Wait. Clay, do you think they have the car? And that's where it is?"

"Has to be."

"I wonder how Poppa and Nana ended up with it."

"We'll find out. Aunt Mitzi said we'd get more info when we get there."

I poke around in the box of keys, looking for the one with number 24 on it. I examine it while it dangles in front of Clay. As I look at the keychain, I notice something about it that poses a question, and I wonder if Clay is thinking the same thing.

"Okay," Clay says, "I get the checkered flags, for the races, but what's that letter?"

"It's a 'D.' I don't get it either. It doesn't seem significant at all. Neither of my grandparents' names start with D. And while there are two Ds in 'Indianapolis, Indiana,' that doesn't seem relevant."

Clay smiles that proud-of-himself smile.

"What is it?"

"It's the Roman numeral for five hundred."

"Indy Five Hundred. Clever."

"I. Am. So. Smart."

"Your sense of humility never ceases to amaze me," I say sarcastically.

"You know, ever since the new millennium, it's been a lot easier to read the copyright date at the end of movies. Before that, there were so many Roman numerals listed it was hard to make it out in a flash."

"Now who's the dork?"

"Whatever. You're an artsy girl. I'm a numbers guy."

I smile and then take a closer look at the key. "This isn't the key to the car. It's not a car key at all. It's too small."

"Let me see." Clay looks it over. "Maybe for a padlock. We'll see when we get there."

"I need to call my grandparents. You need to call Stone. And you can start the truck now."

"You're right. On all accounts."

The truck purrs to life and Clay hits the number for Stone on the dashboard display. The line rings throughout the speakers of the cab.

"Hello?" A female voice answers. Clay and I look at each other. I raise my eyebrows.

"Annie?" I ask.

"Hey, girl. Yeah, it's me. Stone's in the shower. I told him Clay was calling and he said I could answer it."

I look at the time. 9:17 in the morning. "It's early. You and Stone having sleepovers now?"

"Last night was the first of many I hope." I can hear the smile in her voice.

"Really? That's awesome."

"Yeah. I need to get up, but his bed is so comfortable."

"I wouldn't know. Oh! Happy birthday!"

"Thank you. So far it's been better than happy."

"What did he get you?"

"Well, first he gave me multiple…wait. Is Clay listening?"

"I can hear you loud and clear, Annie," Clay says. "You gonna finish that sentence?"

"Oh shit, I'm so embarrassed. I forgot it was your phone that called. This is a conversation for later. With Lynn."

I visualize her ears turning red. "Girl, don't be embarrassed. I told you it would probably be good."

"Good is an understatement. Okay, I've said too much. Stone hasn't given me my real present yet though. He's taking me to an early lunch at Olive or Twist."

"Oooh, all-day happy hour Mondays," I say with a smile.

"Yes, and I love the cocktail roulette."

"I like the flights," Clay says.

"I've never done one of their drink flights," Annie says.

"You should. You won't be disappointed. Okay, look, Annie. It sounds like you and Lynn have a few things to discuss, given your current, uh, position."

"Jesus, Clay," I smack him.

"Just tell Stone to call me after he gets out of the shower, please."

"Will do. Lynn, I'll call you later."

"You better. Did you take off today?"

"No, I took a half day. Going in after we eat, so I won't be drinking too much."

"Gotcha. Have a good birthday lunch. Drink something fruity for me though. Love you."

"Love you too. Bye, y'all."

Clay disconnects the phone. "Well, well, well…sounds like my brother's falling hard. He hasn't had a woman spend the night at his place since he got divorced."

"Seriously?"

"Yeah."

"Wow."

"Don't tell her that. He may not want her to know how he feels about her yet, you know? She may not be on the same page."

"Oh, she's on the same page. Same paragraph. Same line. But I won't say a word. I'll let them figure it out for themselves."

I reach for my phone and shuffle through my *Elements* playlist. "Ocean Drive" by Duke Dumont starts playing, followed by Carole King's "I Feel the Earth Move" and "Seminole Wind" by John Anderson. In the middle of Pitbull's "Fireball," Clay's phone rings.

"Stone. My man. Keeping women in your bed again, eh?"

"Shut up. Don't talk about her like she's a conquest."

"Jesus, I'm kidding. Lighten up, dude. Have you told her how you feel?"

"That's none of your business, Clay."

"So, you have." Clay taunts him by singing "Stone in Love" by Journey.

"No, I haven't. And fuck you. You know I hate that song."

"Well I like it. And fuck you back. I guess I'll keep the Brougham to myself then."

"Dude, you got it?"

"I think so. I'm on my way to get her now. I need your help. Can you meet me in Indianapolis with your trailer, day after tomorrow? It's about a twelve and a half-hour drive from Baton Rouge."

"Yeah. Good thing I'm my own boss. I'm there. What's the address?"

"Lynn's grandparents' house. I'll text it to you. Thanks, bro."

"No sweat. See you Wednesday."

I'll never understand those two. How they went from cursing each other out to being best friends again in less than a second is beyond my comprehension.

CHAPTER 14

Five hours later, we pull into the driveway of Poppa and Nana's two-story house. It hasn't changed a bit, still painted white with black trim. I called them after Clay hung up with Stone earlier and told them we were on our way thanks to Aunt Mitzi's clue and that we'd be here in time for supper. They were so happy I called and said they couldn't wait to see us.

Nana is on the front porch swing crocheting, and Poppa is pruning the shrubs. They are quite agile for their late eighties. I hope it's genetic.

I jump out of the truck and run towards the porch. "Nana! Poppa!" I hug Nana's neck as Poppa makes his way over from the flower beds. "It's so good to see you both. I've missed y'all so much."

"It's been too long, dear," Nana says. "You look beautiful as ever."

"Thanks, Nana."

"How's your sister doing?"

"CeCe's doing great. House-sitting for us, actually."

"That's wonderful." She reaches up to hug Clay while I turn to give Poppa a hug. "And I didn't think it was possible for you to get any better looking, Clay. Is there something in the water down in Louisiana?"

"You're too kind, Nana," Clay says. "You're not so bad yourself. Great to see you again."

"Hey now," Poppa chimes in. "Hands off. That's my woman."

Clay turns with a laugh and gives Poppa the old half hug, half hand-shake male greeting. "Hey Poppa. You're looking well."

"Not too shabby for eighty-eight, eh?" He wraps his thumbs around his red elastic suspenders and stretches them outwards.

"The yard looks fantastic," I say. "I can't believe you can keep up with it all, Poppa."

"Oh, it's nothing. I enjoy it. Now, let's get your luggage and come on in. Laurel's got your favorite dinner ready, Lynn."

"Roast with rice and gravy?" I ask Nana.

"Of course, dear. I've got you covered. With corn on the cob, broccoli casserole, macaroni and cheese, and lemon ice box pie for dessert. Ash even squeezed the lemons for me. Straight from our tree."

"Oh, that sounds delicious. And quite the spread. You've been busy, Nana. You really didn't have to fix all of that. It's just us."

"Nonsense. You know how much I love to cook. And I haven't seen you in ages, so it's a special occasion. Besides, it's already done."

"Well, okay then. Thanks for helping her out, Poppa."

"I wouldn't have it any other way."

"All this talk of food has my mouth watering," Clay says. "And I was praying for your mac and cheese, Nana."

"I've got you covered, too, Clay. I remember how much you love your macaroni and cheese."

"Thanks," he smiles. "You're the best Nana ever." Clay moves his attention to me. "I'll get our bags, Lynn. You go on inside and help Nana get set up."

I go into the kitchen, uncover all the food, and put serving spoons in each dish. Everything is just where I remember it. The smell coming from the various pots, skillets, and blue cornflower CorningWare dishes wafts through the kitchen, creating an aroma that I can only describe as heavenly. The divine scent of a Nana smorgasbord. Clay comes in with our bags and hauls them upstairs to the guest room, comes back down and helps us in the kitchen by filling glasses with ice.

We gather around the table and pass the dishes to each other, trimming our plates with home-cooked goodness. My grandparents update us on what's been going on in their lives. Nana has started a book club and Poppa is the new president of the local garden society.

"But," Poppa states, "we know you're not here to talk about books and bromeliads. It's the Brougham."

Clay's face lights up. "So you do have it. I knew it! Tell us how you came into possession of that beautiful baby."

"We bought it from Sid and Mitzi. Simple as that."

"You've had it all this time?" I ask Poppa. "I don't understand. Did Aunt Mitzi and Uncle Sid buy it back from you to give to us?"

"Not exactly. We kept it for about five years. Traded it in for a Cutlass Supreme back in seventy-two. When Mitzi contacted me a decade ago or so, trying to track it down for you, she told us what she and Sid were doing with their scavenger hunt mystery adventure for you and Clay. I thought that was the greatest thing I'd ever heard. I put my nose to the grindstone for you, following the paper trail of where the Brougham finally ended up. Since we traded it up here in Indianapolis, it was only fitting that I take care of this end for Mitzi and Sid, though they arranged for the pick-up and delivery."

"Where did you find her?" Clay asks.

"Not too far from here, actually. Sandusky, Ohio. I couldn't believe it had only landed three hundred miles away in thirty-five years. The last owner had all intentions of restoring it, but he fell sick and never got the chance. He died and his wife couldn't bear to part with it, until I told her Mitzi's story. Your story. And she agreed to sell it back."

"Can we see it after dinner?" I asked.

"It's quite dark in the garage. Several lights are burned out."

"I told you to change them out, dear," Nana scolds.

"I know, hon. I will. Tomorrow would be better to take a gander at it though. It's not in the best shape, so be prepared, son."

"I know, that's okay. Aunt Mitzi left us a letter and said the Brougham wasn't in great condition. I can't wait to start fixing her up."

"How will you get it back home?" Nana asks.

"My brother, Stone. He'll be meeting us here Wednesday, if that's okay."

"Of course, dear. He's more than welcome to come and stay."

"Thanks, Nana. He has a trailer and will haul it home for me."

"For us," I say. "It's my car too." I stick my tongue out at Clay. I couldn't have cared less about the car in the beginning, but the more I learn what a marvel it was, the more I know I'm going to enjoy it once Clay finishes restoring it.

The next morning, with light barely peeking through the windows, Clay jumps out of bed. "Lynn, wake up. Get dressed. Let's go check out the Brougham."

"Are you crazy? It's the butt-crack of dawn." My voice is rough with sleep. "Nana and Poppa probably aren't even awake yet."

"Of course they are. They're old. Old people wake up early. I smell bacon and coffee anyway. They're up. Come on, Lynn."

I growl and begrudgingly roll out of bed. "Fine."

Clay claps his hands and rubs them together with excitement. "This is gonna be great. Up and at 'em."

"I'm up, but it'll be a minute before I'm at 'em."

We make our way downstairs, and sure enough, Nana and Poppa look like they've been up for hours. There's an entire spread of biscuits, eggs, bacon, and hash browns.

"Good morning, you two. Coffee?" Nana asks.

"Morning. Please," I tell her. "Everything smells great. You didn't have to cook all of this for us though. Again, Nana, it's too much. We'd have been fine with cereal."

"Nonsense. It's nothing. My pleasure. Sleep okay?" Nana gets two mugs out of the cabinet and fills them with coffee. "Sugar? Creamer? Half n' half?"

"Creamer. Thanks."

"Black," Clay says. "Thanks. And yes, we slept great."

"Clay couldn't wait to get out of bed to go look at the car. But I gotta admit, I'm excited too."

"After breakfast," Poppa chimes in, "we'll go take a look at her. But as I mentioned, she's very sick. In need of great care to nurse her back to health."

"Don't worry. I'll have her back to her old self as soon as possible," Clay says. "I'm not sure what she'll need, but I found the parts manual online. A free PDF download. It has diagrams and everything needed, down to the exact nuts and bolts used. I've been researching the cost of each part. Some are reasonably priced, some not so much. But I hope I'll have her back up and running within a year or so after we get finished with our trip. Realistically though, I'm sure it will take longer."

"Maybe we can drive it back up here to show you when he's done," I say.

"Oh, I'd love that," Nana says. "God willing, we'll still be here."

After we eat, I help Nana clean the kitchen and then Poppa takes us outside to his shop where the Brougham has been kept.

"Did you bring your padlock key?" Poppa asks.

"Oh, crap. I didn't give it a second thought after you told us all about the car last night," Clay says. "I can go get it."

"I'm just messin' with ya. I've got my own. Though, you can leave yours with us. Be nice to have my spare back." Poppa unlocks the padlock on the garage door.

"Yes, sir. No problem."

Walking into the garage, a whiff of grease, gasoline, and tools invades my nose. A big shadowy shape sits in the corner, draped with a cover.

"There she is," Poppa says. "Help me with the sheet, Clay."

"Sure thing. I can't believe I'm about to see her."

Clay and Poppa remove the cover. Wow. I'm not sure what I was expecting, but this is worse. It's a total hunk of junk. Half rusted. Seats ripped to shreds. A busted window. But one thing stands out. That roof. That gorgeous brushed stainless-steel roof. It looks brand new. At least that won't have to be restored.

"Whoa." Clay is mesmerized. He runs a slow finger along what's left of the chrome edge trim. "I can't believe it." He turns to me. "What do you think, Lynn?"

"It reminds me of the Greased Lightnin' car before Kenickie and Zuko fixed it up for the race at Thunder Road."

Clay chuckles. "So, you're saying, this car could be…systematic? Hydromatic? And ultramatic?" I laugh as he pretends to take off a leather T-Birds jacket and flings it into the air. We proceed to sing a few lines of the song from the movie *Grease* before Poppa clears his throat.

"What the hell are you two doing?"

We both laugh and get back to the importance at hand. I answer Clay's question seriously this time. "I definitely see the beauty behind the ruin. It's going to be fantastic. I'm glad it's white. That will be a lot cooler in the summer back home. What time is Stone getting here tomorrow?"

"The plan is for him to be here around lunch. He'll leave Baton Rouge after work today, spend the night in Memphis, then leave from there early tomorrow."

"Okay, so what happens when he gets here? I mean, you just load this bad boy up on his trailer and that's it? No special precautions need to be made for its arriving home safely?"

"Um, first of all, it's a she. Got her own perfume and everything. She's yet to be named though. And second, you're right. It's a very delicate piece of American automobile history. I thought better of just putting her on one of his regular trailers, vulnerable to the elements. Called last night when you were in the shower and told Stone to bring one of his enclosed car haulers."

"Good thinking, kid," Poppa says.

"One of the benefits of having a brother that owns a heavy equipment and trailer rental company."

"You ain't kiddin'. The toughest part is going to be rolling her onto the ramp without the front door falling off."

"We'll manage. Thanks for doing everything you did to get this baby back."

"My pleasure. It'd been a long time since I chased a beautiful girl."

Clay smiles. "Now, Poppa, point me to your tallest ladder and your replacement bulbs and I'll change the burned ones out for you."

"Well, thank you, son. But, do me a favor and tell Nana I did it."

"You got it."

I laugh at them and shake my head. Men.

Stone pulls up in the driveway the next afternoon. He jumps out of his truck and we greet him on the porch. Clay introduces him to Nana and Poppa.

"It's a pleasure to finally meet you, Mr. and Mrs. Boudreaux. Thanks for allowing me to crash your visit with your granddaughter and my crazy brother."

"Great to meet you as well, Stone. And think nothing of it. Glad to have you," Nana says.

"Do you have room for one more by chance?"

"What do you mean?" I ask. "You brought the dog with you?"

"Hardly." He whistles towards his truck, the passenger door opens, and out bounds Annie.

"Oh my god! I knew it as soon as you started whistling," I laugh. Hands in her back pockets, she walks with a little more pep in her step than I've seen in a long time. "What the hell, girl? Were you hiding?" I give her a huge hug.

"Stone made me. I told him we should tell you. So, is it okay?" she asks with a sheepish grin.

"Of course it's okay," Nana brightens. "Annie, I haven't seen you since you and Lynn were teenagers."

"Yeah, that was almost ten years ago," Annie jokes.

"Riiiight," Stone teases, and Annie punches him playfully in the arm.

"How are you, darlin'?" Nana asks Annie.

"Doing great. Thanks."

"Welcome to our home, Stone and Annie," Poppa says. "Annie, you look wonderful. Come on in. Just in time for lunch. Hope you don't mind leftovers."

"I'll get your bags," Clay says.

"Thanks, man."

With lunch over, Clay takes Stone out to the garage to show him the car. I use the time to get the scoop from Annie.

"Okay, it's been a month and a half. I know things are obviously going well, but I want to hear it from you."

"Well, we started off wanting to take things slow, you know? We're both pretty much in the same place in our lives, with getting over divorces. But we just meshed so well together. We figured we'd throw caution to the wind. Just see what happens. Have fun and go with it. We're not getting any younger. I know we're still a little guarded when it comes to matters of the heart, but it's not like I don't know him. I know he's a great guy, I've always known that. He makes me laugh. Holds my hand in public. Sends me sweet texts in the middle of the day."

"Are we talking about the same guy? Stone Easton Sinclair?" I tease.

She smiles. "The other night, we were supposed to go out and I had to end up working late. I was so bummed. Told me to text him when I left the office. When I got home, he was waiting in the driveway with takeout from Antonio's. Knew I wouldn't want to cook or feel like eating leftover pizza again."

"That is super sweet."

"I don't know if it's because it's new or because I've known him forever or what, but I have deep feelings for him already. And he told me he could easily fall hard for me. We're so comfortable together. It just…feels right."

"Aww, Annie, that's so awesome."

"Yeah."

I gasp. "Oh my gosh, do you know what this means?"

"What?"

"We could be sisters. Like for real."

"That would be pretty freaking cool. But we haven't said the 'L' word yet. I mean really, it's probably a little soon for that."

"Tell me what he got you for your birthday."

"Well, you know how it started." She looks at the ceiling and blushes, a wide smile flashes across her face. "God, I had no idea sex could be so good. He's so generous, takes his time with me, savors me. Martin wasn't awful, but he was all I really knew for so long. He doesn't compare to Stone one bit. Like not even in the same realm. I mean, you know Stone is only the third person I've ever been with. Rhett in high school, then—"

"Yeah, I know your story. Then you met Martin in college, blah, blah, blah. Get to the good stuff. How'd the rest of your day go?"

She laughs. "Well, after work, he brought me a bouquet of beautiful red roses and took me out to dinner."

"Nice."

"He also got me a bottle of my favorite perfume and a blanket with the text of *Little Women* printed on it. It's so soft, I brought it with me."

"A *Little Women* blanket?"

"Yeah, he said he noticed my collection of copies I had on my shelf at home."

"Well, it is your favorite book."

"I didn't even realize he was paying that much attention to the 'little' details of my life."

I smile. "How observant. Smart guy, that one."

"I have so many versions of that book. He must think I'm crazy."

"Clearly he doesn't."

"Stone said he found a website online that prints the text of classic books on all sorts of things like t-shirts, tote bags, and blankets. Stuff like that. Since we like to cozy up on the couch and watch movies, he got me a blanket. I love it so much. It's perfect."

"Sounds like he did a great job picking out something from his heart. I'm so excited for you. Both of you deserve the very best and it sounds like you might be it for each other."

"Maybe so. I can see a future with him."

I let out a giddy squeal and we hug each other. "I'm so glad you came along for the ride up here. I've missed you."

"Me too. Taking a road trip is a great way to see a person for who they really are, and Stone was great the whole way up here. Besides cussing out a few slow drivers and watching his demeanor dip slightly in a traffic jam, he was pleasant company. Let me pick our drive-thru meals and have control of the radio."

"Oh yeah," I laugh, "you can tell you haven't been dating very long. Clay and I switch up the radio, but he gets antsy for his turn."

A rumble of footsteps up the stairs and laughter of our men enters our ears.

"Girl talk on hold," Annie whispers.

"What are you two plotting?" Clay asks.

"Plotting?" I reply.

"We're not plotting anything," Annie says.

"Okay good. Because Stone and I planned something."

"Oh lord. What are we doing?" I ask.

"Look," Stone says, "I know it's only Wednesday, Annie, and we're supposed to be back home Friday. But do you think you could take off work Monday too?"

"What's going on?" I ask. "Are y'all following us to our next destination?"

"No. If Annie can get Monday off, we're staying here till Saturday."

"I can get Monday off. Shouldn't be a problem. What's this all about?"

"The Indianapolis Five Hundred," Clay beams. "The big race isn't till Sunday, but Friday is Carb Day."

"Carb Day?" Annie asks. "I love carbs. I've been trying to do keto though."

"Oh, that's so hard," I respond.

"That's what she said," Clay and Stone say in unison. Then of course we all crack up.

"It's 'carb' as in carburetor," Clay says. "Not carbohydrates. Anyway, there are races all day, but the best part is, the Steve Miller Band is playing that evening."

"Oooh, sounds like fun," I say. "Wait. Do Nana and Poppa know about this?"

"They've been in Indianapolis for decades, so I'm pretty sure they do."

"That's not what I mean, goofball. I don't want to impose on them all week long."

"It was Poppa's idea. He's the one who told me about it. Asked if we'd ever been to the races. Perfect timing for us to be here. So, we'll give Indianapolis hell for the next few days. If you girls can hang."

"Please," Annie says. "I think we're up for the challenge. You know us better than that."

"And that's why I love you both. Y'all are in charge of finding us someplace cool to go tonight. Stone and I are going to hit the local gym."

"On it," I tell him. "Don't be gone too long."

"Yes, ma'am," Clay says.

The guys grab workout clothes and kiss us goodbye. Annie and I proceed to research the nightlife of Indianapolis. We find a place called Union 50 that sounds right up our alley. The pictures online show a huge backlit bar and a unique menu with all kinds of meat and seafood, as well as an eclectic cocktail menu. Their signature seasonal cocktails are named after all things pop culture. Currently, the list includes Gargamel, Little Buddy, Thundercats Go!, and a few others.

The four of us spend the evening eating, drinking, and laughing, truly enjoying each other's company. I notice the way Stone looks at Annie, as if she's the only woman on the planet. It makes my heart smile for her. They really make a great couple.

Friday comes and we head to the Indianapolis Motor Speedway for Carb Day. It's a lot like tailgating for an LSU game. People are packed under canopies, cooking food and drinking copious amounts of alcohol, dancing to music blaring from huge speakers, playing flip cup and beer pong. Oh, and there's racing. Somewhere. We meet some great people from all around the country and get a bit of a lesson on all things Indy 500. We even met some people that came all the way from Australia just for the races. I'm so glad we were able to experience this, and that both Stone and Annie are here too.

As the Steve Miller Band makes it on stage, we rock out, jamming to all their greatest hits, my favorites being "Abracadabra" and "The Joker." The night winds down and we head back to Nana and Poppa's for a good night's sleep. Today was a blast. Hell, this whole week has been a blast. Tomorrow, Clay and Stone will load up the Brougham and we'll go our separate ways.

CHAPTER 15

"Nice and easy," Clay says to Stone as they roll the Brougham onto the dock ramp of the car hauler.

"I'm doing the best I can, man. The right front tire is wobbly. Thank God I brought the hauler with an automatic lift. I can't imagine trying to get this baby up an inclined ramp without breaking something else."

They get the car centered and Stone presses the power button, raising up to the entrance of the trailer. They guide the Brougham inside and take their time securing it.

Annie uses this opportunity to pull me aside. She speaks in a soft voice. "Stone told me he loved me last night."

"Wait. What?" I can't believe it. I'm so happy for her. "Are you serious? I thought you said it was too soon for that."

"Yes, I'm serious. I thought it was too soon. For him."

"Did you say it back?"

"Of course," she says with a huge smile across her face. "I knew I was falling for him, but I was holding back because I didn't know where he was. And I wasn't sure it was actually love until he said it to me first. My heart just opened completely, and I knew. I'm in love with him."

I get a little giddy and give her a big hug. Stone turns his head at the sound of my high-pitched squeal and catches us. He smiles and shakes his head, knowing she must have told me. At that moment, I think he told Clay, too, because I hear Stone's voice lower and the words 'love' and 'Annie' are discernible. The next thing I know, I hear Clay saying, "Get the fuck outta here. That's great, man." Then he starts singing "Stone in Love" again. Annie and I laugh. I don't think Stone meant for us to know that he was telling Clay about his revelation, but there's a slight echo from them being in that car hauler, and his hushed voice managed to carry halfway across the yard. But Clay? He definitely wasn't trying to be quiet.

The guys finally get the car locked down and lower themselves on the automatic platform.

"That was nerve wracking. We good to go?" Annie asks.

"Clear for take-off," Stone says.

"Dude. Be careful. Please."

"As if, bro. Like you need to tell me. I want this sweet thing home safe and sound as much as you do."

"I doubt that," Clay says. "And please do me a favor. After she's parked safely in the garage, don't touch her again until I get back home."

"Are you shitting me?"

"No, man. I'm freaking serious. Don't do anything without me. Call Frank to help you offload her."

"Frank? Isn't Cecilia at your house?"

"Yes."

"Will she be okay with that?"

"Yeah, they still get along." Clay turns to me. "Lynn, give CeCe a heads up that Frank will be meeting Stone at the house."

"I'm sure my sister would love nothing more than to see her ex-husband," I say with sarcasm.

"What?" Clay says. "They do get along, right?"

"They're cordial. It'll be fine."

I go inside to tell Nana and Poppa the car is loaded and we're all about to leave. They follow me back outside to see us off. Stone and Annie thank my grandparents for their hospitality, hugs all around.

"Thanks for coming up here, man," Clay tells Stone.

"Happy to do it. Now hurry up with this expedition of yours so we can fix her back up."

"May be a couple more months. I'll keep in touch."

They give each other the clap-on-the-back hug and shake hands.

I give Stone a big bear hug. "Take care of my bestie."

"You know I will. She's my girl." He smiles as he looks at her.

"I can't tell you how happy I am about that."

Annie hugs me. "Glad I was able to make the trip. Thanks for everything. We had a great time. Love you."

"Love you too. Y'all be careful driving back. Let us know when you get there."

"Will do."

"Call me if you have any problems," Clay says.

"Sure thing," Stone says.

Annie and Stone get in his truck and he backs the car hauler out of the driveway like the pro that he is. We all wave to them as they leave, and Stone honks his horn.

Clay and I are ready to get back to our travels. We hug Nana and Poppa and say good-bye.

"I hope we didn't disrupt your lives too much this week," I tell them.

"Are you kidding? It's been great having all of you," Nana says.

"Glad you decided to stay the whole week," Poppa says. "Don't forget this." He dangles a key from a keychain. "For the ignition."

"Holy crap," Clay says. "I thought this would be long gone. This is great, Poppa. Thanks."

"Well, you'll still probably need to rebuild the ignition, but this is the original key. Something of a keepsake, perhaps."

"Of course," Clay says.

"You kids be careful on the road."

"We will. Thanks again for everything and for taking care of the Brougham," Clay tells Nana and Poppa.

"One more hug for the road," I say. I give them both tight hugs, as I have no idea when we'll be back. "Love you both. Take care of yourselves."

"You do the same, sweetheart," Nana says. "We love you too." She smooths my hair and kisses my cheek.

"Bye, darlin'," Poppa says. "Clay, you keep taking good care of my granddaughter."

"Yes, sir. That's my number one priority. We'll be back with the restored Brougham as soon as we can."

"Look forward to it. Be safe."

We get in the truck and wave good-bye as we back out.

"That was a great visit," Clay says.

"Like a vacation within a vacation. The races were a blast."

"Sure were. Whatcha got for music?"

"I have the perfect song." I pull up my *Road Trip* playlist and hit "On the Road Again" by Willie Nelson.

"Okay. I can dig it, given it's been a while since we've actually been on the road," he says.

I text Cecilia to check on things at the house and thank her again for staying there while we're gone. And then I let her know that Frank will be dropping by to help Stone with the car. I cross my fingers that she won't be too upset. She replies with a horde of eye-roll emojis. At least it's not a bunch of middle finger emojis.

"Clay?"

"Yes, love?"

"Where are we going?"

"Oh, shit. I have no idea. I was just heading south. Where are our heads?"

"I don't know. I think we're just really tired from going nonstop this week. Pull over and I'll get the clue sheet out."

Clay exits the interstate and drives into a church parking lot. I unfold the papers to read the next clue.

"Alright, here we go. 'In the building of Stella Cohen Peine's death, access the place where she took her last breath. Beware what's around, for the space is cluttered, but there you'll find a libation cupboard. Watch for Stella, as she still remains. Though she moves many things, she doesn't shake chains.' Oh holy crap." Not a fan of the spooky stuff.

"Yes indeed. You ready for some ghostbustin'?"

"I'm a little freaked out."

"We should call Dr. Peter Venkman and crew. Maybe Stella is the Keymaster."

"Stop it," I laugh. He starts singing "Ghostbusters" by Ray Parker, Jr.

"Do you know where this place is? Or who Stella is?"

"No, but I have a feeling we're about to get a lesson."

"What did it say about libations? Does Aunt Mitzi want us to get our drink on?" he laughs.

I look back at the clue. "Libation cupboard."

"So, like a liquor cabinet then. Something inside a liquor cabinet in a messy room."

"Something like that."

"What about the keychain?" he asks. "Maybe that will help."

I rummage through the box of keys and find the one labeled 25. "Twenty-five. Wow. We're halfway through." There's a sadness to my voice.

"What's wrong?"

"Nothing. Not really. Just…I feel like we're almost done."

"Lynn, halfway isn't almost. When we get to forty-eight…that's almost. We still have so much left to do. And you know we can drag this trip out for as long as we want. We just did that by taking the extra week in Indianapolis. Plus all the other side trips we've taken, like Boston, Hershey, and Fallingwater. When we're finished, only the trip is over. Not the memories. We'll be talking about this for the rest of our lives. Telling stories to our friends and family. It will always be in our hearts and minds. Your tree with all the ornaments you've bought will be a constant memento in the house. You said you wanted to keep it up all year, right?"

"Yeah," I sniffle.

"Remember how we said we wanted to go back to some of the places and spend more time there? Like Clarksdale, Mississippi and the bed and breakfast in Glade Valley, North Carolina?"

"I remember. And Birmingham. We've gotta go back to the Empire Building. Take Kitty up on her offer to stay at the Elyton Hotel."

"See? We will. We can revisit the memories in person. It'll never really be over, babe."

My insides warm and my heart swells. I love him so much. I'm so thankful to know that Clay will still want to travel together even after our quest is over. "I love you."

"And I love you." Clay wraps his hand around the back of my neck, pulls me towards him, and presses a soft kiss to my lips. "So, what does the keychain look like?"

I smile and show him. "It's Marlon Brando."

"Brando? Young Brando or big, bald, and crazy Brando? Do you know where he's from? Maybe that's where we're supposed to go next."

"I don't know where he's from," I said. "But look at the picture."

"Black and white. It's young Brando. He's screaming."

"This is the famous scene from *A Streetcar Named Desire*."

"Never saw it. Wait. That's in New Orleans. We can't be going there. What's the deal?"

"It's the scene where he's screaming his wife's name." Clay has a blank look on his face. "Come on, Clay. You have to know this."

"How would I know his wife's name if I never saw the movie?"

"It's only been parodied about a million times. I know you've seen the one with Julia Louis-Dreyfus in an episode of *Seinfeld*." Still nothing.

"Does Brando like, do a weird dance that can only be described as a 'full body dry heave'?"

"Seriously? Oh my god, Clay. You're going to make me do it, aren't you?"

"Do what?" he smiles.

I give my best impersonation of Brando's Stanley Kowalski, screaming 'Stella' and stretching it out for a couple of seconds. Clay starts cracking up. "What?" I ask.

"I just wanted to drive you to start screaming for Stella. That was greatness. Of course I know that scene."

"You ass. I just knew you were doing that to me on purpose," I laugh and smack him on the arm.

"You should've seen yourself." He mocks my impersonation. I can't help but laugh even harder. "And you know we never missed *Seinfeld*. That was one of my favorite episodes."

"Mine too. All that aside, this still doesn't help tell us where we need to go." I pull up the web browser on my phone and search for Stella Cohen Peine. "Paducah, Kentucky."

"Paducah, Kentucky. Ready or not, here we come." Clay puts the city into the GPS, and we continue heading south. "It's a five-hour drive. Should be there by supper time. Tell me who this Stella from Paducah was."

"Okay, hold on. Let me see what I can find." My eyes scan the headings. "Don't need to know where she's buried, don't need her census info…" My voice trails off as I scroll down. "Ah, here we go. The C. C. Cohen Building. That's where she died. It's now a restaurant called Shandies."

"Okay. Find a hotel. After we check in, we'll go have dinner at Shandies and see if we can't find Stella while we're there."

"Um, please don't do anything on purpose to make her show herself."

"You scared?"

"Maybe. I just don't think we should poke the bear, you know? We're already going into her personal space. The place where she died."

"She sounds more like a harmless poltergeist."

"You think poltergeists are harmless? I'm sorry, but, did you see a different movie than I did?"

"Lynn, the movie *Poltergeist* is completely different than what a poltergeist actually is, you know that. They only move things and turn off lights. It's their way of saying, 'Hello' to you."

"It could also be interpreted as, 'Get the hell off my property, you sons-a-bitches.'"

Clay laughs and shakes his head at me. "It'll be fine. I promise I won't provoke her spirit."

CHAPTER 16

D RIVING UP TO the corner where the C. C. Cohen Building is located, I take in all the details that say, 'this building is an antique.' The Italianate structure was probably built in the mid-1860s, around the end of the Civil War, when that style was becoming more popular. The mass production of cast iron and pressed metal made the ornamental elements of Italianate style affordable, and architects of the time really took advantage.

The three-story C. C. Cohen Building's bricks are painted a lovely salmon color. Decorative cast iron columns and pilasters support the weight of the upper floors. A row of evenly spaced dentils is set between fancy corbels under the white cornice at the roof. Vertical windows are set on the top two floors, also trimmed in white. The second-floor windows catch my eye. Arched, they consist of three panes: the top pane is round, the middle is square, and the bottom is rectangle. I've never seen any like that before. The decorative window hoods on both levels display ornate key-stones. Though the windows on the third floor aren't exactly arched, they still exude elegance. Two stacked rectangle panes of glass make up those windows, with most of them having closed shutters on the bottom piece of glass. That must be the floor where Stella lived. And died.

"Man, that is one girly building." Clay parks the truck on the curb right outside of Shandies. "I mean, the ornamental stuff's not so bad, but did they have to paint it pink?"

"It's salmon."

"Raw-fish pink. So much better," he says sarcastically. "You know, 'salmon' is what women say to get their men to wear pink shirts."

"Pink is a color. It's not just a 'girl' color. Do you think blue is just for boys?"

"Well no, but that's different."

"Wrong. See…such a double-standard. Haven't you ever heard the saying, 'Real men wear pink.'?"

"Babe. I don't need to wear pink to prove how much of a real man I am. Do I really need to show you? Right now?"

"That won't be necessary. Just agree that pink isn't just for girls."

"You say tomato…" He reaches over to my side and opens the glovebox while accidentally on purpose brushing his arm against my breasts. "Not that everything girly is bad." He winks at me. Clay never misses a chance to try and cop a feel. He grabs two small but powerful flashlights. "Put these in your purse."

We enter the restaurant and it smells divine. The combined aromas of garlic, grilled steak, and french fries hit my nose and my stomach tells me it's time to eat. I didn't realize how hungry I was until now. The atmosphere is pub style, with a color-scheme of red, gold, and green. I see dark wood tables and beams, stained glass accents, and a lot of brass. A large circular candelabra hangs from the center of the ceiling. Surrounding mirrors create the illusion that there are more than one. Brass railings border a raised bar to the left. We're greeted by the hostess and seated at a table. She hands us menus and tells us that our server will be right with us.

"Welcome to Shandies. I'm Donovan and I'll be your waita fah tonight." The guy has a thick Boston accent. Completely out of place in Kentucky. "Can I staht you auff with a drink?"

"A drink. Yes, absolutely," I say. "What's good? I want something fruity."

"Lights auf Paducah is kind auf populah," Donovan says.

"Lights of Paducah. What's in it?" I ask as I scan the cocktail menu, looking for the drink.

"Peach vodka, lemonade, pineapple juice, and grenadine. It looks like a sunset."

"Perfect. Sign me up."

"I'll try your Kentucky Shandy."

"Great choice. I'll be right back."

Donovan makes his way to the bar and I see him relay our drink orders to the bartender. Clay scans the interior of the restaurant from top to bottom, probably trying to see if we'll be able to sneak upstairs.

"The second floor is wide open," he whispers.

"I noticed."

"I don't think we'll get by without being seen, but…" he trails off and I can tell that he's thinking of a plan.

"What do you want to do?"

"I hear people talking up there. Sounds like a private party. We can probably go up with our drinks like we belong. Then maybe look for a door or another set of stairs to the third floor."

"And pretend we're lost if we get caught?"

"That's the game we've been playing, so, yeah."

Donovan sets our drinks on the table. My Lights of Paducah really does look like a sunset, with a nice golden yellow at the top, a blend of orange in the middle, and fading into a layer of cherry red at the bottom. I take a sip.

"How is it?" Donovan asks.

"Just what I needed. Thanks."

He takes our dinner order. "If you need anythin' else aur have any questions, I won't be fah."

"Great. Thanks," Clay says.

Donovan leaves to bring our order to the kitchen.

"You're so predictable," I tell Clay.

"How do you mean?"

"I knew you'd get the mac and cheese."

He smiles. "And I knew you'd get the steak."

"Touché. How's your shandy?"

"Not bad. I can taste a hint of bourbon." After taking another sip, Clay points to his drink with a raise of his eyebrows, offering me a taste.

I shake my head. "No thanks. I don't think it will mix well with mine."

Clay looks around some more. "I wonder why the first-floor windows are so much different than the upper levels. Why are they so huge and simple?"

"Probably because when this place was first built, it was a department store or general store that needed display windows to show off their merchandise."

"Good point." He lifts his shandy at me, like a cheer for my knowledge. "Did you find out any background about this place? Its history?"

"No, I didn't read further after finding out this is where Stella died."

"Maybe there's some sort of connection to Uncle Sid. This could've been a bank at one time."

"On it." I do a search for more info on my phone while Clay surveys the restaurant's layout and finishes his drink.

Donovan brings our dinner and sets everything down. After Clay orders us a second round of drinks, we thank Donovan and I cut into my juicy steak. Between bites, I continue scrolling to see if I can find anything on the building's past.

Clay takes a bite of his pork chop and chases it with a forkful of macaroni and cheese. "Lynn, guess what I want to say about this mac and cheese?"

"Is it effing delicious?"

"That it is," he laughs.

I laugh and shake my head at him as I pop another piece of ribeye into my mouth. Still scrolling on my phone next to my plate, I find something interesting. "Says here that this building was a clothing store, dry goods store, and then, get this…a liquor dealer and distillery company."

"Nice. So maybe the liquor cabinet we're looking for has something to do with that."

"That's what I'd assume. But that owner only had the building from 1914 until 1921. Or at least that's only how long it was a liquor dealer and distillery."

"Hmm. I guess business didn't do so well after Prohibition kicked in," he laughs.

"Right," I smile. A thought occurs to me. "Uncle Sid was too young during that time though."

"But his dad wasn't."

"Precisely."

"What are you thinking? I see your wheels turning."

"Maybe this place was a speakeasy."

"I don't think so."

"But how could you know? Weren't they all secret?"

"Yes and no," Clay says. "Most of your speakeasies were in big cities like New York, Chicago, Detroit. It's not likely this place was a speakeasy per se, but…" He pauses.

"What? Now it's your wheels that are turning."

"Maybe the distillery sold its liquor illegally to…take a guess."

I think about it for a second. "Holy shit. Al Capone."

"Ding ding ding. So, we have another possible mob connection between Scarface and Mr. Santini. As if it wasn't interesting enough to find out that the senior Santini was one of the whistleblowers on Capone. All those newspaper articles we received at the old bus station in Georgia with the crazy Capone headlines…"

"Yeah, fun read. So, what do you think Mr. Santini could have had to do with the distillery here?"

"No idea. Not even saying he did have anything to do with it. Just sort of coincidental, don't you think? That Aunt Mitzi sent us here looking for a liquor cabinet when this place used to be a distillery right before Prohibition went into effect?"

"Oh, what if Mr. Santini was one of the Untouchables?"

"Doubtful. Not unless Eliot Ness hired him without anybody ever knowing. Ever."

"But he could've. And maybe Uncle Sid knew."

"The whole situation is iffy though. And I think the timeline is a little off. Capone's bootlegging heyday wasn't really until the mid to late twenties. Besides, what would a banker from a small town in Louisiana have to do with trying to catch bootleggers in Kentucky?"

"Exactly. Nobody would suspect a thing." I point my fork at Clay after taking another bite.

"You really want it to be true, don't you?"

"It would just be exciting to find out something like that. And maybe we figured it out without Aunt Mitzi even having to tell us." I can feel my face light up, with eyebrows raised and a broad smile that flashes all my teeth. "Either way, it's kind of fun to think about."

"It kind of is. In the meantime—"

"How's everythin' taste?" Donovan asks, as he's back at our tableside.

"Great," Clay says.

"Can I get you anythin' else?"

"Well," I say, "now that you mention it, you said to let you know if we have any questions, right?"

"Shawr. Ask away."

"Can you possibly let us—" Clay gives me a soft kick under the table and barely shakes his head at me. If we weren't so in tune with each other I would have never known he was giving me a signal to not ask about going upstairs.

"Can we see a dessert menu?" Clay asks.

"Auf cawse. Be right back."

"What did you do that for?"

"We don't need the extra attention, Lynn."

"I was just going to ask what's going on upstairs. People do that at restaurants."

"What if it's a party we can't crash?"

"Yeah, but all we have is the key to the liquor cabinet. What if the place itself is locked?"

Clay nods towards our waiter across the restaurant. "You think Good Will Hunting is just going to let us in? What if it's not locked at all?"

"Alright. Fine."

"Here you awr," Donovan says, handing both Clay and me a dessert menu.

"Give us a second to look it over?" I ask him.

"No prahblem." He walks back over to the bar and puts a drink order in for another table.

I put the menu down. I'm too full to eat dessert.

"You don't want dessert?" Clay asks.

"I thought you just did that as a diversion. I'm stuffed anyway."

"Oh hell no. I want dessert. You sure you don't wanna share the Triple Chocolate Bomb with me?"

"Say what now? Triple chocolate? That's thirty-three percent better than double chocolate!"

"Fifty percent better."

"Don't mix dessert and math."

His voice lowers to a seductive tone. "It's black velvet cake." Then he whispers, "And no math."

I snicker. "Black velvet?" I close my eyes.

"With chocolate mousse."

"Chocolate mousse?" I repeat, matching his tone.

He whispers, "Dark. Chocolate. Shell."

Must. Have. Need.

"What else?" I whisper, eyes still closed.

"Chocolate…curls. Come on, Lynn, you know you want it. Tell me you want it."

"I want it." My whisper is breathy.

"Have we decided aun a dessert?" Donovan asks.

I open my eyes with a start. My face flushes. Our waiter is blushing and trying to hide a smile. Jesus, how long has he been standing there?

Clay chuckles out, "We'll take the Pineapple Upside Down Cake."

The hell we will. It's my turn to kick him.

Clay grins. "Or maybe instead, we'll have the Triple Chocolate Bomb. Two spoons."

"Great choice, sir. It'll be out shahtly."

"You're such an ass," I tell Clay, working hard not to laugh. "Only you would seduce me in the middle of a restaurant with the promise of all my favorite variations of chocolate converged onto one plate. In front of the frickin' waiter no less."

"Was it good for you?"

"I think Donovan liked it. Good lord, I can't believe you did that. I'm so embarrassed."

"No you're not."

"Maybe not *so* embarrassed, but embarrassed just the same. So much for not drawing extra attention to ourselves. Smooth move."

"Nah, that was insurance. If the place upstairs is locked, I'm sure

Donovan will let us in. That little show we just gave him? Combined with the fat tip I'll leave him? He won't be able to say no."

"What am I going to do with you, Sinclair?"

"Anything you want." He winks at me.

After devouring our decadent dessert, we pay the bill and head in the direction of the restrooms, fortunately located near the stairway to the second floor.

"Score," Clay whispers.

"Two minutes," I say as I disappear into the ladies' room. I use the bathroom, wash my hands, and touch-up my face before meeting Clay back at the stairs.

He climbs to the upper floor with me right behind him. There is indeed a private party going on. A banner with 'The Mack Attack is Back!' is hung on the wall over pictures of crew-cut men in full combat gear. Looks like Mack just came home from deployment. I know first-hand how it feels to celebrate such an occasion. The party we threw for Clay when he got back from Afghanistan was a lot like this one.

What's left of a huge cake sits on a table in the corner, the only evidence of its former immensity is an outline of blue icing on a slab of white cardboard bearing the few remaining slices. Miraculously, one is a corner piece. The group is laughing, drinking, telling stories, and are completely oblivious to us. They sound like a fun bunch of people.

Across the room from the party sit three empty Chesterfield sofas along with several club chairs and coffee tables of different styles, all centered around a dark stage. I presume they have live music here from time to time. Possibly even wedding receptions. There's another bar that lines the long wall, but it's not being utilized now, even with the private party going on in the area.

Looking back at Clay, I notice he's zoned out. I put my hand on his arm. "Hey. You with me?"

He turns his head to look in my eyes. "Yeah. Sorry, love. Let's move."

We approach a dark hall in the corner near the stage area. Another set of stairs comes into view on the left side. Treading lightly, we ascend. The large wooden door at the top looms and I feel like it gets further away with every step we take. Kind of like that scene in *Poltergeist*. Hmm…

I'm nervous, as my fingers grip the old brass doorknob. The knob turns, but the door doesn't budge. "It's locked," I whisper.

"Scoot over. Let me try," he whispers back. Clay puts a little more muscle behind it. It opens and he smiles. "After you." He gestures to let me go ahead of him.

"No thanks. You first."

We enter the apartment and Clay quietly shuts the door behind him. Silhouettes of chairs are revealed by the slightest bit of moonlight that slips through the top windowpanes.

Clicking on our flashlights, we scan the room.

"Holy crap. This place is huge." My voice is low, in volume and pitch.

"Yeah. See anything that could be a liquor cabinet?"

"Not so far."

Various types of furniture, framed prints, and several odd styles of bird cages are scattered all around in disarray.

"Shelves, tables, chairs, lamps," Clay surveys.

I see a figure of a person and jump, grabbing on to Clay. "Oh my god, who is that?" I whisper as I close my eyes.

"Nobody. It's a mannequin. Chill out, babe. It's all good."

"Oh, sweet seven-pound nine-ounce baby Jesus, my heart is beating out of my chest. That thing scared the shit out of me."

Clay laughs. "It's like a freaking flea market up in here."

"Well, Aunt Mitzi did say the place was cluttered."

"Look. Over there in the far corner. There's some kind of cabinet to the left of that old dresser."

"Let's check it out."

As soon as I take the first step towards the cabinet, we hear a noise, like a chair scraping across a wood floor. I flash back to the sliding furniture in *Poltergeist*.

I freeze. "What the hell was that? Did you move something?" I ask in a whisper.

"That had to be coming from downstairs, echoing up."

"Sure. Yeah, let's go with that. Unless someone's on to us."

"I don't think anybody knows we're up here."

"Except…Stella. Stella knows we're here."

"Stella?" Clay address her. "We come in peace," he snickers as he holds two fingers up in the hippie sign for peace.

"Jesus, Clay. We're not aliens in a sci-fi movie. Don't make fun. I'm a little freaked out."

"Sorry. Okay. Stella, my name is Clay. This is my wife, Lynn." He points to me. "We apologize for invading your personal space. Please allow us to retrieve the item, or items, in the liquor cabinet without incident." He turns to me. "Happy?"

I nod. We continue towards the cabinet, and the closer we get, I see that it's one of those old Art Deco radio bars. "This is it. Oh my gosh. I've always wanted one of these."

"Hold up. Are you sure this is a liquor cabinet? There's no lock. This thing looks like a big stand-up antique radio."

"It is. But," I open the lid and swing open the sides. "Voilà. It's also a bar."

"Holy shit. This thing is pretty bad-ass."

"They used these during Prohibition, to disguise the fact that it's a liquor cabinet. It just appears to be a big piece of furniture. Plus, party music. For the most part, only the more affluent families and businessmen had them." I shine my light inside and I'm in awe of what I discover next. "Oh my god. It still has all the original glassware." I pick up one of the glasses, its silver rim and sparkling designs glinting in the subtle moonlight. "Oh, Clay. I'm in love. Damn. I wish we could take this whole thing home with us."

"I'll never understand how women fall in love with furniture."

"The same way men fall in love with cars. Also, it's a freaking liquor cabinet. What's not to love?"

"Touché, Mrs. Sinclair. I guess I'm a little in love. Just don't tell my truck. Wait. Why do we have a key if there's no lock?"

"Au contraire, mon amour. The liquor locker is at the bottom. On the side." I put the glass back and point my flashlight to reveal the small locked door.

"Well I'll be damned. Liquor locker? Like, for backup?"

"Sure. I guess you could call it that," I laugh. "That's usually where the actual bottles were kept, since the liquor would be poured into the decanters that come with the bar cabinet. Wanna hear a bit of useless, but interesting tidbit of trivia?"

"Always."

"One of these radio bars was featured in the movie *Angels with Dirty Faces* from the nineteen-thirties, starring Humphrey Bogart and James Cagney. It's an old gangster movie."

"Okay."

"And you know the old gangster movie from *Home Alone* that Macaulay Culkin watches and uses to pay the pizza boy?"

"Yeah. Wasn't that called *Filthy Souls* or something?"

"*Angels with Filthy Souls*. It's not a real movie. But it was based on *Angels with Dirty Faces*."

"No shit?"

"No shit."

"Huh. Never would've guessed."

"Well, now you know."

"Might come in handy if I'm ever on *Jeopardy*."

Bending down, I unlock the liquor locker. Inside, a small duffle bag waits to be unzipped. I reach for it, but the bag gets stuck on its way out.

"Can you get down here and grab it, Clay?"

Clay gets a good grasp on the bag and pulls it out. "Can I open it?"

"Of course."

He unzips the duffle and pulls out a slender wooden box. My eyes can barely focus on the box in the dark, but I can see there are some words, or a logo imprinted in the grain of the wood. Flashing my light over the stamp, I read it, but I'm unsure of its meaning.

Clay's mouth drops.

CHAPTER 17

"No. Fucking. Way."

"A bottle of liquor?" I ask.

"Yeah. But, not just any bottle of liquor." He opens the wooden box. "This is The Macallan. Scotch Whiskey. From the Fine and Rare Collection. Of 1991, babe. The year we got married."

"Holy crap. That's awesome."

"Lynn. This…this…wow…" He trails off and shakes his head. I swear he's about to cry or something.

"What is it, Clay?"

His voice nearly cracks. "This is…at least…a ten-thousand-dollar bottle of Scotch."

"What? Are you serious?"

"Yeah."

"Why is it so expensive?"

"Because it's *fine* and *rare*. But, what I'm really…just totally and utterly in awe of is…this particular vintage stock was only released about three months ago."

"*What?*"

"Yeah."

"Three freaking months ago? How did she…when…*how?*"

"I don't know," Clay says, "but she must have had help, or at the very least, had to know her Scotch. What to look for. How to get it. Maybe she knew somebody in the business. Hell, I don't know."

"This is crazy."

"Yeah. We should go."

"Wait. Maybe that's not even supposed to be for us. Maybe somebody hid it up here. I don't want to commit grand larceny."

"But we had the key."

"Maybe there's more than one key though," I say. "Maybe somebody stole what was meant for us. Look in the bag and see if there's a note or something."

Clay shuffles his hand through the bag. "I've got something." He pulls out an envelope with our names on it.

"Thank God. We can read it later. Let's go." I take the envelope and put it in my purse.

Clay puts the bottle back in the box, zips it up in the bag, and slings the bag over his shoulder. As I'm locking the cabinet, all the lights in the room turn on. We're hidden from the entrance, but that doesn't stop all the blood in my veins from turning cold. Clay slowly crouches down beside me.

We hear the flick of a lighter. Clay's eyes widen. Surely there's no smoking allowed in here. The weight of the bag over Clay's shoulder shifts and it touches the floor, making a sound.

"Somebody theh?" a voice asks.

Clay mouths 'Donovan' at me. Yeah, it sounds like our waiter. That thick Boston accent gives him away.

Clay stands up and moves towards the exit. I follow suit.

"Donovan," Clay says. "Hi."

"What the hells are you two doin' up here?" he asks.

"Is that a joint?" Clay counters, pointing to the lit doobie.

"Shit. Yeh." He tenses up. "Please doan nahk aun me."

"Don't worry. Not gonna narc on you," Clay says.

Donovan relaxes and offers Clay a hit, which he declines. "Seriously though. What's you up here fah?"

As we tell him what we're doing, his face goes from impressed, to surprised, to shocked, and back to impressed. "Un-fahckin-believable," he finally says. "So, what's in the bag?"

Clay tells him, and Donovan gives us another shocked face.

"See, Lynn? Told you this was some good shit."

"Can you get us out of here without being noticed?" I ask

"Yeh. I'll sneak you guys out. You're good people. Great tippahs. Not nahks. An' I appreciated that little show wit' ya dessert." He winks at me and my face flushes. Clay smiles. Donovan snuffs out his joint and puts the rest of it back in a pack of cigarettes. "Fahllah me."

Clay slings the duffle bag over his shoulder, and we follow Donovan out the door and back down the stairs. At the last step, he puts his hand up and we stop. The party is still going on.

Donovan peeks around the corner. "Coast is cleh," he says. "C'mon."

We continue behind Donovan and are immediately caught by an employee coming out of the kitchen behind the bar. "Donnie. There you are. Where the hell you been, man? Did you just come from upstairs? Who's this?" The guy points to us.

"Hey, Lucas. I thought I heard somethin' up there. Wanted to check it out," Donovan says.

"And them?" Lucas refers to us again.

"Long stahry," Donovan says. "I'll fill you in lateh."

"Everything's cool though?"

"Yeh."

"Okay. I'm clocking out. Later, man."

"Lateh."

Lucas heads back downstairs and Donovan turns back to us.

"We good?" Clay asks.

"Yeh. Got you covered. You guys have a good night. Take it easy. I'm goin' to check aun the pahty an' see if they need anythin' while I'm up here."

"Thanks, Donovan," I say.

"Yeah. We really appreciate it."

"So do I, man. Know what I mean?"

"No sweat. Hey, if this was 1984, I might have taken a hit off that doob."

"I wasn't even fahckin' bahn yet. I'm only twenty-eight." We laugh and

Clay shakes his hand. We walk back downstairs, through the restaurant, and back outside to the truck.

"That could've gone worse," I tell Clay as he heads back to the hotel.

"No joke. Good thing Donovan is the one that caught us. I still can't get over having that bottle of Macallan though. Un-freaking-real. Read the letter."

"Oh yeah." I get it out of my purse. "It feels like a greeting card instead of a letter." I open it and there's a cartoon picture of a bunch of dancing high-ball glasses and liquor bottles with faces on the front. It says, 'Hope every hour is a happy hour!' I show Clay. The inside says, 'Happy Booze Day!' Super cute. There's a small handwritten note that I read out loud to Clay.

"'Hope you like this find, my sweet loves.

Always, Aunt Mitzi'"

"That's it? No explanation of how she scored it?"

"Nope, that's it."

"But she just put it there, like a couple of months ago. How?"

"Clay, it's not like she knew when she was going to die. We haven't gotten explanations with everything we've received. Any number of the items could have been waiting for just a few months. There's no way she could have known how well you know that type of scotch."

"I guess that's true. I'm just floored at how quickly she got it and put it there. What if she wouldn't have been able to get the chance before she died? I mean, that cabinet could have been empty."

"Then I guess it would have been another dead end."

"Guess so. Hey, maybe Flo helped her. She knew about the box of keys we found."

"Oh, good point. Maybe so. I'll have to call her. So, you want to open the bottle? Have some later?"

"Hell no. It will only increase in value. Bottles from their Fine and Rare Collection that are from the 1940s are worth like thirty-thousand bucks. Or more."

"I don't care if it's worth a million bucks. I'm not selling it, Clay. Ever."

"Of course not."

"So…let's drink it then."

"But…it's The Macallan Fine and Rare."

"Clearly, it's meant to be consumed."

"Rare, Lynn. Rare. I don't think you fully understand the magnitude of the rarity."

"It's just whiskey."

"It's *not* 'just whiskey,' my dear wife."

"Have you ever had any?"

"Not from this collection. You can get a bottle from one of their more inexpensive collections for anywhere from sixty to eighty dollars. Other bottles, like from the Rare Cask line, are about three hundred or so. I've had some of their triple cask matured."

"Was it good?"

"Extraordinary."

"Then imagine how smooth a shot of this will be."

"Jesus. You don't shoot The Macallan, Lynn. You enjoy it. Savor it."

"Okay. Fine then. Let's each savor two fingers of this Fine and Rare tonight."

Clay sighs and scrapes his hand across his jawline. "Okay, Lynn. I'll compromise with you. We'll wait until we get home. And then, just one drink each alright?"

"Deal. We'll save the rest for special occasions."

Clay gives me a side-eye glance. "You're killing me, woman."

"Oh, come on, Clay. Uncle Sid would roll over in his grave if we never opened this bottle and enjoyed it. I'm willing to bet he's the one who is behind this, some way or another. What about on *fine and rare* special occasions?"

He smiles and shakes his head. "Okay, love. Okay. I'll bend. Man, you are relentless. We'll bring the bottle back out for fine and rare special occasions. But it's just for us." He takes my hand and kisses it as we pull into the hotel parking lot.

I'm awakened by the sound of Clay mumbling. The digital clock on the nightstand reads 2:27 a.m. Clay's mumbling in his sleep gets louder. Turning over in bed, I see him trying to bat something away with his arms. "Clay, wake up." No change. He's nearly yelling, but I can't understand what he's saying. It's all a jumble, or maybe another language. I shake him. "Clay. It's okay. Wake up." He kicks me in my legs so hard that I nearly fall out of the bed. Damn, that hurt. Gasping, I sit up and straddle him, grab his arms, and say his name with force. He awakes with a start. Sweating and panting, he jolts up, breaking out of my hold, and looks around like he doesn't know where he is.

"Lynn," he huffs. "What the fuck are you doing here? The perimeter is unsecure. You have to go." He grabs my shoulders. "*Now.*"

"Clay. You were having a nightmare. Come back." His eyebrows nearly meet in the middle and his eyes dart back and forth like a crazed metronome. "Clay." My fingertips caress his face. "It's okay. Just breathe," I say calmly. "It's alright. We're okay. We're safe." He wraps his arms around me and I hug him back. I can feel his heart against mine, pounding a mile a minute. He's soaking wet. "We're safe. Deep breaths. Come back. We're on Aunt Mitzi's road trip. Kentucky. Shandies. The Macallan. Remember?"

He pulls me in tighter. His breathing slows as he inhales deeply and lets it out. "Oh my god, Lynn. Yeah. Christ. Okay. Shit. I'm sorry." He cradles his face in my neck and breathes me in. "Got dammit. I'm sorry, babe. That was a rough one. It must have been that party from the restaurant. Got in my head. Are you alright? Did I hurt you?" He pulls back and looks at me, giving me the once over. He tucks my hair behind my ears and holds my face, gliding his thumbs along my cheeks.

"No, I'm fine. You have nothing to be sorry for. What about you? Are you okay? Do you want to talk about it?"

"No. I just…" He kisses me softly. "I just want to lay here with you. Come here."

He spoons me and holds me close. We lay in silence for a while. Kissing my shoulder, he says, "I've never told you about what happened…that fucked-up day in Afghanistan."

"It's okay." I know he'll probably never tell me, and I'm alright with that. "I'm ready."

He's what? I turn over and face him. "Clay, are you sure? You don't have to."

"I want to tell you. I have to. I need to."

"Okay." I've always been curious, but out of respect for him, I've never asked. I didn't think he'd ever tell me.

"Just promise you won't hate me."

"I could never hate you."

"You may change your mind."

"I won't. Clay, if you're really not ready, it's okay."

"No. I am. I'll spare you the details, but, you should know that it was my fault. I shouldn't even be alive."

"Clay, don't say that."

"Please, Lynn, just let me get this out."

"Okay, I'm sorry. Go on."

"It was November, almost Thanksgiving. We had a birthday party for Harrison. Cake, candles, horrible singing, the whole deal. Right after the party, we were running route clearance outside the perimeter. There were eight of us total. Four of us in each truck. I was with Harrison, Chambers, and Mack. Fuck. That's it. Mack. Didn't that sign at the party tonight say, 'Mack Attack' or something?"

"Yeah, sure did."

He sighs. "Anyway. We were the lead vehicle. I was in the back of the truck. Mack was telling us all about the layout of a new route he came up with that he thought we should practice. Said he drew it out, patted his pocket indicating he had it with him. I asked him to show it to me. It was a single piece of paper he'd drawn on. I took it from him, and a big gust of wind blew it right out of my hands. 'Shit, man, that's my only copy,' he said. So, Chambers turned the truck around to follow it. When we caught up to the paper, I jumped out to get it, but it blew away again in another direction. The wind out there was fucking brutal. I was running. The guys were following in the truck, laughing at me, and yelling 'Run, Sinclair! Run!' like I was Forrest fucking Gump," he chuckles. "Then for whatever reason, the truck just died. I kept running. I was about fifty yards from them when I caught up to that stupid piece of paper. They finally got the truck started again. Not two seconds later..." He pauses. "They struck a goddamn IED. All of them were gone." His voice cracks. "Right in front of me. Right the fuck in front of me, Lynn." He sniffles.

"Oh god, Clay. I'm so sorry."

"Harrison died on his birthday, ten fucking minutes after we sang to him."

"Jesus," I whisper.

"If I'd only had a better hold on the paper when Mack gave it to me, we'd all still be here."

"You can't know that."

"If I wouldn't have asked to see it."

"Clay," I whisper.

"I should've just waited."

"Don't do this to yourself."

"I can't help it. They all had families, Lynn. I took them away from their wives and children."

"You didn't."

"I did."

"It wasn't your fault. You have to know that."

"But—"

"You are not responsible for their deaths. The bastards that caused the blast are." He squeezes his eyes shut. "Look at me, Clay." He opens them slowly. "It was not your fault. But I understand the guilt you hold. Survivor's guilt. I promise you: the families of those guys do not blame you."

"They would if they knew the whole truth. Because of me—"

"No they wouldn't."

"Yes they would. I would."

"No. You wouldn't."

He takes another deep breath. "It should've been me too."

"Please stop saying that." I let a tear fall down my face and Clay wipes it away.

"I'm sorry. I'm so sorry they died because of me."

"I know you are, and I'm sorry they died too. But it wasn't because of you. And I don't hate you, or think any less of you. How could you even think I would hate you?" He doesn't answer. "If anything, I think I love you even more, for opening up to me, and trusting me with your demons. I know that wasn't easy and I understand."

Clay sighs and nods. He pulls me in for a kiss and holds me close. "My doctor has told me all the same stuff, that it wasn't my fault and all. I still don't believe that, and I won't, not unless I hear it from the families. I probably never will, but I needed to hear that from you. I never wanted to lay the burden of what happened on you. I wanted to keep that part of my life from you to protect your dreams from my nightmares, but not knowing what you would really think of me kept eating and eating at me." He pauses and sighs. "You know when I space out sometimes?"

"Yeah."

"That's usually what I'm thinking about. Something will trigger me, set me back there. And while I've learned how to cope and deal with what happens after the trigger, I've always been left with the question, 'What would Lynn think of me?' and I've feared the worst. That you would leave. That's why I was so withdrawn when I came back from Afghanistan. I could barely look you in the eyes. I was so ashamed of what I'd done."

"Oh god, Clay."

"I'm so sorry, babe. I hated doing that to you. I put on an act until you made me get help. I played the part of 'husband,' but I didn't feel like one. I felt like a terrible human being inside, a monster really. I couldn't tell you about what happened. I just couldn't. I couldn't bear how I thought you'd look at me if I told you. But, I'm sorry. I had to tell you tonight. I just couldn't take it anymore. I had to know. The not-knowing was making me worse. I know that's selfish of me."

"It's okay, Clay. It's not selfish. You are the most generous man I know." I smooth my hand down his back. "And by telling me this, trusting me, you won't go to that place anymore. You know I'll never leave you."

"I love you, Lynn. *God*, I love you."

"I love you too."

"Thank you for listening and lifting that weight off my shoulders."

"Thank you for telling me. I'm sorry you carried it for so long."

"I don't want you to think that I've been hiding anything else or holding anything back from you physically or emotionally all this time. That's all been real. I need you to know that."

"I do know that."

"It's just been that single thought. What you would think. When it wasn't on my mind, everything in my life was bliss. But when a trigger hit, my mind would go to hell for a few minutes. My thoughts would spin out until you innocently snapped me back into place. Every. Time. You didn't even realize what you were doing. And it didn't matter if the trigger happened hours before I saw you again. It's crazy that even though I feared what you would think of me, you're the only one that could bring me back to my present and make me forget about it."

"I'm glad, babe."

"Me too."

We're silent for a few minutes before something dawns on me. "That's why you can't watch *Forrest Gump*. Isn't it?"

"Yeah. Sorry I threw your DVD and soundtrack away. I couldn't even stand to see it on the shelves."

"I noticed. Wondered if it had something to do with that, but didn't want to ask you. Figured it was more about the war aspect of the movie. Never thought it would be just a quote from it."

"Yeah, well…" he sighs. "Close your eyes, love. Let's go back to sleep."

I close my eyes, but I'm far from sleep. My poor husband has been harboring his feelings about what I would think of him for years. I can't imagine the pain he feels inside for what happened out there. I knew when he came home from his last deployment that he'd lost some brothers on a drill, but I didn't realize how close of a call to losing his own life it had been for him. Thank God he made it back to me. My life would be incomplete without him.

Clay was distant when he first got back from Afghanistan. I just thought he was having a hard time adjusting to getting back into the swing of things, being back home, and trying to get back to his 'normal' life while mourning his brothers in his own way. His routine had shifted though. He changed his schedule at the precinct, switching to night shifts. He took on more extra duty work. More weekend hours. I barely saw him. Now it all makes sense. He was avoiding me.

I wasn't sure how to react at first. I almost felt like I was living with a stranger. We were like two ships passing in the night. We'd kiss hello and good-bye as he walked in from his shift and I left for work. I missed him in our bed at night. We hadn't had more than a quickie since he'd gotten home from his deployment.

A couple of months after he'd been back, there was one Friday night when we were actually home at the same time. I made a suggestion.

"Clay?"

"Yes?"

"Since you're off tonight, let's go out to dinner. We haven't been anywhere since you've been home. You've been working so much, and I know it's been an adjustment, but I miss our date nights. I miss…you."

"I'm not off, I'm on-call."

"Oh." I slumped.

"But let's go for it," he said with a smile. "It's a risk I'm willing to take. As long as I don't have any alcohol to drink. I miss you too. And let's go somewhere special."

I beamed. "What do you have in mind?"

"Go put on one of those little sexy black dresses of yours. I'm calling Juban's. They have the best soft-shelled crab."

With a smile on my face, I ran to our room and found the perfect dress. It was a knee-length velvet Bardot style dress. Classy and elegant.

When Clay finished getting ready, I was in still in my robe putting on my makeup. He came up behind me and put his arms around my waist. It felt good to have him so close again. His eyes met mine in the mirror. "You look hot, babe."

"I'm not even dressed yet." I smiled. "And," I pointed to my head, "still have rollers in my hair."

"Doesn't matter. Still hot."

"You're not too bad yourself, Sinclair." I winked at him.

"Tonight's for us, yeah?"

"Yeah. We've got tonight."

"We've got tonight." He smiled and started singing that title song by Bob Seger to me in my ears. So. Freaking. Sexy.

"You keep that up and we're not going anywhere."

"Would that be so bad? Let's just stay in."

"Clay, as much as I want that, we need this time out of the house together. We need a date. And this way, the anticipation of what's to come later will make it that much better."

"You're right." He smacked my butt and whispered in my ear, "I'll wait for you in the living room."

"Give me fifteen minutes."

"Yes, ma'am," he said as he snuck a hand into my robe and squeezed a boob.

That was the Clay I missed so badly. So madly. My insatiable flirtatious man. I really believed he was back to his old self. I started getting butterflies, like it was our first date all over again.

Seventeen minutes later, I was ready. I had picked out a matching black velvet choker, and pearl-drop earrings. My ensemble was completed by the addition of my sexiest pair of black heels. I walked out of the bedroom just as Clay's voice rang down the hall.

"You almost finished, Lynn?"

"Coming."

As I reached the living room, I thought Clay might pass out when he looked me up and down. "Whoa," he said. "You look…"

"Hot?" I asked, smiling.

"Beyond hot. Scorching. God, babe. Let's go so we can hurry and get back. I want that dress on the floor as soon as possible. And I'm taking my time with you."

Finally, I thought. *Please don't get called in to work tonight.*

As we finished up dessert, a group of people a couple of tables over started singing "Happy Birthday" to a grinning man sitting behind a cake lined with tiny candles.

Clay dropped his fork and began hyperventilating.

"What's wrong?" I asked. He ignored me. I had no idea what set him off.

"I gotta get outta here." He jumped up and ran outside.

I called the waiter over to get the check. Told him to please hurry, as we had a family emergency.

I found Clay waiting for me in the truck already. I opened the passenger door and stood there, trying to read him. He was agitated and sweating.

"Babe, what happened? Are you alright?"

"I don't want to talk about it."

"Maybe I should drive."

"Fuck that. Get in."

"But, Clay, you're—"

"Get in the goddamn truck, Lynn!" he yelled.

Holy shit. He's scaring me.

I did as I was told and shut the door. He took off before I could even fasten my seatbelt. "Jesus, Clay! Slow down. Shit. Did I do something to upset you?"

"No."

"Then please tell me why you ran out. You're scaring me."

"I said I didn't want to talk about it, Lynn!" he yelled through clenched teeth.

"But—"

"Leave it the hell ALONE!"

I didn't say another word the whole ride home. Or the whole time I got undressed and got ready for bed. Or the rest of the night. I thought we were finally going to have a passionate night of lovemaking. We hadn't had that since he got home. I cried myself to sleep, alone in our bed.

After I woke up the next morning, I could tell that Clay never came to bed. I thought I would find him on the couch, but he wasn't even home. *What happened last night?* I sat at the kitchen table and cried some more.

Twenty minutes later, he came home.

"You're up," he said.

I just stared at him.

"I went to get donuts, your favorite kind, and…" He set the box of donuts on the table. *Krispy Kreme. That is my favorite.* "I'll be right back."

He left out the door and came back with a big bouquet of red roses.

I rolled my eyes. "You think some flowers and chocolate glazed are going to make up for the way you shut me out last night, Clay?" I shouted. "What the fuck happened to you last night?"

"You wouldn't understand."

"Then help me understand. Please."

He put the roses on the counter and sat down at the table with me. Clay sighed and took my hands in his. "I won't tell you what happened, exactly, but…" He paused for a minute and I didn't push him. "I went through a fuck ton of horrifying shit over there, Lynn. Witnessed something I'll never be able to un-see. Never be able to take back."

"What do you mean you can't take it back?"

"No details, Lynn. And please, don't ever ask me what happened. If I do ever decide to tell you, it'll be on my terms. Just know that some fucked up shit went down and there's nothing I can do about it. I'm sorry I flipped out on you last night. That's the last thing I wanted. Last night was supposed to be about us. I wanted you, wanted to rip that dress off and take you to bed. We should've just stayed home. I never wanted you to see me like that."

"So, that's happened before? Since you've been back?"

"Yes." He let go of my hands.

"Clay, why didn't you tell me?" He didn't answer. Turned his head and looked out the window. I could see his jaw tic. "More than once?" He gave a small nod, still looking away. "More than twice?" My voice cracked with angst.

He finally looked in my direction, but not at me. "A few times, okay? Maybe about six."

"Jesus, Clay. Six times in two months? You know what's going on here, right?" He looked away again, his jaw twitched fiercely. "You need help, babe." He whipped his head around and squinted his eyes at me with such fury that it made me gasp. "I think you're having symptoms of—"

"Don't say it. Don't you dare fucking say it."

A tear fell from the corner of my eye. "I'm sorry, Clay, but I believe it's true. Please go talk to someone. A doctor, a therapist, a priest. Hell, the boy next door. Anybody. If you're not going to let me in, that's okay, but you need to get control of this. There's medication that can help you in addition to talking to a professional. PTSD is nothing to play around with, you know?"

"I told you not to fucking say it." He scooted out from the table with such anger that the chair legs marred the floor. He blazed to the other side of the kitchen and started pacing.

"Clay, it's nothing to be ashamed of. You're not alone in this. There are plenty of other armed service men and women going through the same thing. Doesn't the VA have group therapy sessions where you can go for help?"

"I'm not doing that shit. I don't need to hear everybody else's fucking problems. I'm fine. I can handle it."

"You're not fine. And you're not handling it." He glared at me. "Clay, please, make an appointment. If you think you can deal with this on your own, you're wrong. I've seen families get torn apart over this. Marriages too." I paused. "I don't know if I can live with you like this."

He looked at me like I had gutted him. His eyes watered. He ran back out the door, jumped in his truck, and peeled out.

Shit. Clearly, that was the wrong thing to say. Here he is, trying to apologize for the night before, opened up a little, and I made it about me. I practically gave him an ultimatum. I am such a bitch. I went to lie down on the couch, and I cried until sleep took me.

I was awakened by a kiss on my forehead. My eyes focused on Clay at my side. He brushed a thumb over my tear-streaked cheeks and smiled sheepishly. *Oh good, he's calmed down.* I glanced at the clock. He'd been gone about an hour and a half.

"I'm sorry," he said.

"No. *I'm* sorry. I should've never said that to you. I didn't mean it. We took a vow, for better or worse."

"It's okay. I'm sorry I stormed out, but I needed to clear my head. And I think I needed to hear those words from you. I didn't want to admit it to myself. I don't like it and I didn't like it when you said it. When you said it, you made it real. I got pissed. But the longer I drove around, the more I thought about everything else you said too. I can't live without you, Lynn. You're my world. My safe place. My home. I need you. And I'll do whatever it takes to make you happy. To keep us together. I can't lose you. I won't lose you over this. If that means I need to sit down with a shrink once a week for the rest of my life and take some drugs that get my head straight, then so be it. I'll call Monday morning and make an appointment with somebody."

I touched his face and started crying. Again. "Thank you. That's all I ask. And thank you for the flowers and donuts."

"You're welcome." He smiled.

"Will you please bring me a couple? Did you get any cream-filled? Or raspberry jelly ones? I finally have an appetite."

"Later. Right now, I've got an appetite for you."

He kissed me, scooped me up off the couch, and brought me back to bed. He finally made love to me. Sweet, long, beautiful love.

Clay hated going to his therapy sessions at first, but he kept at it. I think once his meds got into his system, he started to get better, but it was several weeks before he really started getting anything out of his meetings with his doctor. He was learning to identify his triggers. Learning how to control them, cope with them, and avoid them. He had a couple of breakthroughs and actually began looking forward to his appointments.

Part of his therapy is going to the gym. He works out at least three times a week, sometimes more. The last fifteen years has been somewhat challenging for him to keep his demons buried, but he's got a good hold on them now, for the most part. Until they rear their ugly heads and enter his psyche, creating nightmares like the one he just had.

I finally let my mind rest and fall asleep.

CHAPTER 18

SUNLIGHT PEEKS THROUGH the edge of the curtains at the window. I check the clock. It's 10:20 and checkout is at 11:00. The cadence of Clay's breathing tells me that he is still sound asleep. I grab my phone and call the front desk to ask for a late checkout, speaking in a hushed tone so as not to disturb Clay's sleep. I don't want to wake him after the night he had. I set my alarm and place my phone back on the nightstand.

"What are you doing?" Clay asks, surprising the hell out of me.

I smile and turn my head in his direction. "Sorry. Didn't mean to wake you up. I was trying to be quiet."

"That's okay. Who'd you call?"

"Front desk. Got us a late checkout. It's almost eleven. We have till one now."

"Okay. Come back here." He opens his arms to me.

I snuggle into him, my back against his chest. He wraps me in his arms and pulls me closer. "Love this position," I tell him.

"Me too. Thanks again for last night. I needed you," he says, kissing my cheek.

"Anytime."

"I love you, Lynn."

"I love you too, Clay."

While we're eating lunch in our hotel room, I take the clue sheets out of my purse and get into clue-solving mode. "What state do you think we'll be sleeping in tonight?"

"You tell me. What does the clue say?"

"Let's see." Unfolding the papers, I scan for the next clue in the list. "Okay. 'In the state that gave us cotton candy and Moon pies, you'll find a Smoky place for you to close your eyes. In the birthplace of Dolly, you've got to coordinate. This isn't a folly, what awaits you is great.' The word 'smoky' is capitalized, just FYI. She's probably referring to the Smoky mountains."

"Well, since the Smokies only run through two states, we're going to Tennessee, seeing as how we've already been to North Carolina. I had no idea Tennessee was home to cotton candy and Moon pies though, did you?"

"No. I love Moon pies."

"I know you do. Especially with—"

"An RC Cola," we say in unison.

"Okay, now that we know what state we're going to," Clay says, "I'm assuming the Dolly she's referring to is Dolly Parton."

"Obviously."

"Do you know where she was born?"

"Pigeon Forge maybe. At least, that's where her Dollywood theme park is located. I'll double check though." I search online for Dolly's birthplace. "Not Pigeon Forge. Sevierville. About fifteen miles north of Gatlinburg."

"What are we supposed to coordinate when we get there?" Clay asks.

"I don't know. A meeting with Dolly Parton?"

"How are we supposed to manage that? Did Aunt Mitzi know her?"

"Not that I know of. Though, it wouldn't surprise me."

"Well, even if she knew her personally, we don't have any way to get in touch with her. Aunt Mitzi would have left a number or something. Dolly may not even be there. She still tours a lot. What about the keychain?"

I find the clue's corresponding keychain. "Whoa." I hold it up to Clay and dangle it.

"What the hell?" He grabs it.

The keychain is a small slice of lacquered wood about a half-inch thick and two inches in diameter, with bark around the outer edge. Must have been one small tree. Or part of a branch.

"What do you make of it?" I ask, smiling.

"These are coordinates."

"Yes."

"Burned into the wood."

"Yes."

"You about done eating?"

"Yes," I smile.

"I guess we know what we'll be coordinating. Let's get the hell outta here, babe."

We pack up and check out. Before we pull out of the parking lot, Clay enters the coordinates from the keychain into the GPS. It's about a five and a half-hour drive to our destination. We'll be there around 7:00 tonight.

"What do you want to listen to?" I ask Clay.

"Something from my arsenal of rock." He smiles and picks up his phone, pressing the play button. "Machinehead" by Bush starts playing.

"Where do you think the coordinates will bring us?" I ask.

"I have a good idea. I bet you do too."

"Mountain cabin?" I say bouncing up and down in the seat like a kid.

"Could be. You said they loved the mountains. And whatever awaits us is great. What could be greater than our own vacation home in the Smokies?"

"I really hope that's it."

"Me too, babe. That would be awesome, wouldn't it?"

"Yeah," I whisper with a smile plastered across my face.

"Don't get your hopes up though. It could be anything."

"I know."

"Put the coordinates into Google and see if it comes up on Google Earth."

"Good idea." I do what he says, but can't really see much. "The resolution is awful. You can only zoom in so far. But the pinpoint is around a lot of greenery, so it's probably trees. Fingers crossed there's a cabin somewhere in the middle of all that green."

"Fingers crossed, love."

"We've got an hour and a half before we reach the border. If I fall asleep, please wake me up so I can snap a picture of the 'Welcome to Tennessee' sign."

"You know I will." Clay smiles at me, grabs my hand, and kisses the back of it as he winks at me. I wink back at my sexy husband.

Goldie Hawn smiles at me from the cover of the People magazine I picked up at a gas station on the way out of Paducah. Grabbing it off the seat, I flip to the back to work on the crossword puzzle as Bon Jovi's "Livin' on a Prayer" begins to play.

A couple of hours pass and Clay's phone rings throughout the cab of the truck. It's Stone.

"Hey, bro. Everything okay?"

"Yeah, man. Made it home. Our baby is in the garage, all safe and sound."

"Sweet. And no problems, I presume?"

"None whatsoever."

"Awesome. Frank able to meet you there?"

"Yup. Said he wants to help restore it with us. Told him that was your call."

"Hmm…he does have a tool we need. May have to throw him a bone or two."

"Leave me out of it if you all you want him for is to throw boners in exchange for his tool."

We all crack up at that.

"Hey, Stone?" I ask as the laughter settles.

"Yeah?"

"Thanks for bringing Annie up to Indianapolis with you. And for being so good to her."

"No sweat. We had a great time. I'm glad she got to go with me."

"Me too. And I love that you love her."

"Yeah, well, she's lovable."

"She is."

"Wish we would have made the connection twenty-five years ago. Could've saved each other a lot of heartache."

"Aww, Stone, that's so sweet."

"Okay, I'm going to turn one of my man cards in now for talking about my feelings while my brother listens. Clay, call me tomorrow. Need to talk to you about something."

"Alright. Later, sis," Clay laughs.

"Later, ass clown."

"Lynn, we're here," I hear Clay saying as he squeezes my thigh to wake me up.

"What? Why didn't you wake me sooner? I missed the welcome sign!"

"Love, you were sleeping so hard. I couldn't wake you."

"But—"

"Check your phone."

I check my phone and there's a text. From Clay. With a picture of Tennessee's welcome sign. "You're the best."

"I know." He smiles. "I don't know how you can sleep so soundly in this truck. Figured you must have needed the extra shut-eye."

"Thank you."

"Welcome."

"So, we're here? This is it?"

"This is it."

We're parked in front of a cozy little log cabin with large logs the color of caramel. "I knew it." The smile that forms makes my face hurt. "It's so cute, Clay! I can't wait to see inside. Let's go." I jump out of the truck and stretch. Grabbing Clay's hand, I pull him to the front door. A rustic bench with a backrest made from a huge wagon wheel sits on the porch. So charming, if not all that comfortable. I unlock the door and push it open just enough for me to reach my hand inside and feel for the light switch. Once the lights are on, I open the door and we step inside. I can't believe what I'm seeing. "Holy. Crap."

CHAPTER 19

"Wow," Clay says.

"This is not what I was expecting when I opened the door."

"Me either."

"It looks so small from the outside looking at the front."

"Looks can be deceiving."

The cabin far exceeds my expectations. The front door opens to a large living room with a stacked stone fireplace on the right and a chef's dream kitchen on the left. A beautiful oak dining table with seating for at least eight people separates the two rooms. A staircase to the right of the foyer leads to a lower level. The cabin is decked out in light wood: the walls, the floors, the log beam rafters running along the vaulted ceiling, and stair railings.

"This is hardly what I'd call cute. This is…" I'm at a loss for words.

"Fucking luxurious," Clay says in a serious tone.

"Okay," I laugh, "I'll agree to that."

"This is a cabin in the same sense that the Queen Mary is a boat. I mean, look at this place."

As we walk further into the not so humble abode, I set my purse down on the dark granite countertop of the kitchen. Looking towards the living room, the view from the floor to ceiling windows is breathtaking. The sun is setting over the distant mountains, casting the sky with colors of orange, pink, and purple.

I notice another staircase at the far-right wall leading to the top floor. My eyes follow it up, landing on a loft bedroom.

"Is this really ours, Lynn?"

"I guess."

"I wonder how long it's been vacant though, just waiting for us to get here. It's so clean. The furniture isn't covered in sheets like you see in the movies."

"This isn't the movies. Maybe we'll find a letter somewhere, but right now, I want to check the place out."

"Where do you want to start?"

"Down the hallway right here. That's probably where the master bedroom is since this is the main level."

"Babe, most of the bedrooms in these cabins are usually all considered masters, with each having their own bathroom."

"Well, then…the master master."

"After you," he gestures.

Walking down the hall, there's a half-bath and laundry room on the left. The end of the hall leads right into a bedroom with a king size bed with a frame and headboard made of the same logs that were used to build the house, a stone fireplace in the corner, and a cozy sitting area. The dresser also has some of the log elements from the house. A small Bluetooth sound system rests on top of the dresser. Aunt Mitzi thought of everything. The room is decorated in rich tones of browns and greens, and a live ivy plant stands in a tucked away nook. Its leaves climb the corner and border the entire perimeter at the top near the ceiling. I guess whoever cleans the place also waters the plants. Dark chocolate mosquito netting hangs from the rim of an emerald green chandelier above the head of the bed, creating an enchanting tree-like appearance. A door opens to the wrap-around porch with white ladderback rocking chairs and that gorgeous view of the Smoky Mountains. The en suite bathroom is lavish, consisting of a spacious slate walk-in shower with two shower heads, a jetted tub, and a long counter with a vanity spaced between the two sinks.

I sit on the edge of the bed and bounce a little.

"Testing its durability, are you?" Clay laughs.

"No, goofball, its comfort."

"Ah." Clay sits next to me and does the same, but his bounce is stronger. "Comfy. *And* durable." He falls backwards, lying down with his legs hanging off the side. "I think I could pass out right now."

"No, sir. Get up, we've got two more levels to explore. Then we can test out that huge shower together and go to bed."

We make our way to the second floor where the loft bedroom is. A wrought iron queen size bed and a couch upholstered with a sailboat print take up most of the space here. A kite hangs in one corner while a bookcase shaped like a windmill is in another corner. Small hurricane lamps are set on the bedside tables, and the ceiling is painted sky blue with white puffy clouds.

A short hallway leads to the bathroom just off the bedroom area of the loft. It's your basic bathroom, nothing too over-the-top, but bigger than I expected. No tub though, shower only.

Heading down to the bottom level, we see that it's the game room. But not just a game room. It's also part movie theater, complete with theater seating for ten and a red velvet curtain that covers the giant movie screen. There's another couch and a few bean bag chairs. A closet stocked with board games, tons of DVDs, and thousand-piece puzzles is in the corner.

The walls are covered in framed movie posters of *The Sound of Music* (one of Aunt Mitzi's favorite movies, as well as mine), *WarGames* (no doubt a nod to Clay from Uncle Sid), *Star Wars*, and of course, *Footloose*, and *The Breakfast Club* (two more of my favorite movies).

Cinematic metal signs stating 'Tickets,' 'Now Showing,' and 'Lights, Camera, Action' are spaced throughout the room on the walls. Even shadow boxes with movie memorabilia are hung all around. Our showcases include a prop gun from *Men in Black*; a group of gold nuggets, coins, and jewels from *Pirates of the Caribbean*; a tribal stone face carving from the ancient temple in *Raiders of the Lost Ark*; and a pair of sunglasses that John Belushi wore in *The Blues Brothers*. Certificates of Authenticity are framed next to each item. Unbelievable. It's like we have our own little Planet Hollywood. Seeing all of it makes me want to add to the collection.

In the back of the rec room, we have an air hockey table, a pool table, a poker table, and a standing arcade machine with a bunch of classic Atari games pre-loaded into it, like *Donkey Kong*, *Frogger*, *Pitfall*, and more. And finally, the pièce de résistance, a Harlem Globetrotters pinball machine stands next to the arcade.

In the corner near the poker table is a wet bar with a counter and bar stools. A dorm-sized refrigerator is tucked underneath, just waiting to be loaded with drinks and snacks. I'm sure it would be stocked with food already, but whoever keeps this cabin up had no idea when we'd be arriving, as this entire trip wasn't set in motion until Aunt Mitzi died. Then it was contingent on us finding the box of keys.

Rounding out the bar area is a small microwave and even a red and white striped popcorn cart on wheels. Bottles of top-shelf liquor are presented on lit mirrored shelves behind the bar, and cabinets underneath the bar house any kind of barware one would need. A neon sign with the word 'Concessions' in script hangs on the wall behind the bar.

Double doors lead out to the porch with two swings and a hot tub. Nice.

"Babe," Clay says, "this place is un-freaking-believable."

"You can say that again."

"This place is un-freaking-believable," he smiles.

"Let's go check out the other bedrooms down the hall."

"Right behind you."

"And then we need to get our suitcases out of the truck."

The first bedroom on the left is painted Caribbean blue, with a mural of a coral reef on one wall. The bed is, oh my gosh, I see what's going on here.

"Is that a waterbed?" Clay asks.

"I'm pretty sure it is."

We sit on it, laughing as our bodies bob up and down with the motion of the waves inside the mattress.

"I didn't even know they still made these things," Clay says. "This is insane. I love it. Look at this room. I feel like I'm at the beach, not the mountains."

"Clay. Don't you get it?"

"Get what?"

"The elements."

"What do you mean?"

"The four classical elements of nature. The master bedroom was decorated like earth, with the dark colors and the log bed with the tree above it and the ivy climbing around the border of the walls. The loft bedroom was wind, with the ceiling painted like the sky and the kite hanging in the corner. The windmill, the sailboats, and the hurricane lamps. This is water. I bet the last one is fire."

"Holy shit. Like the pins she left us at the typewriter museum."

"Yeah. I can't believe she did this. It's unreal."

"It's real, Lynn. She was one amazing woman. Come on." He takes my hand. "Let's go see the fire room."

The last room, at the end of the hall, boasts walls painted in hot colors, ombre style. Starting with red at the bottom, blending into orange in the middle, and yellow at the top. An apropos fireplace is in the corner near the doors that lead to the porch. Huge flames carved out of wood make up the headboard, which was no doubt custom made just for this room. The bedspread matches the walls.

"It's beautiful." I sit on the bed and start to cry.

"Aww, love, what's wrong?"

"Nothing, I just…I'm so…it's all…"

"I know." Clay puts his arm around me, brings me into his side, and rubs my back.

"I'm okay. Happy tears. Overwhelmed. C'mon. Let's head back up. You go grab our bags while I shower."

"On it."

***

The next morning, my stomach wakes me up. I'm starving. And I bet there's not a lick of sustenance in this cabin.

"Clay." I nudge him. "Wake up. I'm hungry."

"Mmm. Okay, babe." His voice is groggy, but he lands a blind hand on my boob and starts to rub.

I push his hand away. "No, goofball. Not hungry for sex. Hungry for food. Famished. Need to eat."

He puts his hand back anyway. "Bummer." He squeezes. "Okay. I'll go cook some breakf…oh. Shit. We don't have any food. Do we?"

"I didn't check the fridge or the pantry, but I'm kind of thinking we don't. Get dressed so we can go shopping."

Two hours later, after a quick breakfast at McDonald's (we wanted to hurry and get back to the cabin, so we decided against a full-service restaurant for our first meal in Sevierville) and a trip to the grocery store in town, the cabin is stocked with a couple of days' worth of nourishment. We decided to stay through Tuesday and leave Wednesday morning, which gives us two more nights.

After I cook us a lunch consisting of lasagna, garlic bread, and Caesar salad, we drive around for a while and explore the city. It's a beautiful town, close enough to visit Pigeon Forge and Gatlinburg, but far enough away from the tourists and traffic congestion of those two cities. Knoxville is less than an hour's drive north and there's a ton of stuff see and do there as well. It's a college town, so there's always live music playing somewhere. They've got great parks and theaters too.

As we come around a bend, we spot an old abandoned grist mill on the highway. I make Clay stop and we take some pictures. I love how rustic it is. I'm going to frame one of the pictures and hang it in the kitchen of the cabin.

We drive some more and come across Forbidden Caverns, one of the many caverns beneath the foothills of Tennessee. We decide to stop and take the tour, which ended up being really cool. They have one of the largest walls of cave onyx known to exist. Colored lights were set around here and there showing off some of the other natural formations, like the one they call 'Valley of the Moon.'

With the busy day behind us, we're now back at the cabin. I put a baked potato casserole in the oven and Clay is grilling steaks in the outdoor kitchen. That's right, outdoor kitchen. I failed to mention that earlier. We also have a fire pit with bench seats arranged around it made of tree trunks.

I'm now sitting in one of the chaise lounge chairs under the cover of the outdoor kitchen, drinking a glass of sweet tea, watching my husband cook our steaks.

"Great day today, huh?" Clay asks as he flips a steak.

"Yeah. What do you want to do after we eat? Watch a movie in our theater with a big bowl of popcorn?"

"I was thinking more along the lines of Strip Pinball."

I laugh. "Strip Pinball, huh?"

"Strip Pinball."

"What are the stakes?"

"Steaks are right here." He points to the grill, laughing at his own joke. "And they're done." He puts them on a plate, and we go inside.

I take the potato casserole out of the oven. "You didn't answer my question, Sinclair."

"Let's just see who can best handle the long plunger and set of balls."

"Nice innuendo."

"Thank you very much. First one naked loses."

"That's usually how a game of 'Strip Whatever' works. What do we lose, besides clothes?"

"Not sure yet. Still thinking."

"Fine. Me too."

After we eat dinner and clean up the kitchen, we walk out to the porch, sit in the rocking chairs with a glass of wine, and watch the sun set.

"I'm so full," Clay says.

"So am I. Great steaks as usual, babe."

"Thanks. Your potatoes were awesome."

"Thank you," I smile.

"Good thing we came out here to let our food settle because I'm about to school you on some pinball, missy."

"Is that so, mister?"

"I believe it is."

"Guess we'll just see about that."

"Looking forward to it."

"I bet you are." He winks at me and I shake my head at him. Changing the subject, I say, "I could get used to this," pointing my head towards the sun dipping behind the mountains.

"No joke. It's great out here. Definitely see us making more than one trip a year up to this place."

"I bet between Sevierville, Gatlinburg, Pigeon Forge, and Knoxville, they go all out with decorations for the holidays."

"Let's plan to come back for Christmas then. We can stay long enough to put up a tree and stay through New Year's."

"Really? That sounds wonderful," I say.

"Stone and Annie can come too. I'm sure they'll stay as long as they can."

"That would be so much fun. But no Strip Pinball."

"Uh, no. No Strip Pinball. No Strip anything. Unless it's just you and me in our bed."

We finish our wine and head downstairs to the game room.

"You ready to lose your ass?" I ask.

"Funny. I was just about to ask you the same thing. You want another glass of wine?"

"You trying to get me drunk so my equilibrium will be off kilter?"

"Maybe."

"Scared?"

"No. Just wanna see you topless with your tits shaking over the machine to that catchy theme song as you strike the ball with the flippers. That's all."

"You're incorrigible."

"I certainly can be."

"You know what? Go ahead. Pour me another glass, Sinclair. I'll still kick your ass."

"It's so on. I mean…off." He winks at me as he pours me another glass of wine. He fixes himself a Crown and Coke.

"Flip a coin to see who starts?"

"No need. Ladies first."

I smile and start up the pinball machine. Upon hearing the Harlem Globetrotters' signature song, a whistled version of "Sweet Georgia Brown" by Brother Bones, Clay thinks he's Meadowlark Lemon. He throws a pretend basketball all around his body and through his legs, then makes a shot to a goal post that doesn't exist and yells, "Nothin' but net! And the crowd goes wild! Suck it, Generals!" I laugh at his antics. "Remember their Saturday morning cartoons in the early seventies?" he asks.

"No, but I remember when they were on *Scooby-Doo*."

"Oh yeah, those episodes were good too. Ready to play?"

"Born ready," I say.

"Give it hell, babe."

I pull the spring-loaded plunger back and let it go. The ball flies through the shooter alley and into the playfield with careless abandon, landing right in the saucer for a bonus off the bat. Skill shot accomplished. The ball is kicked out of the saucer and bounces back and forth against the pop bumpers, creating dinging and chiming sounds. Rolling down the playfield, the ball goes under the spinners, ricochets off the kickers and slingshots, and comes towards me near the flipper. I strike the drop targets one after the other (four in a row) and get the extra bonus.

"Ha. How ya like me now?"

"Not bad."

"Scared yet?"

"Nope."

"Maybe you should be." The ball hits the spinners again, but this time with fierce velocity and my points climb.

"I know what I want when I win."

"Oh yeah? And what might that be?" I score another bonus.

"I want you to do a strip tease for me."

That's it. I've lost my concentration and the ball goes past the flipper and down the hole.

"Look what you made me do. Not cool, Clay."

He laughs. "Sorry, love."

"No ya not sorry." I push him in the shoulder, making his drink spill.

"Watch it, woman. You're making a mess."

"Why are you trying to sabotage me?"

"We didn't lay any ground rules against it."

"Touché. Now, what is this supposed strip tease you want? If you think you're going to win, I'll already be naked. What's the point of a strip tease?"

"I want you to get redressed. And then do it. To music."

"You're insane."

"Mmm. Am I?" He smacks my butt. "Go ahead. Your next ball is ready."

I send the ball back into the playfield and ignore Clay's attempts at trying to make me lose control. "You're cheating," I tell him as he takes a pool cue and rubs it between my legs. "But it's not working."

He replaces the cue with his hand. "How 'bout now?" His voice is in my ear, low and seductive.

Oh, he is really trying hard to make me weak. It's effective. My knees go warm. "Stand down, Sinclair." My voice is strong and confident. I deliver another bonus to my score. He bites my ear while the ball waits in its saucer as my points increase. Bells chime and ding. Lights blink and flash. I nearly come undone with what Clay is doing to me. But I straighten and elbow him in the ribs. He backs off with an "oomph" and retreats to his bar stool, laughing. But I lose my grip when I head back for the flipper and the ball is gone.

"Two down, one to go," he says with triumph as he soothes his side. "Damn, you have some pointy-ass elbows."

"Serves you right. Jerkface."

"'Jerkface'? What are you, twelve?" he laughs.

"I can call you an asshole if you prefer."

"Jerkface is good."

"Mmm hmm. Just wait till your turn. Two can play at this game. Leave me alone for this last ball. I freaking mean it."

He holds his hands up in surrender. "Okay. I'm sorry." But then he whispers, "Not sorry."

Clay doesn't bother me for my last round though, true to his word. He's as quiet as a monk in training while he works on his Crown and Coke. I'm killing it on the pinball machine. I end my first round with a score of 459,648.

"You sure play a mean pinball," he says, and then starts singing "Pinball Wizard."

"Thank you." I bow. "Beat that, Sinclair."

"I fully intend to."

"Knock yourself out."

Clay downs his drink and takes his stance at the machine. He lets the ball rip. He misses the skill shot, but the ball bounces all over the place, from bumper to bumper and back again. When his ball reaches the right flipper, he aims for the side targets on the left and hits all five of them in a row, awarding him the special bonus. Then he lands the ball right in the saucer over and over and gets two bonuses in a row. Dang him. He's halfway to my score and he's only on his first turn. Time for some distraction.

I walk up behind him and reach my arms around to unbuckle his belt and slide it through his belt loops lightning fast.

"What the hell are you doing?" he asks.

"Like you don't know." I lower my hand and reach for his package through his shorts.

"Lynn?" He questions my name in a warning tone. "I wouldn't do that."

"Oh, I'm doing it." I rub him and feel him start to rise.

Clay drops his hands and lets the pinball hit the drain. He spins around and grabs me, kisses me so hard that I think this game is over and he's going to take me right here, right now. But then he stops.

"You're a dirty tease," he murmurs.

"As are you," I say breathlessly.

Clay walks me back to my stool at the bar and gives me my glass of wine. "I'm trusting you to behave."

"Whatever. I do like your idea though. If I win, you have to do a strip tease for me."

"Straight men don't strip," he says as he releases the plunger on his second ball.

"Some do. And you will."

"Not gonna happen."

"Oh yes. It is. And you're gonna do it to Ginuwine's 'Pony' just like Channing Tatum in *Magic Mike*."

"The hell I am."

"So you *are* scared."

"Nope. Just not gonna happen because you'll be the one stripping." He says that just as he lands a free throw bonus.

Jeez, even I didn't get that one. Or the special bonus. He's close to beating my score and still has a round to go. I get up and lick the back of his neck while unbuttoning his shorts. He tries to shake me off. "Stop fighting it, Clay," I whisper in his ear. "You know you want it." I put my hand down his shorts and rub him through his boxers.

"You wicked little vixen." He drops his hands from the game again, turns around and rips my shirt open, pulls it off my shoulders, and drops it to the ground. A sound that's half scream, half laugh escapes me as buttons fly into the air. I hear them land on the floor, the bar, the pinball machine. It sounds like a string of pearls just broke.

"Clay Weston Sinclair! I don't believe you just did that."

"Believe it. You were about to lose that shirt anyway. Keep your hands to yourself, woman, 'cause I'm about to beat the pants off you too." He goes back to the game, but not before he bites my boob through my bra and slaps my ass.

I let him play his last round without incident. I'm too stunned to move anyway. Grabbing my wine, I watch as his score skyrockets above mine when he hits the extra special bonus, giving him an extra ball to play in addition to the one he already has. I'm toast. Both balls are flying from one end of the playfield to the other. He racks up a score of 874,330 before he finally misses with the flipper and his pinballs are no more.

"Holy shit."

"Who's the Pinball Wizard now?"

"You are. That was awesome, babe."

"Thanks. Lose the pants."

"No. You don't get two for one. You already got me out of my shirt before you even finished playing."

"That was retribution."

"I didn't punish *you* when you got *me* all in a tizzy."

"You elbowed me."

"Oh shit, I sure did. Alright. Fine." I shimmy out of my jeans and kick them to the side.

Clay looks me up and down. His eyes stop at a huge dark bruise about the size of a baseball on my thigh. "What the hell happened to your leg?"

I look down. "Oh. That must be from when you had your nightmare the other night."

"Oh god, Lynn. I did that to you?"

"It was an accident, before you woke up."

"You said I didn't hurt you."

"You didn't mean it."

"Jesus, babe. Come here." I walk over to him and he hugs me. "Why didn't you tell me?"

"It's no big deal. Just a bruise."

"I'm so sorry. Christ. That had to really hurt. I kicked the shit out of you." He pulls back from me and I see fear in his eyes.

"Hey. I'm fine. It's okay." I really am okay, but I can tell he feels terrible.

His face is full of anguish. He scrubs his jaw with his hand and then rakes his hand through his hair. "That's like the third time I've done something like that while I was having a nightmare, but it's the most severe. What if something worse happens next time?"

"Clay, you were asleep. You couldn't help it. If anything, it's my fault for getting in the way."

"That was not your fault."

"Well it certainly wasn't yours. Please, it's okay. I'm fine. Come on." I take his hand and lead him upstairs, grabbing my clothes in the process.

"Where are we going?"

"I believe I owe you a strip tease."

His voice relaxes. "Oh yeah?"

"Yeah," I whisper.

We go to our bedroom and I take out another button-up shirt from the dresser. After getting redressed in the bathroom, I scan my *Animal Instincts* playlist to look for the sexiest song I can find. Got it. Joining Clay back in the bedroom, I see that he's already in bed. He's sitting up under the covers, shirtless, leaning on the stack of pillows at the headboard with his hands clasped behind his head. Probably totally naked.

"Let's get this party started," Clay says, rubbing his hands together.

I turn off the lamp, leaving only the light of the moon to eclipse me into a silhouette. After connecting my phone to the Bluetooth sound system, I press the play button on my phone and Paula Cole's "Feelin' Love" starts playing.

Believe it or not, I've never given my husband a strip tease before, so I'm a little nervous. I stand back from the foot of the bed and sway my hips as I begin to slowly unbutton my shirt. When I'm halfway through, I turn around, my back to Clay. I look over my shoulder at him, keeping eye contact, as I continue with the buttons. When the last button is undone, I raise my right shoulder slightly, letting the shirt slide down, exposing my shoulder. I take my arms out of the sleeves and turn to face

Clay, simultaneously moving my shirt over my bra, blocking his view. He swallows. I drop the shirt.

"Sweet Jesus," he whispers.

I turn sideways and stand up straight, circling my hips, making sure he gets a good look at the profile of my lace-covered breasts in the moonlight. I unbutton my jeans and take my time bringing the zipper down.

Giving him another view of my back, I take my jeans off in slow motion, bending over as I do so, all the while swaying my hips back and forth to the sultry sounds of the music. I peer at him through my legs. His mouth is parted. His stare is burning.

I put my hands on my butt, keeping my hips moving. I raise myself slowly and turn back around to face him. My eyes on his, I reach around and unhook my bra, letting it slide gently down my arms until it falls to the floor.

"Shit, Lynn. I'm dying over here," Clay says in a hushed tone. I can barely hear him over the song.

My center begins to ache. I can feel how wet I am. Didn't think I'd get this turned on giving a strip tease. I grab the sides of my panties with my thumbs, pulling them down in no hurry.

Now fully naked, I show off my profile again. I undo the elastic band holding my ponytail and shake my head, letting my loose curls fall around my shoulders. Arching my back, my boobs are nearly pointed at the ceiling as I bend, the tips of my long hair grazing the back of my knees.

"God, Lynn. I'm so hard for you right now. Are you wet for me?"

Soaked. But I don't answer him. Instead, I trace a languid finger around the side of my breast and circle the tip.

"Get over here before I explode."

I saunter to the end of the bed and climb over the footboard just as "Moments in Love" by Art of Noise starts. Another very sexy song. I'm prowling towards him on my hands and knees. He throws the covers back, ready for me, as I expected. Naked. Rock hard.

He puts his hands between my legs and feels how slick I am.

"Holy fuck. You're drenched. That was the hottest goddamn thing I've ever seen, Lynn," he says in a sexy low growl. "Ride me."

I straddle Clay and slowly fill myself with him. The feel of his length inside me charges my body with anticipation. I start moving. "You liked it?"

"Fucking loved it."

I pick up speed.

"Shit, slow down, I don't want to finish faster than a teenage boy. I want to relish this." I rein in my pace. "You got me so worked up, Lynn. I couldn't take it anymore. That's why I called your sweet ass over here. You're so sexy. So beautiful. I love every inch of you."

"I love you too, Clay." I continue to rock my hips on top of him. When his breathing increases, I begin to pick up the pace. He grabs on to my butt and slams himself into me a few times, his angle hitting my G-spot, initiating an inevitable wave of euphoria over me. We both cry out in pleasure as we release and enter a satisfying state of bliss together.

CHAPTER 20

IT'S TUESDAY MORNING. Our last day here. I don't want to leave. I know we don't have to, but I'm anxious to get to our next destination.

Down the hall wafts a scrumptious aroma. Bacon. Delicious bacon. No mistaking that smell. Clay must be trying to cook the rest of the breakfast food so we don't have to throw it all away. I get up, brush my teeth, put some clothes on, and head to the kitchen. I hear Clay belting out Warrant's "Cherry Pie" in a low voice. I stop in the hall and listen to him for a minute. His near whisper-singing makes me smile. He's in an exceptional mood this morning. Maybe I should give him a strip tease more often. I proceed into the kitchen.

Clay removes his ear buds when he sees me. "Mornin', love. Coffee?"

"Please. I'm guessing you slept well since you're up before eight." He puts my mug full of morning fuel in front of me at the island bar. I add creamer and stir, the spoon clinking on the ceramic.

"I slept unbelievably well. Haven't slept that soundly since we left our house."

"Wow, really? That's great. I mean, not that it's been that long, but just that you had a good night's sleep."

"Well, everything leading up to it was good. Better than good. You rocked my world last night. Seriously, Lynn. That was ten kinds of sexy. And those songs…I've never even heard them before, but, damn."

"Sexiest songs on the planet. In my opinion anyway."

"I think I'd have to agree with you."

"Glad you enjoyed it all." I smile.

"Understatement." He flips the eggs over and walks around the island to give me a kiss. "Hi."

"Hi."

"What do you want to do today?" He strolls back to the skillet and slides the two eggs onto a plate next to a few slices of bacon.

"Since it's our last day here, I want to drive into Gatlinburg and go to the winery and jelly store."

"Great idea."

With breakfast done and our bellies full, we drive to the Smoky Mountain Winery in Gatlinburg. Clay and I taste a few different wines, and while I usually gravitate towards my old standby of Cabernet Sauvignon, we opt to buy several bottles of their strawberry wine. It's so good.

"I wanted a whole case," I tell Clay, "but now that we have a place here, we'll just come back after we finish these at home."

"Works for me."

We put the wine in the truck and walk over to the Smoky Mountain Farms Jelly House. We sample some of their more popular jams, jellies, honeys, and butters. But I came here for their banana-pineapple jelly. My favorite. I buy a few jars.

Our next stop is Lorelei Candles, where I purchase a candle to match each bedroom in the cabin. We then head to Sparky's Glassblowing and pick out some Christmas ornaments, some of which I decide to leave here for decorating a tree when we come back for the holidays. After lunch at Pancake Pantry (which is a must-do when in Gatlinburg), we make our way back to Sevierville for our last night here.

Clay's phone rings while we're on the road. It's CeCe. Clay pushes the button on the dashboard to answer the call.

"Hey, CeCe. What's up?" he asks.

"Hey, Clay. Tried to call Lynn, but she didn't answer."

"Oh, sorry," I pipe up. "My phone's in my purse. Didn't hear it ring. Is everything okay?"

"Yeah, I think. Um, it's just that, you got a delivery."

"What is it?" Clay asks.

"Uh, it's a really huge Hooters sign?" she questions. "Like one from an actual Hooters restaurant."

I smile and look at Clay while what CeCe just said registers with him.

"Yeah," I tell CeCe. "I was expecting it."

Clay looks at me. If his ears weren't in the way I think his smile would wrap around his head.

"Where should I tell the guy to put it?"

"In the garage is fine. Thanks, CeCe. Sorry, I forgot to let you know it was on its way. Everything else going well?"

"Yep, everything's fine. Lemme go so I can direct him to the garage. Talk to you later."

"Okay, thanks, sis."

"No problem. Be safe. Love you."

"Love you too."

Clay pushes the button to hang up. "Do you know how much I love you right now?"

"It was supposed to be a surprise."

"I am definitely surprised."

"Good." I smile.

"Thank you. Seriously. I love it."

"You're welcome. I knew you would."

"I swear, woman, if I weren't driving right now, I'd take you right here. I can't believe you did that for me. You gave me so much shit about wanting that sign," he laughs. "You constantly stun me, Lynn Sinclair. Don't ever stop."

"Likewise, Clay Sinclair."

"I'm going to have to get you some little orange shorts for your next show." He grins at me and I roll my eyes.

We pull up in the driveway and bring our wares of the day inside. We head down to the theater section of the game room. Clay looks for a movie to watch while I pop popcorn and make us each a root beer float.

"What are we watching?" I ask.

"Don't know yet. Thinking comedy. Not sitting through a chick flick. There must be at least a hundred movies in this cabinet."

"I bet Aunt Mitzi had fun choosing which ones to stock."

"How about *Spaceballs*?"

"Perfect. Popcorn's almost done."

"Smells delicious. Make mine with extra butter. And throw some Snow Caps in there."

"Is there any other way to eat popcorn?"

Clay puts the movie on while I close the blinds to darken the room. We sit down and enjoy our floats, munch on our popcorn, and quote practically the whole movie while it plays.

After Lone Starr defeats Dark Helmet and is subsequently able to marry Princess Vespa (if you haven't seen *Spaceballs* by now, you deserved that spoiler), we decide to have a sandwich as our dinner. Clay prepares mine for me. Even though it has everything on it that I like and it's the way I would have made it, somehow it tastes better than if I would have made it myself. Isn't that always the case?

Before we go to bed, I clean out my purse and put all the things I don't need but don't want to throw away onto the bedside table. I notice that the drawer is cracked open just a bit. It takes a little effort to open it up. I gasp.

"Clay. There's another letter from Aunt Mitzi in here."

"Holy shit. How have you not noticed it? We've been here three days."

"The first time I tried this drawer, it was stuck. So, I thought it was just one of those fake decorative drawers that didn't open. But then I noticed it was slightly ajar, so I tried again."

"Well damn."

"I know."

"Read it to me while I brush my teeth."

I open the letter. "Okay. Here we go.

"Dear Loves,

'I hope you are enjoying your trip and that you like the cabin. Sid and I did our best to decorate it, but please feel

free to change it to your hearts' desire. You may be wondering how it's stayed so clean. A local company has been checking on it weekly to keep it up. It's called Foothill Property Management, so you'll need to contact them and let them know that you've found the cabin. It's up to you if you want them to continue the weekly cleaning and upkeep, but it's paid for as long as you own the cabin. Sid was friends with the owner, Charlie, and bailed him out of trouble years ago. Charlie was having a hard time keeping the company afloat, so we helped him get back in the black by becoming silent partners. As such, Sid told Charlie to make sure the cabin was kept up weekly after we built it for you. Of course, Charlie was happy to do it. He arranged everything. Over the years, the property management company has prospered, and upon Sid's death, I sold our share of the company back to Charlie and his wife, Linda. However, I worked out a deal for the service to continue, reminding Charlie and Linda that without our help, they wouldn't be where they are today. A contract has been signed between Charlie, Linda, and me, for the provision of lifetime housekeeping, so don't worry about a thing. If you'd like a copy of the contract, all you have to do is ask when you call. They will be happy to oblige and would probably love to meet you.'"

"Wow," Clay says, rinsing his mouth. "For some reason that thought didn't even cross my mind. Damn glad you found that letter, babe."

"Yeah, really. Man, they thought of everything."

"That was a badass thing Aunt Mitzi did."

"What do you mean?"

"In no uncertain terms, she reminded the couple that owns the company what their future could have been like without her and Uncle Sid. She put the smackdown on them."

"Shit, you're right. Kind of out of character for her. Go, Aunt Mitzi, with ya bad self!"

Clay laughs. "Sorry, keep going."

"'As you probably know, most cabins in the area are named. However, we left that part up to you. I know you will both come up with something meaningful and/or fun.'"

"How about Cabin McCabinface?"
"Negative," I say.
"Hashtag Mountain Mama Mansion?"
"Hashtag no effing way."
"Okay," he laughs. "After your performance last night, what about The Southern Strip?" he laughs again.
"That's a hard no, you hear me?"
"Hard no. Pass. Got it," he snickers.
"Now, would you please be quiet, Sinclair?"
"Yes'm."

"'Lynn, I hope you found your grandparents well and they were both still there to receive you. If not, know that we are all up here looking down proudly at you. Another clue was set into place in case that has happened. Regardless, you would still have been led to the Brougham. And speaking of the car, Clay, I hope you were able to find a way to get it home safe and sound. I know you're probably so excited about it. Sid and I will be watching your progress. Until then, he wants you to enjoy The Macallan.

'My love always,

Aunt Mitzi.'"

"Huh," Clay utters. "Guess you were right."
"Told you he'd want us to drink it."
"I can't wrap my head around the fact that she mentioned The Macallan, which, as I said the other day, was only released a few months ago. And then to mention it in this letter…that means she had to have put the letter here

recently. And how could she tell us that Uncle Sid wants us to enjoy it? He died three years ago, before the bottle we have was released."

"Maybe there was a cheaper bottle of The Macallan at first, and when she found out about the ninety-one release, she wanted us to have it since that's the year we got married. Maybe she made a phone call to her contact at Shandies or the liquor distributor and had them switch it out. We'll probably never get a real explanation."

"That's a good assumption. Makes much more sense. Still need to call Flo though and see what she knows," Clay says.

I walk into the bathroom to brush my teeth and Clay gets into the shower.

"Join me?" he asks. "I need to thank you properly for that Hooters sign." I look at the ceiling and tap my lips, like I'm seriously contemplating his request. "Come on, you know you want to. Last night here. Big huge space. Waterfall shower heads. Body jet panels."

"Okay, you've convinced me. I'll be right in. Get it nice and steamy for me."

"Yes, ma'am."

Once we've showered and are in bed, I think about the past three days. I think about what to name the cabin. I think about what could possibly be next. I'm so overcome with awe and admiration for everything Aunt Mitzi and Uncle Sid have done for us. Never in my wildest dreams could I have imagined any of this would ever happen.

"What's goin' through your head, love?" Clay asks as he swipes his thumb across my cheek.

I smile at him in the dark. "Just thinking about everything. It's so incredible, you know?"

"Yeah. Overwhelming. They loved you so much."

"They loved us both so much."

Clay kisses me. "What do you want to name the cabin?"

"I've been tossing a few names around in my head. What do you think about Key Elements? It has a double meaning. Since we acquired it during this trip with all the keys, and the bedrooms are decorated in the four classical elements of nature."

"So, Cabin McCabinface is completely off the table?"

"Yes," I smile.

"Then I freaking love it. Key Elements it is. We'll have a sign made up to hang outside the front door by the next time we come to visit."

"That's a great idea. I love you."

"I know. Let's get some sleep. Early day tomorrow."

Clay kisses me again and we drift off to dreamland.

CHAPTER 21

s Clay packs the car, I brew some coffee and wash out the coffeepot. We decided to keep the property management thing going (why not, right?), so I call and speak to Linda and let her know we've discovered the cabin and we'd appreciate them keeping it up. I tell her that we'd like to have a copy of the contract and we'll stop by to pick it up and introduce ourselves on our way out of town.

I'm sitting at the kitchen table when Clay comes back in. I have the cipher out, waiting for him to help with the next clue.

He sits down at the table and picks up his coffee mug. "What's it say?" he asks before taking a sip.

"'Find the only hotel with each floor on the ground. The smorgasbord in the room of balls holds something for you that's been kept safe and sound.'" Clay smiles. "Why are you smiling? What is it? You have an idea?"

"I know this one," he says proudly. "I've been to that place. Mom and Dad took us there on vacation one summer when we were in high school. It's a cool establishment. Interesting history behind it. Stone and I got into a little bit of trouble while we were there. He dared me to—"

"Clay?" I'm losing patience.

"Yes, love?"

"You gonna beat around the bush, or tell me what and where it is?"

"I should make you figure it out." He winks at me and I glare at him. "Never mind."

"Smart man. Using your head."

"You're taking the fun out of it. What happened to your inner Nancy Drew?"

"My 'inner Nancy Drew' is about to start using enhanced interrogation techniques."

"Fine. It's the Basin Park Hotel in Eureka Springs, Arkansas."

"See? Was that so hard?"

"Stop doing that."

"Stop doing what?"

"You just said 'balls,' 'bush,' 'head,' and 'hard' in the last thirty seconds. You can't keep saying things like that and expect me to just sit here calmly and ignore it. I want to throw you over my shoulder, bring you to the bedroom, and have my way with you."

"You're such a cave man."

"I am what I am."

"Now you're Popeye?" He laughs, nearly choking on his coffee. "Let's get back on track, shall we? How does this hotel have a ground floor on every level? Is there only one floor or something?"

"No. It's built on the side of a mountain. The first hotel on the property burned down in the late eighteen-hundreds. When the owner decided to rebuild, he took an extra safety precaution and had iron catwalks built on every floor leading to the mountainside."

"So, they would have to climb down the mountain if there was a fire?"

"Nah. There are stairs leading down from the catwalks, fire-escape style."

"Nice."

"Now, regarding the second part of the clue, I know there's a ballroom in the hotel, so that's probably the 'room of balls,' but I'm not sure about the 'smorgasbord' part."

"All I can think about is Templeton from *Charlotte's Web* where he sings that song after gorging himself on food at the fair." We both laugh.

"Well it obviously has something to do with food," he says.

"Maybe we're supposed to order something from their restaurant."

"In the ballroom though? That doesn't make sense. What about the keychain?"

I dig it out of the box, look at it, and give it to Clay. It's about one-inch square with the phrase 'A-ha!' printed on it in frilly lettering and surrounded by pastel roses.

"What's the significance?" I ask. "Is it about the band from the eighties that sings 'Take On Me'? I love that song."

"Somehow I doubt Aunt Mitzi had Norwegian synthpop in her repertoire. I'm pretty sure this refers to the word 'Eureka' which literally means, 'I found it.' And usually, when you find something you've been looking for, or when you finally figure out a solution to a problem, you say—"

"A-ha! Cute one. I've never been to Eureka Springs. How far are we?"

"Hmm…probably close to twelve hours."

"I'm not sitting in the truck for twelve hours today."

"I'm not driving for twelve hours today. It's already eight. We can go a little out of the way and spend the night in Memphis. That's about halfway."

"Ooh, can we go to Graceland?"

"Sure thing, little mama," he says in his best Elvis impersonation.

As we climb into the truck and say good-bye to our freaking awesome mountain cabin, it starts to rain.

"Oh, I have the perfect song for right now," I tell Clay.

"What is it?"

I search in my list of country songs and hit the play button. "Smoky Mountain Rain" by Ronnie Milsap begins and I sing along, much to Clay's dismay since he's not a huge fan of country music, but he indulges me as I belt out the lyrics.

After stopping to eat lunch in Nashville, we continue to Memphis and check in to the famous Peabody Hotel. I've always wanted to stay here and watch the famous mallard ducks make their daily red carpet appearance.

"The last tour at Graceland is at four-forty-five," Clay says. "You still want to go? We'll miss the ducks."

"Of course I still want to go. It's freaking Elvis, babe. Book the tickets.

We can see the ducks before we check out tomorrow. Lucky for us they make their march twice a day."

"Guess that makes us lucky ducks," Clay laughs at his lame joke as he punches a few numbers into his phone. "Done. Let's rock and roll."

We tour Graceland, and a few things surprise me about the place: the gates are way smaller than every picture makes them look, the jungle room isn't *that* tacky, and, for all his money, Elvis sure had a lot of family photos in dime store frames. Not saying that's a bad thing, just expected a little more gaud from the King of Rock n' Roll.

We end up at the gift shop looking for ornaments. There are so many to choose from, I have a hard time deciding. Then I see the one I know I'm going to purchase.

"Oh my God, Clay. Look at this one. It's in the shape of a key! We have to buy it."

"Perfect. Let's get it and go so we can get back to the hotel please. I'm beat."

As we settle back into the truck, I open the box of my souvenir and examine the ornament closer. The key is a metal antique style, gold in color. The Graceland logo, which is a stylized image of the house over its name in a simple cursive font, is embossed at the key's filigree head. The bit at the end is fashioned into a beautifully detailed feature of Graceland itself. I love it so much. This will make a great addition to my scrapbook Christmas tree.

Back in the hotel room, we shower and head straight to bed for some much needed shut-eye.

CHAPTER 22

A s we arrive at the Basin Park Hotel in Eureka Springs, we check into the Sunroom Suite and freshen up before grabbing dinner at the Balcony Restaurant inside the hotel. The restaurant overlooks Spring Street in historic downtown Eureka Springs and has a great view of the scenic Ozark Mountains.

As I'm eating one of the best burgers I've ever had (it's literally called 'The Best Burger' on the menu, with a blend of brisket and sirloin; sautéed mushrooms, onions, and bell peppers; and Swiss cheese, on a deliciously sweet brioche bun), Clay is looking on his phone to see what kind of night-life is to be had in town.

"You think we should try and sneak into the ballroom tonight or tomorrow?" I ask Clay.

"Funny you should ask. I just found the perfect cover for us."

"So, you're basically saying, 'Eureka.'"

"I suppose I am. How 'bout that?"

"Well, tell me. What are we doing?"

"There's a ghost tour in the hotel that starts in the Lucky Seven Billiards and Bar on the sixth floor."

"Okay. It better be worth it. You know how I feel about ghosts, babe."

For me, ghosts are best encountered in books and movies. I can always close the book and I probably wouldn't go to the movie anyway.

"It covers the ballroom."

"Totally worth it. What time does it start?"

"Eight. We have time. Already bought the tickets." He shows me his phone with a creepy nighttime image of the hotel attached to the receipt confirmation. "Don't rush to finish eating."

"How long is the tour?" I take another bite of my burger.

"A little over an hour. It also goes to the rooftop and ends up in an underground cave."

"Nice. Probably where the natural springs are."

"No doubt. And they'll also give us a sample of the bootleg liquor that was once served here."

"Bootleg, huh? Just how 'bootleg' can it be if they're advertising it on their web page?"

Clay laughs. "That's what it says."

I swirl a couple of fries in ketchup. "Yesterday you said something about you and Stone getting in trouble here. Tell me about that. What did he dare you to do?"

Clay stops mid-air when he's about to take a bite of his burger and looks at me. "You really don't want to hear about that."

"You started to tell me yesterday. Why the change of heart? Spill it, Sinclair."

He takes the bite of burger, stalling for time. "Just goofy teenage boy, Stone being a dick brother type of stuff."

"Details."

He sighs. "It's so embarrassing. I don't know what I was thinking by bringing it up in the first place. It's not one of my favorite memories."

"How old were you? You said you were teenagers, but are we talking closer to thirteen or nineteen?"

He looks up to the sky, like he's trying to remember exactly how old he was. "Fifteen, I think. Maybe sixteen. I'm not telling you the story."

"Seriously, Clay. It can't be that bad. Just tell me already."

"Ugh. Okay." He takes a sip of his Coke. "Stone dared me to streak down the hall."

"Oh my god," I laugh. "I take it you got caught?"

"Yeah, and not by my parents, which would have been bad enough. But, I got caught by the hotel manager, who happened to be lady about a hundred and twenty years old."

I belly laugh at that. "What did she do?"

"At first she gasped. Put her hands over her face and said, 'Young man! This is not a nudist colony.' I covered myself with my hands and apologized. Meanwhile I could hear Stone around the corner laughing his ass off. Motherfucker."

I laugh. "Sounds like Stone. Then what happened?"

"Um, well, then she…she…"

"She what?"

He sighs. "This is the embarrassing part. She walked up to me, moved my hands out of the way, and proceeded to um, admire me."

"Holy shit! She touched you?" My face is serious now.

"Hell no. I would've never let that happen. She just, um, looked. And then she said, 'Impressive, young man. You'll make some woman very happy one day.' Then she winked at me and asked me where my room was. I thought she was going to attack me, for Christ's sake." Clay's face is beet red.

"You poor thing," I snicker.

"This is why I didn't want to tell you." He rolls his eyes and then smiles.

"What did she do after that?"

"She grabbed me by my ear, (which hurts like a bitch, by the way), hauled me back to our room, and knocked on the door. When Dad answered, she asked him if I belonged to him. Dad cussed under his breath and pulled me in the room by my arm, apologized to the perverted old lady, shut the door in her face, and gave me the what-for while I got dressed. Asked where Stone was. Thank God Mom had gone to the bar to get a couple of drinks. He never told her about what happened."

"He just let it go?"

"Yeah."

"Did you tell him she checked you out?"

"Fuck no," he laughs.

"What happened to Stone?"

"He came back a few minutes later, laughing of course, until Dad told him to shut up and not to ever mention it in front of Mom."

"Wow. You could have sued that woman for sexual harassment."

"Please. Nobody did that shit back then."

"But weren't you the least bit offended?"

"Offended? Not really. Grossed out? Yes."

I shake my head and can't help but smile.

"What?" Clay asks.

"She liked what she saw."

"Christ, Lynn," he laughs. "The last thing I wanted was for a dirty old lady to wink at my junk."

"Well, it is impressive."

"I know." He winks at me with a cocky smile.

"Ah, there he is, ladies and gentlemen…my humble husband, Clay Sinclair."

"Can we please change the subject now?"

"Okay. So, you and your family didn't take this ghost tour when you came here back then?"

"No. It might be something they've added recently. But Mom was always a scaredy cat, so that could also be the reason we didn't take it."

"Wow. Something your mom and I actually have in common."

"Oh, come on, Lynn. Y'all have more than that in common."

"Yeah, we do. We both love you."

Clay's mom and I have never really seen eye to eye. We tolerate each other for Clay's sake, but she's not my favorite person and I know I'm not hers.

When Clay got home from his first tour overseas after Operation Desert Storm, we got married as soon as legally possible. We had only been dating a few months before he left, and he was gone for eight months. She thought Clay and I were rushing into things and he was making a mistake.

The day before our wedding, I overheard her telling Clay something that nearly broke my heart. I was about to knock on his front door when I heard her shrill voice yelling at him.

"She's too young for you!"

"Too young? That's ridiculous, Mom. She's only three years younger than I am. Which makes her older than Alexa, and you didn't have a problem with her being younger. I love Lynn and we are getting married. Tomorrow. So, you're going to have to get over it."

"She's the wrong fit for you. You need to think long and hard before you marry that girl. You don't know what you're doing. You hardly know her."

"I do know her!" he shouted. "You're the one who doesn't know her. We've been together over a year. Give her a chance."

"You haven't been together. You've been halfway across the world in another country with remote access to the outside. You barely knew her before you left."

"It's enough to know I've never felt this way about anyone ever before, Mom. *Anyone.* She waited for me. For almost a year. Why would she do that if not for love? Lynn got me through the worst times while I was away. All I had to do was picture her."

"There's more to a marriage than just a pretty face, Clay. Have you talked to Alexa lately? I really liked her. I saw her a while back. She was a mess. She misses you."

"Well that's her problem. I don't miss a single thing about that bitch."

"Clay, don't be ugly."

"'Don't be ugly'? You wanna talk about being ugly? Alexa egged my house while I was away, Mom." I heard her gasp. "That's right. I didn't tell you about that because she's not worth the breath. She also threatened Lynn."

"Well. I'm sorry to hear that. I just want what's best for you."

"Lynn is what's best for me. She's going to be my wife. Make your peace with that. I love you and I love her. I would appreciate it if you would just take some time to get to know her. Dad likes her."

"Your dad likes everybody."

"No, he doesn't. He's a great judge of character, and you know it."

"It's her or me."

"Don't do that. You won't like the outcome. What's that Bible verse about a man leaving his father and mother and clinging to his wife?"

"Fine. It was worth a shot."

"That's what I *thought.*"

"I'll get along with her for you, but not because I like her. I'll fake it till I make it. But you're making the wrong decision, Clay."

"I don't believe that. I'll never believe that. This conversation is over, Mom."

I smiled, took a deep breath, and finally knocked on the door. Clay opened it and I put my best face on, trying not to give away what I'd over-heard. His mom walked out in a huff.

"Hi, Mrs. Sinclair," I said in a cheery tone. "It's good to see you again."

"Hello, Lynn. I was just leaving. I guess I'll see you tomorrow."

"Yes, ma'am. You sure will."

Clay stepped out and watched his mom get into her car as he wrapped me in a hug. "You heard."

"I did."

"I'm sorry."

"Don't be. You're her baby. I get it. She doesn't know me and she's just trying to protect you."

He pulled back and took my face in his hands. "I love you."

"I love you too. So, no second thoughts?"

"None whatsoever." He kissed me. "Come on, let's get to Aunt Mitzi's so we can help her prepare for our wedding day."

Over the last twenty-six years, his mom has softened to me somewhat, but I'm never sure if she has actually warmed up to me or if she's just gotten better at putting on a performance. I only have to see her for family wed-dings and funerals, an occasional Sunday dinner, and a couple of holidays a year, so I'm fine with it.

Clay brings me back to reality. "Ready to head back to the room?"

"Sure."

"We've got about forty-five minutes till the tour starts."

"Good. I can change my shoes."

"What's the game plan?" Clay asks as we make our way to the pool hall and bar room for the ghost tour.

"You tell me. We don't even know exactly what we're looking for."

"I think it might be a commercial buffet. You know, one of those big stainless-steel ones like they have in restaurants. The hotel has weddings and parties in the ballroom, so I'm sure they serve food there. Smorgasbords."

"Good thinking. Okay, so since there's no wedding tonight, it's probably tucked away in a corner, not in use. You'll have to create a diversion if there's no free roaming."

Once we get to the Lucky Seven, we gather with the rest of the group. I count a dozen people, including the two of us. Shouldn't be too hard to break away without bringing much attention to ourselves.

The tour guide is dressed in full cowboy regalia, complete with a southern twang. He gives us some history about the town and the hotel. Turns out, even Al Capone's sister spent some time at the Basin Park Hotel. Clay and I had a good chuckle over that little nugget of knowledge.

We progress to the rooftop for more stories and accounts of ghost sightings and activities that have been reported in the hotel. The tour guide tells us that our next stop includes a surprise.

When we finally get to the ballroom, Clay and I scan the huge room for a big buffet server. However, the room is sparse, holding only a few folding chairs against a wall and…eureka! A dark wood antique buffet table sits alone near one of the corners. I point it out to Clay. He nods and winks at me.

Our guide says we can download a free ghost hunting app on our cell phones for a potential encounter of our own with the other side. That's the surprise. It gives me chills, but the best part about that news is we'll be able to wander around the room for twenty minutes as we please. Score one for the Sinclairs.

"Well isn't that just the icing on the cake," Clay mumbles with a smile in his voice.

"Right on," I muse.

We download the ghost detector app and separate from the rest of the group.

Clay and I pretend like we are searching for spiritual activity with our phones, swaying them slowly around ourselves as we inch our way towards the buffet table. Clay starts humming the Johnny Cash song "Ghost Riders in the Sky." He probably wouldn't even know that song if it weren't for the Nicolas Cage movie *Ghost Rider*. Clay's phone screen scrambles with a blip. It shows that an entity is present. The name 'Matilda' pops up.

"Holy shit," he whispers.

My insides quiver and my pulse races. Heat washes over my body like I'm about to break out in hives. I take deep breaths, trying to calm myself down. "Don't you dare bring that to anyone's attention."

"Yippy ai ohhhh," he sings.

"Stop it! That can't be real. It's just part of the 'show.' Smoke and mirrors. We have a job to do, Sinclair. Get over there and block everybody's view of me as I crouch down to the cabinet door."

He salutes me. "Whatever you say, sarge." He laughs as I whack him in the arm with my phone.

The first thing I do is open the drawers of this beautiful mahogany buffet. They aren't locked. Silverware and napkins are stored inside. As I stoop down, lifting my heels and resting on the balls of my feet, I tug on the right cabinet of the buffet. Locked. I insert the key and twist it, letting out a sigh of relief when the key releases the latch. Opening the side door a few inches wide, my hand roves around inside. Nothing.

"Anything?" Clay asks.

"Not on this side."

"Shine a light in there. Maybe there's something written on the sides."

I turn on the flashlight on my phone to illuminate the inside of the cabinet. Still nothing; at least nothing I can see through the narrow opening.

I scooch down to the left side and pull at the handle. Also locked. Relief showers me. At least I know there's still a chance to find something. I repeat my actions from the previous end of the cabinet. My hand lands on a glass. I grip it and pull it out discreetly. It's not a glass per se, but an old Mason jar. Full of buttons. At first glance I know they are Aunt Mitzi's buttons. I smile at the memory of the games my cousins and I played with them. After locking the cabinet back, I put the quart-filled jar in my bag.

"What is it? Are you good to go?" Clay asks, still guarding me.

I stand up. "We're clear. It's a jar full of Aunt Mitzi's buttons."

"Buttons? What the hell for?"

"Cecilia, my cousins, and I used to play with them when we were little, whenever we would go over to Aunt Mitzi and Uncle Sid's. Usually, we'd be outside playing. But when it rained, Aunt Mitzi would break out her buttons. We'd put the pile in the middle of the floor, go around one at a time, and pick our favorites."

"Then what?"

"Then we would trade with each other, putting more value on some than others. There was one that all of us desired the most, and whoever got to pick first knew they would get it."

"I don't understand."

"The prized one was big and thick—"

"That's what she said," Clay laughs.

"Goofball. Anyway, it was a dark blue and white swirl pattern. It reminded me of a hurricane. I think it must have come off an old peacoat or cape. One of the prettiest buttons I've ever seen to this day.

"One time, when it was just Cecilia and me at Aunt Mitzi's, we got the buttons out and CeCe said the big button was automatically hers since she was older. I told her that wasn't fair since we usually pick a number to see who goes first. We fought over the dang button until Aunt Mitzi took it away from us. We never saw it again."

"Ouch. Aunt Mitzi really was a badass."

I laugh. "Yeah. Our cousins were so mad at us when they found out the next rainy holiday that we were all there together, but the button wasn't."

"Rough."

"Right? I made CeCe tell them what happened and that it was her fault. Naturally, by default, everybody's second favorite button became the new first choice. It was shiny turquoise, the color of the Caribbean Sea, with mother-of-pearl specks. About the size of a nickel."

"So, what's the point of all of it?"

"Just cousins being cousins. Girls being girls. Trying to find something to do since we couldn't go outside. Using our imaginations. Made up our own game."

"Did you get to keep the buttons?"

"No, we'd put them all back in the jar after we were finished playing with them and do the same thing the next time we were all there on a rainy day."

"Did you at least throw dice or something for them?"

"No, I told you, we just picked the ones we wanted traded them with each other."

"And then fight over them enough to get your favorite one taken away?"

"Yeah," I chuckle, remembering how much fun it was. Ahh, the simple times.

"Girls are weird."

"Boys are weirder."

"I mean, it was just a button…"

"Didn't you tell me you cried when your mom accidentally threw out your Archie Manning rookie card?"

"Well, that's different. It—"

"I mean, it was just a piece of cardboard."

"Touché."

Chapter 23

Back in our hotel room, we shower and get ready for bed. Pulling the jar of buttons from my purse, I dump them on the bedspread. Clay gets under the covers and grabs the TV remote.

"What are you doing?"

"Jimmy Fallon is about to come on."

"So?"

"He does 'Thank You Notes' tonight."

"No, that's on Fridays. Today's only Wednesday."

"Wow. Life on the road is getting me all mixed up. My days are all running together."

"Good thing you have me to keep you straight. And besides, don't you want to see if the big button is in this pile?"

"Uh…sure?" he asks, gauging the gravity of my tone.

"Yes. You're sure. Then we can figure out the next clue. And then we can watch TV."

"You're not the boss of me," he says with amusement, turning to adjust the pillows behind him at the headboard. All I do is look at him. When he lifts his head back up at me and recognizes my half-squinted eyes with their impending implication, he sits up a little straighter. "Jeez, Lynn. You don't have to break out your mean eyes. Okay. Fine. Let's see what we have here." He rubs his hands together with bogus enthusiasm. Such a good sport, however forced it may be this time.

"Thank you, husband of mine with phony excitement, for indulging your lady in looking through this big pile of antique shirt fasteners."

Clay smiles at my attempt of one of my own Jimmy Fallon-style thank you notes. "You're welcome, wife of mine with an odd penchant for old apparel closures."

I slip in next to him, careful not to let any buttons fall off the bed. My hands spread the large pile of buttons and the childhood trophy emerges, its blue and white swirls circulating in their stormy glory. "This is it! I can't believe it. Well, yes I can." I search for the other most wanted treasure in the lot. "Here's the other one. Aren't they great, Clay?"

"I can see how happy they make you, so yes, they're great. I'm a fan of anything that puts that kind of smile on your face, especially something so simple. Sorry I was such a buzzkill. I know everything we find is important to you, and I can see how special this jar of buttons is to you. Glad you got your prized button back." He kisses me on the forehead and rubs his thumb across my cheek.

"Me too."

"You know what you should do?"

"What?"

"Text a picture of it to CeCe."

"Oh my god, that's brilliant."

"Yeah, show her you've got *both* buttons now." He sticks his tongue out and bobs his head back and forth. "Suck it, CeCe, you doo-doo head."

"'Doo-doo head'?"

"Well, I mean, since we're being so mature and all..." he trails off with sarcasm.

We laugh as I snap a photo of the pile of buttons with the two cherished treasures on top. I text it to CeCe with the caption, 'My latest fortune,' and the tongue sticking out emoji.

"You think she'll see it tonight?" Clay asks.

"Doubt it, it's kind of late for her."

"Alright," Clay says, "time for the clue?"

"Yes." I take the cipher out and scan for the next one. "Number twenty-eight. 'The King of Beers was born in this city. A case for suits with the Blues awaits without pity. In this gallery of artifacts, you'll find legends of names. Like King and Waters and Berry and James.' Wow. Okay, I'm guessing St. Louis, Missouri? Budweiser is the King of Beers, right?"

"Right. At least, according to the commercials. You know I'm a Corona man. Anyway, yes, the Anheuser-Busch plant is in St. Louis."

"The word 'Blues' is capitalized."

"Then it's got to have something to do with the Blues genre of music, given the capital 'B' and the names she mentioned."

"Yeah. I'm assuming she means B.B. King, Muddy Waters, Chuck Berry, and Etta James."

"Those are definitely legends. Is there a Blues museum in St. Louis?" Clay asks.

"I'm not sure. Do you think 'a case for suits' means a garment bag?"

"My first thought was that it might have something to do with the Blues Brothers, because they had those cool suits. But they were from Chicago."

"And fictitious."

"Yeah, so it's probably not Jake and Elwood. I bet it's a suitcase. Garment bags typically don't have locks on them, though I suppose they can. I've just never had one with a lock. What does the key look like?"

I dig in the box and look for the one labeled with 28 on it. "The keychain is the Budweiser bowtie logo. The back of it says—"

"Let me guess," Clay says. "'Enjoy responsibly.'"

I smile and show him. "Yep. And you see this tiny little key on the ring? Definitely looks like it will unlock a suitcase."

Clay pulls up Google on his phone and searches for Blues museums in St. Louis. "Well it doesn't get any more obvious than this."

"What?"

"The National Blues Museum is in St. Louis."

"Okay then. That's where we'll head in the morning. How far is it?"

"About five hours," Clay says.

"Not too bad. We should have a pretty easy day tomorrow then." I'm surprised by my phone buzzing with a text notification. I check it. "It's CeCe," I say with a smile. She replied with 'No way! Bitch.' It's followed by a winky face emoji, and then, 'Awesome!' with a thumbs-up gif. I laugh and show it to Clay. He gets a kick out of it and hands my phone back to me as he turns out the light.

"I thought you wanted to watch Jimmy Fallon."

"It's a rerun. I'm sleepy anyway. Goodnight, babe."

"Night."

He kisses me and we try to fall asleep.

CHAPTER 24

WE EXIT EUREKA Springs and head toward St. Louis. I thumb through my playlist to find some good music. Pressing the random button on my phone, "Chandelier" by Sia starts.

"Cool song. I dig Sia," Clay says.

"Best wigs since Dolly."

Clay laughs. "Hey, can you book us a room in St. Louis? We should be there before lunch."

"Already ahead of you. I booked us a room before I fell asleep last night. You conked out as soon as your head hit the pillow. I don't blame you though. Driving takes a lot out of you. Are you sure you don't want me to drive at all?" I smile and bat my eyelashes.

Clay looks at me with a smirk. He knows I'm joking. He's pretty possessive of his truck. "Don't be silly. I got this."

"I know. I just like getting under your skin."

"Mmm. I like you under my skin. And on top of it. Sideways. And, speaking of swinging from chandeliers, that sounds fun."

I can't help but laugh. "I totally set myself up for that, didn't I?"

"That you did."

My phone rings. It's Annie. It's odd for her to be calling me so early on a weekday. I answer the call. "Hey girl, what's up? Everything okay?"

"I think Stone and I may have broken up last night." There's a crack in her voice.

"*What?* What happened?" Clay looks at me with concern. I cover the phone with my hand and whisper, "Stone and Annie got into a fight."

"He went a little crazy," Annie says.

"Crazy how? Start from the beginning."

"My car wouldn't start after I got off work yesterday. I tried calling Stone to come pick me up, but he didn't answer. Called again, no answer. Texted him. Nothing. So, I figured he must have left his cell at home or something. I was about to call his office phone, but Jim saw me standing next to my car. He asked me if I was okay and I told him my car wouldn't start. He offered me a ride home."

"Which Jim? Jim, the John Stamos look-alike? Or Jim, the rotund guy with the bad comb-over?"

"John Stamos."

I scrunch my face and suck in air through my teeth (that thing you do when you stub your toe) because I know this isn't going to be pretty. "Oh boy. Okay. Keep going. Where did it get crazy?"

"Jim pulled in my driveway and as I was getting out and thanking him, he asked if he could come inside to use the bathroom."

I didn't like where this was going. "I'm assuming you let him."

"Yes. I sat down at my kitchen table, rubbing my temples, trying to get rid of a headache. I didn't hear him come out. Before I knew it, he was behind me, massaging my shoulders, asking me if our boss was working me too hard. Said if he was, Jim would talk to him and get our team deadlines pushed back. I told him no, I just had a headache. At that second, Stone was inside. I gave him a key after we got back from Indianapolis and told him he was welcome to come in anytime, twenty-four-seven."

"That's a big step, Annie."

"Yeah. I thought it was the right one at the time. Anyway, he came in, saw Jim rubbing my shoulders. He asked what the hell was going on and proceeded to punch Jim in the face before I could even answer."

"Jesus. Over a massage?"

"Yeah, a little extreme, don't you think?"

"Slightly, especially without giving you a chance to explain first. So what happened?"

"Jim punched Stone back."

"Shit. What did you do?"

"I screamed at them to stop. I apologized profusely to Jim. Stone had given him a bloody nose, while Jim had given Stone a bloody lip. Jim left, telling me he'd see me tomorrow, which is today, in a few minutes actually, and I'm freaking out. I should have called in sick."

"What happened with Stone after Jim left?"

"He wanted to know who the fuck Jim was, why the fuck he was there, and what the fuck possessed him to think he could give me a fucking massage. His words."

"Sounds like Stone," I said.

"I mean, it's not like I was laying across the couch and he was giving me a foot rub with my legs across his lap, you know? It was just an innocent little shoulder massage."

"Exactly."

"But apparently, it's not so harmless in Stone's eyes. I couldn't understand why he was so pissed, and he couldn't understand how I didn't see that it was a big deal. He said it looks like Jim has a thing for me. Wanted to know if he flirts with me at work, does he ever take me to lunch, and so on."

"So how did you leave it with Stone?"

"We talked. I answered his questions, but he didn't seem to like any of my answers. I mean, yes, Jim flirts with me a little, but he flirts with everybody. That's just his personality. But I don't flirt back. And, of course we go to lunch sometimes. But it's all about business. We're both leading the same team project. I'm not sleeping with him, Lynn."

"What? I know that!"

"Stone left," she cries. "He threw my key back at me, walked out slamming the door behind him, and peeled out of my driveway. Didn't call at all last night," she sniffles. "If we don't spend the night together, we at least talk on the phone before we go to sleep. I don't know what to do. What this means. It feels like a break-up."

"Clearly you need to talk to him, Annie. Maybe he just needed to sleep on it and has cooled off this morning. He was a total ass for what he did and needs to apologize to you. And Jim."

"Yeah. I think so too. Shit, I need to get inside."

"How did you get to work this morning?"

"Called my brother and he said I could borrow my nephew's car since he's in a submarine somewhere in the ocean right now. Cody's car has been sitting in Brett's garage for a few months. He said it needed to be driven anyway. I can keep his until I get mine fixed. I'm going to call when I get inside and have mine towed to the shop today. Thanks for letting me vent."

"No problem. Call me later and let me know how things are going. You'll work it out. Love you."

"Love you too, Lynn. Thanks."

I hang up and let out a long breath. "Wow."

"What did my numbskull brother do to screw things up with Annie?" Clay asks.

"Stone can be such an idiot."

"Agreed."

"Annie thinks it might be over." I told him everything Annie said.

Clay scrubs his face and lets out a breath. "I don't know, Lynn. I probably would have reacted the same way Stone did."

"What? Why?"

"If I caught somebody else rubbing your shoulders, they'd get a beatdown from me too."

"I don't get it. I don't see anything wrong with a simple squeeze of the shoulders if it helps relieve a little tension. I get massages all the time. You know that."

"Yeah, in a professional atmosphere. At a spa. And Hope is the one you make appointments with, not any dudes. Sorry, Lynn. I'm with Stone on this. He didn't overreact."

"Annie's not cheating on him."

"That may be. But for my brother to do that, whatever he walked in on must have looked along those lines. Not that he might've thought Annie was cheating, but just the fact that another man had his hands on her. A massage is sensual, regardless of the part of the body it's performed on, especially if it's given by the opposite sex outside of a professional facility."

"I still think Stone owes Annie an apology. She didn't do anything wrong."

"She let her co-worker massage her, Lynn. Jeez. Haven't you been listening to a word I've said? You know the meaning of 'sexual harassment.' I know you do. You had to watch as many stupid videos for your job as I did for mine. Annie may have been innocent in her thoughts, but her actions showed Stone something different. It's about perception."

"He took it the wrong way. If Jim has a thing for Annie, then that's on Jim. It's not Annie's fault."

"No, I'll give her that, but I can tell you, as a man, Jim knew better. He took advantage of her." He pauses. "Do you remember that Christmas party we went to about ten years ago and some of your work people were there?"

"Yes. What's that got to do with anything?"

"Your old boss was there."

"Alex?"

"Whatever. I was on the other side of the room when he came in and saw you near the door. He hugged you."

"That's a normal reaction. I hugged a lot of people that night, Clay. Other men included. It was Christmas. A merry time of year. The air was bright and cheery. You hugged other women at that party, even kissed a couple on the cheek. I didn't get my panties in a wad."

"I didn't smell their hair."

"What?"

"Alex? Your boss? Smelled your hair when he hugged you. That's a blatant come on."

"My lord, Clay. When you hug someone, you can't help but smell their hair half the time. It's right by your nose."

"No, Lynn. That fucker closed his eyes and breathed you in. I watched him. I wanted to punch his lights out right then inside of that doorway. There are some things you just don't do to other women when they're taken. Like breathing them in and giving them massages."

"You're absurd."

"Really? How long after that party did you switch jobs?"

I start to think. I remember shortly after that Christmas party that Alex had given me the cold shoulder. I wasn't sure why, but I didn't feel like I should ask. I knew I hadn't done anything wrong on any of my assignments at work. I thought he was just keeping his distance because of the promotion I had applied for; he told me in confidence (a week before the Christmas party) he was going to make sure I would get it. But after the party, our conversations dwindled to strictly business and mundane niceties. He was curt with me and started giving me projects that he would have normally given to more junior people in the office. I did ask him about that part. He'd told me that he was just 'spreading the love' and 'giving others a chance to shine.' And then, I didn't get the promotion I was promised. The board 'decided to go in a different direction.' How freaking cliché, right? It wasn't long after that, I began to feel less challenged. Less needed. Less important. Figured it was time to move on to something else.

"Did you…did you say something to him?"

"You bet your sweet ass I did."

"What the hell, Clay!"

"You were in the bathroom. I cornered him and told him he better keep his hands, eyes, and *nose* off of you or he'd be sorry."

I shake my head. "You're the reason. The cause of his standoffishness. I felt so underappreciated at work after that. I was up for a promotion. I didn't get it. Because of you. I loved that job, Clay. I quit because of…I can't believe you did that. Alex never touched me, Clay!"

"Damn right he didn't."

"This is a lot to process. Pull over."

"Lynn, come on. That was so long ago. You moved on to a better job where you were challenged every single day. Your dream job. The one you retired from. You worked your way up all on your own. And you didn't have to deal with a hair-sniffing perv."

"Pull! Over!"

Clay exits the highway and drives to a gas station. He parks on the side of the building near the dumpster, away from the storefront where we can have a little privacy. I jump out and take a few deep breaths. He rounds the front of the truck to my side and tries to tug me into him. I wrench my hands away. The putrid smell of garbage invades my nostrils.

"You're being ridiculous, Lynn."

"Regardless of where I ended up, and how much I loved my last job at the museum, the fact that you interfered and who knows, could have sabotaged me from something great…that really pisses me off, Clay. You had no right to do that."

"The fuck I didn't!" he yells in a whisper. "You're *my* wife, and nobody breathes you in but me!"

"Are you listening to yourself?"

"I'm not apologizing for protecting you. That scumbag could've forced himself onto you at some point."

"God," I raise my hands in exasperation and look up at the sky. "I'm going in to get me something to drink." Clay starts to follow me. "Stay here. I just need a few minutes to breathe and wrap my head around this. I don't care how long ago this happened."

"Fine," he says calmly.

Before I round the corner of the building, I look back at Clay to glare at him. But his hands are on his hips and he's looking at the ground, shaking his head. Is he thinking about what he did? Or is he mad at me because I'm mad at him?

I go into the store and grab a bottle of water (although I feel like I could down a bottle of wine). I look for a snack, all the while thinking about what I'd just learned. I peruse the snack aisle and decide on a couple of trail mix varieties, peanut butter cheese crackers, and a Slim Jim.

What had Clay done by saying that to Alex? Where might our lives have ended up without the butterfly effect of Clay's actions? Of Alex's actions? If Clay hadn't seen him do that, would I have gotten the promotion? Would I have ever even left that job?

I get into the long line at the register. When I'm finally able to check out, I see Clay walking up and we make eye contact through the door. I look away as I grab my water and bag of munchies from the counter and head for the exit. Clay catches my arm after he enters the store and scoots us out of the way. I pull away from his grasp, this time with a little less abrasion. I don't want to cause a scene.

"I'll be in the truck," I tell him without looking at him.

"Yeah, okay," he says softly. Out of my peripheral vision, I see that he notices the lone bottle of water in my hands. "I'm gonna pick up some more drinks. And some peanut butter M&M's."

My favorite kind of chocolate candy. Clay gives me a small apologetic smile. He could buy me a truck load of peanut butter M&M's and it wouldn't make much of a difference in how I feel right now. I'm still pissed. My eyes finally meet his, but my expression remains vacant. He lifts his hand to touch my face, but I turn my cheek and walk out.

Back at the truck, I fumble with my keys and they fall on the pavement with a jingly crash. I bend over to grab them and as I stand back up, an arm wraps around my waist and pulls me backwards, forcing me to drop everything, including my purse. My water bottle rolls under the truck. Frantic, and noticing it's not Clay's arm, I start to scream. But a red bandanna comes over my mouth and nose, smothering my plea. It's a weird, strong smell, like rubbing alcohol and gasoline. Ether. As I'm panicking, I begin to get a little lightheaded. My limbs feel heavy and it becomes too hard to fight back.

A man's voice is at my ear. "Stop struggling or I'll kill you." I immediately steel myself. He lets go of my waist and points a gun at my side. "Go with me quietly or you're dead." I do as he says, as he leads me to a beat-up Mustang parked next to Clay's truck. "Get in and keep the rag over your face." I slowly open the passenger door of his car, hoping Clay will be rounding the corner any second. But I remember how long that damned line is.

The man, his face still hidden to me, slams the door and walks around the front of the car to get into the driver's seat. I'm still getting woozy from the ether. I see his profile through the windshield as he strolls around. He seems familiar, but the combination of ether and adrenaline is battling inside my body for a state of consciousness, and my mind is nothing but a thick cloud of fog. I can't think clearly.

The disheveled man gets inside the car, continues pointing the gun at my side, and smiles at me. I've seen that smile. Oh my god. This man, this loner, this kidnapper…is the handsome stranger from Hildene in Vermont.

To be continued…

About the Author

Rosie Politz is a down-home Cajun girl who loves to travel and hates to cook. She has a Bachelor of Arts degree in Anthropology from LSU and works in the tourism industry. She's a seasoned photographer, a 1980s pop culture trivia fanatic, and an avid list maker. Some of her favorite pastimes include playing board games, planning parties, and singing karaoke. She collects flamingos, wind chimes, and commemorative glasses from her travels. Rosie is married to her husband, Tommy, and they reside in the deep South, where Tommy does most of the cooking.

Rosie is busy working on further installments of her Key series. In the meantime, please visit rosiepolitz.com for up-to-date information about the series and join her mailing list for exclusive material. She would love for you to follow her on facebook.com/rosiepolitzauthor, Twitter @rosiepolitz, and Instagram username rosiepolitz.

If you enjoyed this book, please visit amazon.com and write a review.